DANGEROUSLY
Bad

EDEN BRADLEY

BLACK
LACE

Black Lace, an imprint of Ebury Publishing,
20 Vauxhall Bridge Road,
London SW1V 2SA

Penguin
Random House
UK

Black Lace is part of the Penguin Random House group of
companies whose addresses can be found at
global.penguinrandomhouse.com

First published in the US in 2017 by Berkley, an imprint
of Penguin Random House LLC
First published in the UK in 2017 by Black Lace

www.penguin.co.uk

A CIP catalogue record for this book is available
from the British Library

ISBN 9780352347893

Printed and bound in Great Britain by Clays Ltd, St Ives PLC

Penguin Random House is committed to a sustainable future
for our business, our readers and our planet. This book is
made from Forest Stewardship Council® certified paper.

MIX
Paper from
responsible sources
FSC® C018179

To my very dear friend, author Felice Fox.
I needed you to crack that whip, and you do it so well!
But more than that,
thank you for the rambling nights of worry and doubt,
the dirty pictures and the laughter,
the shared insanity that is being single and dating.
Sometimes no one gets me like you do.

I also must thank the adorable Emily McGuire
for being my beta reader on this one, and simply for being her
wonderful self.

And, as always, I have to thank my readers.
You are why I do this.

DANGEROUSLY
Bad

"BE CAREFUL THERE, Frankie—that's my baby you're lubing," Duff called out.

The short, stocky mechanic he was considering hiring for the new motorcycle branch of SGR Motors looked up, a retort on his lips, but he seemed to think better of it. "I'll take good care of her. Hey, you from Ireland?"

Duff laid a hand over his heart, as if he were mightily offended. He was—a bit. "Irish? I'm a good Scotsman. Well, maybe not so good. But I arrived here from Edinburgh a couple o' months ago to go into business with my cousin Jamie next door—they rebuild vintage muscle cars over there. He owns the auto shop and has half a hand in this place, too. And don't say 'Irish' to him, neither—he was born in Scotland, same as I was."

"Ah. Sorry 'bout the mistake. Couldn't place your accent."

Frankie ran a hand over the sleek black fender of the '48 Harley WL Bobber. "Did you bring the bike over with you? She's a real beauty. They sure don't make 'em like this anymore."

"Yep. That's why we're opening SGR Motorcycles—we'll be working exclusively on vintage bikes, so your skills had better be up to it if you want to work here. My cousin and I both appreciate the way they used to build machines. We'll expect our mechanics to have the same respect. And the knowledge." He leaned against the counter at the edge of the work bay. "How's that chain look?"

"Good, good. No runout. Tight as a teenager. Looks almost new."

"It is. Nothing but the best for my baby. Be sure you take her off the jacks like she's made of china. And be sure you treat all our customers' bikes the same way—and mind the crude remarks. This place won't be just another bike shop."

Frankie looked up, one blond brow raised. "That mean I have the job?"

"Yeah, it does, at that. Go talk to my cousin Jamie next door and he'll have you fill out your paperwork. After the bike is off the jacks, of course."

"Of course. Boss." Frankie cracked a gap-toothed smile.

Duff stroked his chin. "I like the sound of that. 'Boss.'"

"I'll bet you do."

He whirled around at the unexpected feminine voice—and was stunned into sputtering silence when he saw Layla Chouset standing in the doorway of his half-built shop.

Oh, yeah, he knew exactly who she was. The woman he'd seen on his first trip to The Bastille, New Orleans's most exclusive and notorious BDSM club. The woman he'd seen there twice more, locking gazes with her each time. The woman who'd starred in his darkest, hottest fantasies as he'd wanked off to her image nearly every night since he'd first laid eyes on her.

He went hard, took in a breath and willed his treasonous cock down.

She was all creamy chocolate skin and burning spitfire. Green eyes and sass. Gorgeous curves and breasts he wanted to fill his hands with. And she was a Domme. Which only made him want to bury his fists in those twining curls that spilled around her shoulders like dark silk and *pull* until he had her on her knees.

Not happening.

Maybe . . .

He cleared his throat and moved toward her, but his six-foot-seven frame did nothing to intimidate the delicate beauty—she stood her ground, her chin lifting.

"Can I help you, Layla?"

"You seem to think so. I'm here to tell you to back the fuck off."

He cracked a smile—he couldn't help it—and enjoyed watching the fire in her eyes flare. She took a step toward him.

"You think I'm funny?" she demanded.

"It wasn't a smile of amusement, darlin'. I was simply pleased."

"Darlin'? Seriously?"

She took another step toward him, and he realized up close how tiny she was, no more than five foot three or four. He could have picked her up and tossed her over his shoulder easily enough. Or over his lap. His cock wanted to growl.

He felt Frankie's attention to the conversation from behind him.

"Let's move this into my office," he said, gesturing with one hand.

She crossed her arms over her chest, but it only made the tops of her breasts spill from the lacy edge of her black tank top. After a moment she huffed and dropped her arms. "Okay. Fine."

He led the way into the unfinished office at the front of the shop. A wide window looked out onto the quiet street outside, and he distracted himself—and his damn hardening dick—a moment by letting his gaze rest on the coffee place across the way before settling onto the enormous metal desk he and Jamie had moved in the day before. The room still smelled faintly of paint and was piled with boxes of office supplies and the new computer he hadn't set up yet, but there were two chairs in front of the desk.

"Sit down if you like," he offered.

Layla's shoulders squared. "I don't need to sit—this won't be a lengthy visit. I'm just here to tell you—"

"To 'fuck off'?" He moved closer, until he could smell her perfume—or maybe it was simply her skin that smelled of fresh flowers and the night. Like something he wanted to lap up, savor, swallow. "You can tell me again, if you like, but I'm fairly certain you wouldn't be here if that was your only purpose."

"Oh, really? And what do you assume is my other purpose?"

He took one more step closer, then another, until he was almost on top of her. He had to give the woman credit—she didn't even flinch. "I think . . ." He kept his voice low. "I *know* I saw you watching me at The Bastille. More than once. Which is all right by me, since I was watching you."

From the corner of his eye he saw her hands ball into fists, then release. Oh, yes, she was a little shaken up, which was exactly where he wanted her. Well, fuck if that wasn't a lie— he wanted her naked and bent over his desk, but this would do for a start.

"Did it ever occur to you," she fumed, "that I felt your eyes on me and felt the need to see who the hell was stalking me?"

"Sure, it did. But I saw the way you looked at me, darlin'." He lowered his tone even more, his gaze flicking to her throat, where her pulse beat a strong, unsteady cadence. "I saw the question in your eyes. The desire. The same as I see it now." He lifted a hand to one of the satiny spirals resting on her shoulder and took the end between his fingertips.

She went to slap his hand away but he caught her slender wrist.

"Who do you think you are?" she demanded, her pupils going wide.

He answered without hesitation. "I think I'm the one Dominant man you burn for, Layla. I think I'm the one who makes you wonder what the other side is like. The bottom side." Her nostrils flared the tiniest bit, but she hadn't moved. And her pulse beneath his fingertips was running hot and wild. "I think you feel the same undeniable chemistry I do. All you have to do is give in."

She bit her lip, took in a long breath. He'd have bet good money she wasn't even aware of what she was doing.

"You're wrong about me—you and your ego. All you male Doms think no woman can top as well as you can, that we have no place."

"Not true. I've met many a good Domme in my time. I don't doubt you're a good Domme. But you feel it. I know you do. But there can be only one Top here, and I sure as hell am never bowing down for anyone."

A small smile teased at the corners of her gorgeously full lips. "No, I don't imagine you ever would. But I don't bottom for anyone. Not since . . ." She trailed off, glancing away for a moment.

"Not since what?"

"Nothing. Never mind. Look, it's not happening. Not with you. Not with anyone."

"Would you like to know what I think, Layla? No, what I *know*. It'll only be a matter of time. Meanwhile, you're going to be mulling over this conversation—it'll be impossible to forget. And just to make sure you don't forget . . ."

He bent and crushed his mouth to hers, one hand going behind her head and diving into that silky hair. And Christ, but her lips were soft and sweet as she moaned quietly, just the tiniest sigh issuing from her throat. Her mouth began to open under his, but he let her go and stood back, trying not to gloat.

"I'll see you then, shall I, when that time has come?" he asked.

Her eyes narrowed and she wiped her mouth with the back of her hand. "Goddamn it, Duff! What the hell was that?"

"That was what I'll leave you with, darlin'. Think about me, will you?"

She crossed her arms over her chest once more, accentuating her cleavage. Her face had hardened into tight lines—all but her mouth, her lips looking soft and well kissed. "Fuck you, Duff," she muttered before turning and stalking from his office.

He leaned against the edge of the desk, a grin on his face and a raging throbber in his jeans. "Let's hope so," he said loud enough for her to hear. Her retreating shoulders stiffened.

He watched her cross the street and get into a red convertible Mustang—a late 1960s model if he wasn't mistaken. The black top was down and he could see the curve of her shoulders, her lovely skin shining in the sun.

"Hey, Duff."

He glanced over his shoulder at his cousin, who'd just walked into the office through the door connecting SGR Motors and SGR Motorcycles.

"Not now, Jamie. I can't talk to you while I have a hard-on."

"Jesus. Sometimes you're an oversharer—you know that, cousin?" Jamie asked.

"One of my many charms," Duff muttered, his gaze still on Layla as she sat in the car. Why wasn't she starting it, driving away in a huff? Made a man think. Made a man think that perhaps she really was more interested than she let on. "Lord, the way the sun hits her skin. I'd pay to have that skin under my hands."

Jamie chuckled. "I seriously doubt you've ever had to pay for it in your life."

Duff grinned. "You're right enough there. And I don't intend to pay for this one, either."

"Have you forgotten—"

"That she's a Domme?" Duff interrupted. "Not for a single moment. But that only makes her more of a challenge. I like a good challenge. I like her fire. Her stubbornness. She sort of hinted that she's been a bottom before, but even if she hadn't, I *feel* it in her. Still, she's damn brave, that one. And courage is fucking sexy. Now I just have to capture that fire. Contain it. Contain *her*."

"I'll sit back and pop some popcorn. You contain away— or try to."

Duff turned to him. "Do you doubt my abilities, Jamie? And here I thought we were family."

"We are. But that fire you're talking about? It's there, all right—in spades. And someone could get burned."

"Nah. I'm not the burnable type. And look at her, man. She's too fucking delectable to resist. Might be worth a little singeing."

Jamie laughed, shook his head. "Just don't come running to me for Band-Aids, cousin."

"I'm not the running type, either, *cousin*."

Jamie stepped closer and gave him a good slap on the back. "True enough. Now, are you done ogling the girl so we can get back to work?"

Duff waved him off, turning back to the red convertible that still sat parked across the street. "In a minute. Don't mind feeding my hard-on for later."

"Jesus. I did not need to hear that. Come find me when you've recovered. I really don't want to talk business with a man sporting an erection, anyway."

"Smart boy."

"Watch it," Jamie tossed over his retreating shoulder. "I have my toy bag in my truck and I just acquired a new set of canes."

"Yeah, yeah," Duff muttered. "Keep the Domly-Dom stuff for your girl."

"I would anyway. I have no desire to touch your hulking, hairy ass."

"I'll have you know my ass is as smooth as a baby's bottom."

"Again with the TMI."

"You asked for it, cousin."

Duff grinned to himself as Jamie left his office. He kept his gaze on Layla in her hot red Mustang as she slammed both hands onto the steering wheel, and he didn't mind if it was out of frustration with him or pure anger. She was responding to him like crazy one way or the other. And if he could make her feel something—didn't really matter what it was at this point—then he knew he had her. She'd shown up at the shop, hadn't she? If she'd simply been irritated with him, he had no doubt a strong woman like her would have marched up to him at the club to confront him. No, this was an excuse to see him, he was certain. What he wasn't as certain about was the odd melting sensation swarming his belly as he simply watched her through the window. The raging heat that had gone through him when he'd held her delicate wrist in his hand. The way he'd been almost unable to pull away after kissing her.

As besotted as a teenage boy, that's what you are.

It was true. But it was also true that he would have her. He'd damn well find a way.

* * *

You idiot!

She'd thought she could go face-to-face with Duff Stewart, but Jesus fucking Christ—he had been so much more than she'd bargained for. He hadn't been in New Orleans more than a couple of months, but he'd already developed a reputation as a bit of a man-whore, so she'd written off what she'd heard about him being a natural Dominant who made all the submissives swoon. That fact had only fueled her fire—she wasn't about to be looked at as anyone's plaything, damn it!—and she'd come storming into his shop, guns blazing, only to discover the man was the real thing, wearing his dominance like a second skin. And only to have her body completely betray her in the face of his linebacker build, his ridiculously handsome face and what she was having a hard time denying was charm. And the Scottish damn accent! Why was an accent always so sexy? She'd been on the road for a full ten minutes, but even the purr of her beloved '66 Mustang had done nothing to soothe her. If anything, the rumbling vibration of the big engine she could feel against the backs of her thighs—and elsewhere—was making things worse. Or better. Depending on how one looked at it.

Stop it.

"Okay," she muttered to herself over the music blasting from her stereo, "he may be the most insanely desirable man I've ever seen, but I have enough self-control to ignore that. Don't I?" She hit the brakes just in time to prevent herself from running a red light. "Damn it."

She gripped the steering wheel, trying to calm her buzzing body, every nerve on high alert. But all she could think of was his wicked, sensual mouth. The spectacular, strong bone structure set off by his shaved head, the muscular breadth of his shoulders, his hazel eyes glinting with a dangerous metallic gleam, gold and silver simultaneously. She'd never seen eyes like that on a man, framed in dark, sooty lashes. And Jesus, dimples on a man like that were simply not fair.

The light changed and she hit the gas a little too hard. She eased off so she wouldn't get a ticket, then cursed again and grabbed her cell phone from her purse, hitting the button that dialed her best friend.

"Allure Salon," her friend answered in her soft Southern drawl.

"Kitty, it's me."

"Hi, honey. What's up?"

"Do you have a client in the chair? Can you talk?"

"I'm in the middle of a highlight. Can I call you back in . . . No, I'm booked for another hour after that. Are you okay? You sound funny."

Layla sighed. "I feel funny, and not in the 'ha-ha' kind of way. Can you meet me after work?"

"Oh crap, hon—I can't today. You know I'd drop anything for you if I could, but I'm teaching tonight at the beauty school. One of their instructors is on maternity leave. I'm sorry."

"Tomorrow night?" Layla asked, taking a deep breath. She'd just have to handle things by herself until she had a chance to talk to her friend.

"Of course. Our usual place?"

"Sounds good."

"Okay. See you there about five thirty. You gonna be all right until then?"

"Yep. I always am. I'll see you when you're done with work tomorrow."

They hung up, and Layla headed toward the Pontchartrain Expressway to catch the 10 out of town—hitting the road hard for a while would cool her off. It was either that or go home and pull out her collection of vibrators and spend the next two hours coming as hard and as many times as she could.

"This is ridiculous." She accelerated onto the on-ramp, the big engine picking up speed with a satisfying rumble. "I am in control," she reminded herself. "I am in control," she repeated, hoping to convince herself of the blatant lie.

The long, fast drive along with some blasting music and a firm talking-to with herself finally helped to calm her down. She kept driving, taking the 10 through Baton Rouge, moving with the music, letting her car take her down the highway. She was most of the way to Lafayette when she realized she'd better head home. By the time she got there, she was exhausted. With driving. With thinking. With the sensual rage simmering in her body.

She didn't dare go to bed—bed was too tempting. Instead, she flopped down on the big white sofa in her living room, tossing some of the exotic brightly colored pillows onto the floor as she reached for the TV remote. Flipping through the channels, she settled on an old romantic comedy, scooting aside a small bronze sculpture of the Hindu god Kali—one of her own pieces—to rest her feet on the edge of her coffee table, which was a slab of thick glass framed in reclaimed barn wood.

"This movie sure as hell couldn't be further from *my* life," she murmured to herself, settling back into the pile of cushions.

She'd never had a "normal" life, certainly not according to her father. She'd grown sick and tired of hearing him ask why she couldn't get a normal job, like a secretary or a school-teacher. Why she didn't do what he felt was a woman's duty in life and settle down with a good God-fearing man, get married and have babies. Those ideas had been shoved so hard down her throat, she'd gotten into the habit of rejecting them purely because they were *his*—that and his lack of expecting anything else from her—anything more—because she was female.

Most of her thirty-one years had been spent fighting those ideas, first by dating musicians and losers, then, in a more positive effort, by becoming a strong, self-supporting woman. She'd built that strength like a shield around her. And now Duff was trying to get in.

It was not happening. Even if every inch of her skin ached for his touch. Even if her stomach fluttered every time she let his name roll through her brain.

Not. Happening.

She massaged her forehead, flipping the channel until she found an action film, and lost herself in flying bullets and speeding cars. And to the sound of ringing gunshots, she fell asleep.

TUESDAY MORNING AND afternoon dragged as Layla tried to busy herself with packing up some new pieces of sculpture to ship to a gallery—she'd been making her living as a full-time artist since her early twenties—but finally it was time to meet Kitty at The Ruby Slipper Café on Magazine Street.

They'd been going to the café since meeting there five years earlier while waiting to get in for Sunday brunch, chatting until their friends showed up. Then a few months later she'd run into Kitty at The Bastille. Kitty had been new to the kink life at the time, and Layla had taken her under her wing, mentoring her, and they'd become fast friends.

Layla pulled open the door to the café, and the hostess greeted her, along with the homey scents of good, strong chicory coffee and grilled food—comfort food.

"Hi there, Layla. Kitty's in the back."

"Thanks, Rochelle."

She moved past the high polished-steel counter that made a U-shaped curve in the middle of the café, seeing Kitty's pale blond head bowed over the menu at a table by one of the tall windows. Kitty looked up as she approached, the sun lighting her blue eyes.

"Hey, honey." Kitty stood and gave her a quick hug before settling back into her chair. Her friend was a gorgeous, proudly curvy girl who always wore corsets to accent her hourglass figure at the club, but today she was dressed in work attire: black slacks and a sleeveless pink silk blouse.

Layla sat down across from her. "You're looking at the menu? Don't we both have it memorized by now?"

"Of course I do, but I always like to think I'll order something different than my usual barbecued shrimp and grits and some iced coffee. What about you? You having that salad you like?"

Layla shook her head. "It's a bananas Foster French toast kind of day."

Kitty put down her menu. "Uh-oh. That can only mean you either have something to celebrate or something bad has gone down, and I take it from the tone of your phone call yesterday this isn't celebratory French toast."

"It's not." Layla looked out the window at the traffic going by, at a woman walking a dog past the café. "I don't even know where to start."

"Honey, you start at the beginning, right? I'm not going anywhere."

Layla sighed out a long breath. "Okay. You remember that night a while ago when that guy—that big Dom—first showed up at The Bastille with Jamie?"

"The Scottish Dom? How could I forget? That man fills up a room like another wall, only more solid. And that black kilt was just *hot*. Isn't he Jamie's cousin?"

Layla nodded. "Well, I've run into him a few more times, and, Kitty, I swear he stares at me like he can see under my clothes or something."

Kitty shivered. "Was he wearing the kilt again?"

"At the club, yes, every time. He looks just as good in jeans."

Her friend shook her head. "Now, that's just not fair. I saw him staring at you. And personally, I don't think I'd mind that one little bit."

"I mind. I mind it a lot."

The waitress stopped by their table, interrupting the conversation, and they gave her their orders.

Kitty leaned into the table. "Layla, why on earth would you mind a hot man being interested in you?"

"Because I'm a Domme, which is obvious to anyone who's been at the club for more than five minutes. He's watched me play. *Watched* me. It's unnerving. And poor protocol."

"Is it really poor protocol, honey? Or is there some other reason why it bothers you so much? Either way, I still think it's flattering."

"It might be if I were a bottom."

Kitty was quiet a moment. "Layla, let me ask you this. You're pretty much straight, right? Not into girls?"

Layla shrugged. "Pretty much, yeah. I mean, you know I only play with girls these days, but it's not about sex for me."

"But if a woman came on to you, you'd still be flattered, wouldn't you? Even if she knew you didn't swing that way?"

"I guess so. Yes. I would be."

"Why is this any different?" Kitty asked, her blond brows arched.

"It just is," Layla insisted. The waitress returned with their iced coffees, giving her a minute to think about Kitty's reasoning. "Maybe you're right, Kitty, but he just . . . pisses me off. I can feel his eyes on me at the club. It's so intrusive."

"Does he stand there and watch you while you're in scene? Is he stalker-y?"

"No, that's not it. He goes off and does his own thing. It's hard to explain."

"Apparently," Kitty teased, pouring milk into her coffee and taking a sip.

"Yeah," Layla agreed, busying herself with her own coffee, adding milk and more sugar than she usually allowed herself—

she needed it today. She stirred it with her straw, watching the milky swirls disappear into the dark coffee. She caught herself and looked up at her friend. "I'm sorry. I'm brooding."

Kitty smiled at her. "Yes, you are. You gonna tell me what's really going on?"

Layla sighed. "In retrospect I sort of can't believe I did this, but I went by his motorcycle shop yesterday and told him off. Or tried to."

Kitty's brows raised. "You did what?"

Layla wrapped her fingers around her glass, keeping her gaze on the moisture clinging to the sides. "Jamie's a regular at the club, and everyone knows he owns SGR Motors, and that his cousin is here to open a motorcycle branch. It was easy enough to find him."

"You know that wasn't what I was asking. What did you do, exactly?"

"When he suggested I bottom for him, I kind of told him . . . to fuck off."

Kitty laughed. "Oh my God. Really?"

"I'm afraid so." Layla looked up, leaning in and keeping her voice down. "And here's the thing. I realize I'm annoyed because Duff got to me. That's why I went to see him, and it was even worse after. I feel like such a fool, but he hit a sore spot." She sat back in her chair, shaking her head. "You know my history, Kitty—you're one of the few people I've ever told the whole story to. Adrien and Marcel. Vincent. And Jimmy . . . Fucking Jimmy. You know why I can't get involved with a Dom, why I pretty much swore off men almost a year ago. It's been eleven and a half months since I did anything more than fuck some guy for my own pleasure—and that was just the one guy right after things ended in that shitstorm with Jimmy. I sure as hell haven't submitted to anyone. I can't do it. I can't. Never again."

She hated the tears burning behind her eyes. She hated that her long string of bad boys—her long string of mistakes—still had some power over her.

Kitty reached across the table and laid a hand on her arm. "Honey, are you trying to convince me or yourself?"

"Both?" Layla blinked hard. "I don't know. This guy has my head spinning. He's arrogant and sarcastic and . . . fucking gorgeous. And I can *feel* the power in him. As soon as I was in the same room with him, up close, it was as if there was something drawing me in. It wasn't simple chemistry. And as hard as I fought it, I couldn't—not entirely. I had to get the hell out of there. I had to catch my breath. I don't know what's wrong with me."

"I don't think there's anything wrong, hon. Maybe you've just finally met your match."

"Oh!" It came out on a puff of air, forced from her throat by shock and the realization that Kitty could be right, as much as she hated to admit it.

The waitress stopped at their table to deliver their food, giving her a chance to calm down a bit.

As soon as the server left, Kitty leaned across the table toward her. "I am about to tell you something important, Layla Adele Chouset. There is not a damn thing wrong with giving in, with giving yourself over. Isn't that what you told me when you were holding my hand through my early days in kink?"

"But you're submissive."

"Yes. But it's more about the connection than anything else, isn't it? Who we are, the good and the bad, goes into making the connection and the energy people generate between them. That's my understanding of what you told me power exchange is about. Did I get it wrong?"

She huffed out a breath. Kitty was simply parroting the words she'd said to her when she'd been mentoring her friend through her introduction to BDSM, but she didn't want to think about it now, not applied to herself. Instead of addressing the issue she said stubbornly, "I haven't known him long enough to establish a connection. I don't know him at all."

"Maybe you should. Connection can sometimes start as powerful chemistry. And I'd say you two have it in spades, because I have never seen you like this. Never."

Layla shook her head, her cheeks going hot. "I do *not* want to deal with this . . . this *situation*, chemistry or not."

"I think you're gonna have to, honey. This Duff guy is setting down roots in our town, establishing himself at our club. Sooner or later you're going to have to deal with whatever it is between you two. I think you're going to have to face your response to him. Something this powerful? It can't be ignored forever. Especially when you're bound to run into him."

She was afraid Kitty was right, afraid of what Duff brought out in her. Long-buried feelings were rising to the surface, reminding her of times that were better forgotten. People who were better forgotten.

But Duff . . . what was it about him that put all her issues with men in her face? Just another bad boy. Just another Dom. Except no one could ever say Duff Stewart was "just" anything.

He was exasperating. Irritating. And she didn't owe this man a single thing, but maybe she owed herself.

Fuck.

"I can't believe I'm saying this, but I probably need to apologize to him. No, I know I do. As a Dominant myself I should have more self-control. I should be able to exercise better manners. I'll have to swallow my pride and go see him again." She rubbed her forehead. "God*damn* it."

Was it pride that was making her behave like such a bitch? And had she been hiding behind the title of Domme to allow herself to be bitchy with him? Despite the fact that they'd just met—had one conversation!—Duff was making her look at herself and discover some things she didn't like. She could cuss him out all she wanted—to his face or in her own head—but the fact was his mere presence had made her see she still had issues to deal with. And first on the list—always—was personal responsibility for her behavior.

"Kitty, I have to go. Will you forgive me?"

"Of course. Especially if I can have your French toast. Right now it's looking a lot more tasty than my shrimp."

Layla smiled. "It's all yours. Pour some extra syrup on for me." She stood, dropping some cash on the table before leaning over and kissing the top of Kitty's blond head.

Her friend looked up, blue eyes wide. "You sure you're gonna be okay? Because I don't care if the man is nine feet tall and the scariest Dom alive, I will kick his tight, muscular ass into next week if he messes with you."

Layla cracked a smile. "I know. Thanks for having my back, but I'll be okay."

"Just sayin'. I'll let you know how the French toast is. You let me know how the scary-hot Dom is."

Layla shook her head as she made her way toward the door. No one could cheer her up like Kitty. But the smile her friend had put on her face was temporary, at best. She had some big stuff to deal with, and she didn't mean Duff's unusual size.

But oh, his unusual size, and the way that in itself made her feel overpowered by him, made her want to melt into him. *Under* him.

"Fucking world, anyway," she muttered, moving down the street to where her car was parked. "Fucking world. Fucking men. Fucking *me* and my daddy issues that always get me into these messes."

On the drive to Duff's shop she blasted some hard-ass, head-banging grunge metal, trying to drown out her thoughts. It didn't help much. By the time she found parking a few doors down from SGR Motorcycles, her heart was pounding.

She approached the door carefully, reached out to push it open, paused and pulled her hand back, giving herself a moment to cuss under her breath once more.

If the man gloated she'd have to kick him in the balls.

That thought cheered her, and she grabbed the door and swung it open, stepping through.

Duff had his feet up on the desk, leaning back in his chair, a laptop on his knees. He wore the big black boots she loved most on a man, which she did her best to ignore.

"Surfing for porn?" she asked.

He glanced up, doing a double take. "Huh. I didn't expect you to come back so soon."

"I didn't expect to come back at all," she admitted truthfully.

He nodded, and there was some hint of respect in the gesture before he shook himself, closing the laptop and setting it on the desk as he got to his feet. "I'm glad you did."

Lord, he was tall. And gorgeous. And tattooed, which was always a bonus—she could see an amazing steampunk biomechanical piece that looked like a graceful combination of a tree and a compass covering the inside of his right forearm. A forearm that was solid muscle. And the size of his hands . . .

Calm. The fuck. Down.

"Are you?" she asked.

"Yeah, I am. Our last visit didn't go as well as it could have."

She dropped her head. "I know." Looking back up at him—and up and up—she told him, "That's why I'm here. I need to . . . take responsibility for my actions. I'm sorry I was such a roaring bitch."

He cracked a grin, his dimples flashing as he shoved both big hands in the front pockets of his dark jeans. "Were you, now? Could have been much worse, in my estimation."

Her cheeks heated. "You're teasing me."

"Aye. I do love to tease a pretty girl."

She rolled her eyes. "Come on, Duff. We're never going to get through a conversation if you talk to me like I'm one of your adoring subbie girls."

He came around from behind the desk until he stood maybe a foot from her. Lowering his tone as he looked down at her, he caught her gaze with his. "Are you telling me you adore me, Layla? Because I could live with that." He finished with a wink, one corner of his mouth quirking. She was about to argue when he stepped even closer, and God, she could see how long and thick his eyelashes were. How beautifully sculpted his chin was. And he smelled just *right*.

"But you know what I'd like even more?" he went on. "I'd like for us to put this rough start behind us and begin all over again. What would you say to a reboot?"

She blinked. "A reboot?"

"Yeah, a reboot. I'll start." He held his hand out to her. "Hallo. I'm Duff. Recent transplant from Edinburgh, cousin to Jamie, who you appear to already know. Dominant, hedonist and general buffoon, or so my little brother tells me." He grinned. "Your turn."

He motioned with his hand, and she took it, her mind a jangling battle between the pure chemical need to touch him and the wildly ringing alarm bells going off in her head, telling her she was moving into deep water. But when his fingers closed around hers, his enormous hand dwarfing hers, there was a comforting warmth underlying the *zing* of electricity that went through her like a small shock. She had to take a moment to review some of the things she knew about him, having seen him at the club—that he was a responsible Dominant, an excellent player. That he was as tender with his bottoms as he was wicked, which was something she felt was crucial. And there was that edge of gentleness about him and his good humor, contrasting with his hulking frame and natural alpha dominance, that was unlike anything—or anyone— she'd ever run into before. And which frankly made her knees weak.

She swallowed, and let out a breath. "Okay. This is silly

but . . . Okay. I'm Layla. Lifelong New Orleans resident. Hedonist, which you already know. And Domme, as you also already know."

His grin widened. "Very glad to meet you." He leaned in toward her, lowering his voice. "We'll put the head-to-head Dom battle on the back burner for now, yes? Yes."

He straightened up and let her hand go, and she found herself curling her fingers to hang on to some of the warmth, then shook her hands out when she realized what she was doing.

"So, Layla, my shop is closed and I've no need to stay any later tonight—will you allow me to take you to dinner?"

"Dinner?"

"Yeah, dinner. You know—that American custom where people eat in the evening. Or 'tea,' as it's properly called."

She shook her head, cracking a smile. His charming affability was hard to resist. "Is that some sort of peace offering?"

"I was thinking of it more as the first phase of a rather clever seduction, but I fear you've seen through my ruse. Still, it's only dinner. What can it hurt? Say yes."

She cocked her head. "Said the sadist to the fly. But yes, I'll have dinner with you."

The word *danger* flashed through her mind like a chant, but something about the danger itself was alluring.

You are losing your mind.

Maybe. But she was going to have dinner with him anyway.

"I knew you liked me," he said.

"That remains to be seen."

He stepped nearer, until he was towering over her. Bending closer, he murmured softly, "Does it, now? Because I'm fairly certain I felt it when I kissed you yesterday. I'm about to do it again. This is your chance to say no. To use your safe word, if you will. And we'll keep it real simple, given the circumstances. All you have to do is tell me to stop."

God, he smelled like a clean man, like soap and a T-shirt fresh out of the laundry. And beneath it was a faint trace of something dark and earthy that made her mouth water. She couldn't speak. Couldn't pay any attention to the voice screaming in her head to tell him no, to run away. All she could do was tilt her chin to be kissed.

He moved in slowly, pausing when his mouth was a mere inch from hers, his breath warm on her skin. She breathed him in—she couldn't help herself—and even his breath was fresh and sweet in a way that made her dizzy, making her want to drink him in.

She raised her chin a notch. He pulled back the tiniest bit. When she swayed closer he inched back once more. He was making a dance of it. A challenge. Making her allow him to *see* that she wanted it. Part of her wanted to rebel, to be angry, but her body was burning with need.

He moved in once more, his mouth nearly touching hers, and she closed her eyes. Waited. Felt his soft exhale against her lips. Her skin tingled all over. When her eyes fluttered open she found his stunning hazel gaze on hers.

"I thought you were going to kiss me," she said, her voice a husky whisper.

"I am. But it will be in my time. *My* time, Layla."

"Don't . . ." she started.

"Don't what? Don't try to dominate you? I can't help it, you know. If you don't want it, you know what to say. But this is who I am, down to the finest particle."

She shook her head the slightest bit. She couldn't get her brain to work. Her body was taking over completely. No. Duff Stewart was taking over. And something in her fucking loved it.

Don't do this.

He was quiet a moment, watching her, his gaze traveling from hers down to her mouth and back again. She saw him swallow hard and wondered briefly if he was feeling as out of control as she was. But as he wrapped a hand up in her hair and pulled her in to kiss her, her mind emptied.

His fingers burrowed against her scalp, and he pulled hard, commanding her, but his lips were soft and gentle. Just a small kiss, a brushing of lips across hers and her nipples went hard. He did it again, and again and again, and lust shivered over her skin, into the pit of her stomach. When he took her in his arms, she felt the massive weight of his muscles holding her, the hard planes of his unbelievable body as he held her close. And still his mouth was sweet against hers as he licked her lower lip, then traced her top lip with the tip of his tongue. Gently, he opened her mouth, his tongue slipping between her lips, exploring. And she was letting him do it, was kissing him back.

How was it possible that these sweet kisses made her feel more taken over than if his kiss had been brutal? How was it possible that her body was melting into him, her breasts crushed to his massive chest, her hands going to his biceps, which were enormous and dense as granite? And she could feel through his shirt that one of his nipples was pierced, making her want to touch it, pull on it. Take it in her mouth.

When he lifted her and set her on the cool metal desk, she

sighed. He parted her thighs and moved in between them. Kissed her harder, finally. But she wanted it. Needed it. He moved in, pressing his body between her spread legs and she felt the solid ridge of his cock—impressively hard, impressively big—against her mound and found she was wet for him.

She groaned into his mouth. He tilted his hips and ground against her.

Oh, God. Yes.

She felt all control slipping away. All power over the situation, over her own body.

No!

The alarms started to scream in her head and she felt it like a hard kick in her gut. She tore her mouth from his and pushed him away—or tried to. He lifted his head, licked his lips.

Looking down at her, he watched her face for a moment while she tried to swallow past the inexplicable lump in her throat.

"Don't be afraid," he said finally. Quietly.

"I'm not afraid," she lied. "I'm just . . . This is getting out of hand."

He stepped back. "Forgive me." Releasing her, he stepped back a bit farther, offering his hand to her. "Shall we get dinner?"

She was a bit shocked by his immediate apology. By the sudden shift. And assured by the raging hard-on beneath his jeans when she glanced down. She didn't mind that he'd been a bit out of control, too. Not that a Dom was above reproach. But that *this* Dom was a little out of his head—oh, yes, she loved knowing it. Loved it, and felt it gave her a little of her personal power back. Having a man at the mercy of his lust for her was always a bit of a heady power trip.

She closed her thighs, straightened the strap of her tank top, which had fallen down, and pushed off the desk. "Okay. Dinner."

A grin quirked one corner of his mouth, making his cheek crease with that ridiculously charming dimple. "I wasn't sure just then if you'd still have dinner with me."

"Honestly, Duff? I wasn't, either," she answered.

CHAPTER

Two

S HE'D AGREED TO ride on the back of his bike to the restaurant, a Thai bistro in Uptown called SukhoThai, and some
part of him never wanted the ride to end. Her arms were tight
around his body, her soft breasts crushed against his back and
the soft wind of the New Orleans evening blowing across his
skin. He never felt more alive than when he was on his bike,
unless it was when he played at the clubs. But something about
riding with Layla, the trust she put in him to deliver her safely,
her small body close behind him, felt just right.

Maybe it was that hyperresponsibility shit again, part of
what drove him to be a Dom, the kind of Dom who lived by
the Safe, Sane and Consensual credo, as well as Risk Aware
Consensual Kink. But no—it was damn well more than that,
although he couldn't begin to understand it. But what did it
matter? The girl was on the back of his bike, riding through

the night. He had half a hard-on and he was about to fill his belly. Life was fucking good, all right.

He turned onto Magazine Street and parked in front of the restaurant. He held the bike up as she got off; then he kicked the stand down and swung his leg over. Layla was fumbling with her helmet and he reached out to help her unbuckle it, letting his fingers brush her smooth cheek as he slipped the helmet from her head, releasing her glossy black curls. She blinked up at him, her gorgeous, full lips parting; then she licked them—which made him bite back a groan. He was glad to have to take a moment to buckle both helmets to the bike—his throbber had gone from half-hard to full-bore in moments.

Get ahold of yourself, man.

He'd have liked to get ahold of himself, take his rigid dick in his hand and stroke until he came. Relieve some of the unbelievable sexual tension making his whole body vibrate. Damn, but this woman was something.

"Duff? Are we going in?"

"What? Yeah, sure. Of course we are."

He slipped a hand to the small of her back, where the warmth of her skin came through her cotton tank top.

So, so not helping.

Opening the door to the restaurant, he gestured for her to go in before him. As he followed her in she swept her hair to one side, allowing him to check out the tattoo on the back of her neck, a long line of Tibetan script running from the base of her skull to somewhere between her shoulder blades. Beautiful against her caramel skin. He'd have loved to put his mouth there, to lick that line of ink, see if he could make her shiver . . .

He bit back a groan, and had to stay close behind Layla as the host led them through the place to seat them. Duff held Layla's chair, and she looked up at him with a raised brow before settling into her seat.

"What? Is it such a surprise that I'd hold your chair for you?" He sat down across from her. "The majority of American men seem to have lost all taste for gallantry, seems to me. It's a sad state of affairs."

"It is. And they have. Thank you."

He shrugged. "My parents brought me up right. I can say that much for 'em, at the very least."

"I take that to mean you don't have a good relationship with them?"

Shrugging, he folded his napkin into his lap. "Let's just say we don't see eye to eye."

Layla rested her elbows on the table and her chin in her hands, leaning toward him. "Oh, really? And why is that?"

"Nosy lass."

She smiled. "Yes, I am. Are you going to tell me?"

"It's a sad bit of history—I don't know if you want to hear it."

She looked puzzled for a second, her brows drawing together. How had he never noticed how heavy her dark lashes were, framing the big almond-shaped eyes?

"I do want to hear it," she told him.

"Really?"

"Yes, really. Why wouldn't I? This isn't a mercy date, you know."

He let out a chuckle. "You're so used to your subbie boys, aren't you?"

She shrugged. "Subbie *girls*. For the last year, anyway."

"Perhaps sometime you'll tell me why it's only been 'subbie girls.'"

"Perhaps. Don't try to change the subject. You said you'd tell me more about your family."

"Did I? I suppose I did, in a roundabout way."

The waitress came to deliver two glasses of water and hand them menus. Duff thanked her.

"You mentioned you had a brother?" Layla asked when the waitress had gone.

"Yeah, Leith. He's a young one—only twenty-nine."

"That's not so young—he's only two years younger than I am. How old are you, Duff?" she asked.

"Ah, I'm an old man of thirty-three." He paused. "And yeah, I suppose he's not that much younger—it's just that I've always felt so protective of him. Responsible for him. Perhaps more than I should, at times."

Layla sipped her water. "I've never had that problem."

"No? Why is that?"

"I'm the youngest. The baby, I suppose, and certainly treated that way. And my older brother, Charles, is a preacher, like my dad. I'm kind of the black sheep. No one . . ." She looked down at her fingers on the glass, those long lashes resting against her cheeks for a moment before she glanced up once more. "I guess no one expects anything of me. I mean they *do*—or they did—but I've sort of let them down." She paused again, letting out a sharp laugh as she ran a hand through her hair. "God, I don't know where all that came from. Tell me more about your family and Scotland and how you ended up here."

He mentally tucked away the bit of information she'd shared for later, then picked up a menu. "Shall we order first? What do you like?"

"I like everything. What are you in the mood for?"

He waggled an eyebrow. "Dangerous question." He'd been teasing, but his dick wanted him to mean it. Hell, he *did* mean it. The woman was dangerous. To him. Maybe to herself.

She shook her head, laughing as she went back to perusing the menu, and after a minute or two the waitress came back to take their order.

"So," he began once they'd ordered, "to answer your question, I came here to go into business with my cousin Jamie."

"I knew about that. Well, everyone at The Bastille knows who Jamie is, and that you're here to open the motorcycle shop—which is how I showed up there—but I wasn't sure if there was another reason for you to come to the U.S."

"There might have been other incentives. But Jamie and I, we've always been close, even though he's been in the States since he was a kid. If I remember correctly, his family moved here soon after he lost his brother—his twin, Ian—in an accident when he was seven or eight. My dad and Jamie's mum are brother and sister—Americans who came to live in Scotland as teenagers, when our grandfather remarried a woman from Edinburgh, so my cousin and I both have dual citizenship. We were kids together in Scotland, although he's a bit younger. There was a time when we lost touch for a while, but we've always shared a love for speed, for a good engine, and that brought us back together. I've visited here a number of times. I've always liked it here. Loved it, really. There's a magic to this city, but I guess you know that. There's a magic to

Scotland, too, with its castles and myths and legends. But I got damn tired of the cold winters in Edinburgh. And some places hold ghosts." He caught himself before he could finish the sentence. That wasn't a place he wanted to go with Layla. Or at all, truth be told.

"So," he went on, "Jamie opened SGR Motors a few years ago, and he's done well. Rebuilds muscle cars, and does a gorgeous job of it. He's in love with your Mustang, by the way. Anyway, he asked me to join him here to open up a joint venture. I arrived a couple of months ago and we've been focusing on getting the new shop put together, which is a huge pain in the ass, but now I'll be doing what I did in Edinburgh—rebuilding vintage bikes, especially Harleys, only I'll be working for my-self. I've spent pretty much every penny I had on opening the business, but I'm fucking thrilled about it. I think we'll make a good go of it."

"It's a wonderful thing to live your passion. Not many of us get to do that."

"Spoken like a woman who well knows the truth of those words." He leaned forward. "Tell me about your passion, Layla."

He swore he saw a faint blush under the flawless mocha skin, but she blinked it away quickly enough.

"I'm a working artist—a sculptor. One of the many reasons why I'm such a disappointment to my family, even though I make a decent living at it. But they don't understand what a challenge it is to do any sort of art full-time. The last couple of years have been pretty good to me, and I'm grateful. I'm showing in a few galleries—here, in San Francisco, in Dallas.

I've even had some interest from New York. I know how lucky I am."

"Aye, that you are. What medium do you work in?" Layla raised one dark brow at him. "What? Just because I'm a mechanic means I know nothing about art?"

"No. No, of course not. It just took me by surprise. Not that you know about art, but that you expressed any interest in it. Most men couldn't care less about what I do, in my experience."

He reached across the table and took her hand. "Then you've experienced the wrong men. I'm interested in everything about you. Every single detail. And I don't mean to sound like a creep. It's simply the truth."

She watched him, her gaze taking him in, trying to sort him out, he thought. He was trying to sort out his interest in Layla Chouset, too. It had been a long time since he'd courted a girl—if that's what this was. He'd done nothing more than play with girls at the clubs, take them home and fuck them. Nothing more since Bess, with good reason. And little else before her. She'd been his second try at a real relationship and he'd fucked it up good. Again. But why was he even thinking about all of that now? Why was he thinking of the past when this beautiful woman was right in front of him?

"Duff, come on. Don't lay any lines on me. I'm not going to bed with you tonight."

"I never said you were." He stroked her palm with his thumb. "All right? This is you and me getting to know each other. Nothing more."

Her eyes narrowed. "Somehow I don't quite believe that. But . . . I'm okay with us getting to know each other."

He let her hand go as their appetizer—a beautifully presented plate of chicken satay, the skewers laid out over a bed of jasmine rice and Thai basil—was delivered.

"I can live with that," he said, smiling at her over the food. "As a start."

She picked up a skewer of the fragrant chicken, dipped it in the peanut sauce and blew on it. "You think this is the start of something?"

There was challenge in her voice. He'd have been a bit disappointed if there wasn't. But she'd also lowered those heavy lashes, peering up at him through that dark veil. She was definitely flirting, and he liked it.

"Don't you?"

She bit into the chicken, and even the way her lush lips closed around the small bite made his dick hard, as he imagined those lips wrapped around it. He had to shift in his chair.

She chewed thoughtfully. "I don't know, Duff." She gestured at him with the skewer. "I'm not sure I can trust you to behave."

"That all depends on what you consider 'behaving,' my lovely."

"Not talking to me or treating me like one of your little subbie girls, to begin with. Not trying to talk me or seduce me into submitting to you, because that's just not who I am."

There was strength in her voice. Determination. And a small smile on her pretty lips.

"Even though you've had some experience from the bottom end before, I gather from your earlier remark?" he countered.

Her lashes fluttered as she glanced away, then back to him. "A little. And yes, even so."

He tasted the satay, which was quite good. Taking another bite, he licked a little peanut sauce from one fingertip, found her gaze riveted to his mouth.

"You know, they do say the best Tops are those who have bottomed, experienced the sensations if not the mind-set," he said.

"You're going to tell me you've bottomed?"

"Me? Fuck no. Well, not aside from letting another trusted Top or two hit me with a flogger, a whip, a cane, a wooden paddle. While I felt I needed to know what the toys felt like, I sincerely doubt there is any chance I will ever reach subspace. Now Topspace—that's another matter."

"I have a feeling you mostly live there," she muttered into her napkin.

"Ha! I heard that. And yeah, it's probably true. I understand that you do, too—believe me, I get it. The sensation of being energized. The hyperfocus where the entire world narrows down to you and your partner. The need for perfectionism is a high in itself, and even though that's not necessarily a common aspect of Topspace, I have the sense you feel it, too. But you've also been a bottom. Enough that you must have experienced the difference in energy, that floating space. You weren't only a sensation bottom, I feel certain. You were a submissive, even. Yes?"

He held her gaze, trying to see *into* her, to read her unspoken response through pupil dilation, through the slight flaring of her nostrils. Finally she licked her lips, which was another sign in itself, and he knew he'd gotten through the tough shell she wore. A little, at any rate.

"Yes," she said quietly.

He gave a small nod of his chin. "And I can see it didn't sit well with you, or doesn't now, in any case. But . . ." He wiped his hands on his napkin, then steepled his fingers as he leaned toward her, lowering his voice. "I have a thought. What do you say we play a game? We'll pretend you're a bottom. A submissive. Now, it's only pretend, mind you. You can tell yourself it's okay—you can justify it—because you know it's only a game."

Her features hardened. "*Your* game."

"No, it's yours, too. Because we can't play without your consent. That's the only way people at our level of kink can play. The ball is in your court, and *you* have the power. You know that's how it works."

"Why do I feel like you're trying to trick me into something?" she asked even as her features began to soften.

"Layla, I am not hiding my interest in you, sexual, kinky or otherwise. I'm assuming there's some interest on your end, as well, or you wouldn't be here having a meal with me and definitely not having this conversation."

She bit her lip. "Okay. That's fair. But I am really not a submissive. Not anymore, if I ever truly was, which is something I question."

"Okay."

"Okay? Just like that?"

Leaning even closer, he smiled at her. "Are you telling me you want me to continue pressing the issue? I'm more than happy to do that, you know." Her mouth was hanging in a stunned little *O* as he lifted her hand and brushed a kiss across the back of it. He wanted to lick it, to suck each of her delicate fingers, one at a time, slowly, swirling his tongue over the tips in a way that would let her know exactly what it would feel like when he went down on her.

His cock filled, aching with need. But that was all right. He could take it—kind of wanted it, even, this delicious torture. And at that moment, his entire focus was on this exquisite woman before him. Her fire and sass. Her gorgeous green eyes and succulent cleavage. And whatever parts of her body were yet to be discovered.

She exhaled, a slow breath with a small gasp in it. Her voice was so quiet he had to strain to hear her. "Why are you looking at me as if you want to eat me alive?"

"Because that's exactly what I want to do." He kissed her fingers once more, letting his lips linger at the tips for several long moments before looking up at her. "Let me."

LAYLA WASN'T EVEN sure how she'd get through the rest of the evening, but the food came just in time, distracting her from having to answer that last plea. That world-rocking, mind-blowing plea that had left her brain in turmoil and her panties damp.

"Let me."

God, if he'd had any idea of the effect those softly spoken words had on her. But he probably did know. This man was the real thing. A true Dom. And every fiber in his being was geared toward every word, every touch, every glance having a desired effect. Toward breaking a person's walls down. It was working beautifully.

Letting her hand go, he leaned back in his chair as the waitress set their plates down. But he kept his steady hazel gaze on her. Oh, yes, he was very good at this game. She knew he'd be every bit as good at the one he'd just proposed. Better, no doubt.

"You can give me your answer later," he said. "Change of subject while we enjoy our food, shall we?"

She bit her lip again. "Excellent idea."

They started on their meal, and while they ate, he asked her again about her sculpting medium, and then about her musical preferences. They found they had a lot in common, which surprised her—that they both loved hard-driving metal, alternative rock, punk, soul and R&B, and even some rap. But Duff seemed to be full of surprises, and she had to remind herself not to judge a book by its cover. A huge Scotsman could be into rap, couldn't he?

"Now that I'm here," Duff continued, "I really want to get a dog once the buildout on the shop is done and we're open for business." He took a bite of his curry and paused to chew. "Plus, I'm living at Jamie's place for now. I'll need to house hunt at some point, and I mean to find something with a yard."

"I've always wanted a dog, but I can't have one at my place. I want to get a French bulldog and name her Lolita. They have such funny faces. I love the absurdity of it."

"No kidding? Seriously? I've wanted to get a bulldog or maybe a mastiff and call her Lolita." He laid a hand over his heart. "I swear it."

"No—you're making that up," she accused, half teasing him.

"On my honor. Boy Scout's honor."

She narrowed her eyes at him. "You were never a Boy Scout, Duff."

"No, but it did sound good, didn't it? But it's true, about the dog's name."

She laughed. "At least you own up to your lies."

"Ach. White lies meant to amuse you, my lovely."

She couldn't help but smile. "It did amuse me. *You* amuse me."

"Somehow that last sounded a bit condescending, but I'll take it. Might be all I get."

"It might be."

Duff insisted on paying the check, and she had a childish urge to run to the ladies' room and call Kitty for advice. But she was a big girl, damn it, and she could handle this—and him—on her own. Couldn't she?

"Ready to go?" Duff asked.

Maybe she'd get away without finishing the conversation tonight after all. She could use some time to think about it, to figure things out.

"Um, sure."

When she stood he slipped a hand around her waist as they walked outside—a single hand that spanned her entire lower back and the curve at her side. Amazing, the size of his hands. Strong. Powerful. She could only imagine what he could do with them.

Stop it.

She focused on getting into her helmet and onto the back of his vintage bike, which was really quite beautiful, so sleek and shining black, with pewter pinstriping detail. Even the pipes were black, which made the big bike look even more badass. Perfect for him. He started the engine and she held on as he raced through the streets. The thrill of riding on the back

of a Harley was something she'd always loved. Even better
with his big body to hang on to. She'd never touched a man
of his size—had possibly never seen a man of his size, not even
her friend Rosie's Dom, Finn, a hulking blond Australian. But
she had to admit she liked Duff's size—she loved it. There was
a natural command in a guy this big, especially in one with
his utter confidence.

She liked that he was confident enough to make a little fun
of himself—she couldn't bear a man who took himself too
seriously. And she liked that they had so much in common.
They laughed a lot together. She thought she'd laughed more
over dinner tonight than she had all week. Maybe she was the
one who took herself too seriously.

He pulled up next to where her car was parked by his shop
and they both got off the bike. Layla handed him her helmet.
"It's beautiful, Duff. A really fine piece of machinery. Thanks
for taking me for a ride."

He turned back from buckling the helmets to the bike, one
dark brow raised. "I haven't even begun."

"More sexual innuendo?"

"Or an offer for another ride on my bike." Pausing, he
grinned, his dimples flashing, making his full mouth look even
more lush and inviting. "Nah—it was totally sexual innuendo.
But . . ." He paused once more, bit his lip and moved in closer.
"I'm going to kiss you again—and I don't plan to be sweet
about it. Not one bit. I don't think I can be. We'll have to see
where things go from there. Brace yourself."

She'd barely had time to gasp before he pulled her roughly
into his arms, and there was definitely nothing gentle this time.

He pulled her into his body, bringing her up on her toes. His hand went into her hair and *gripped* as his mouth came down on hers in a crushing kiss. She could only sigh as his wet tongue opened her lips, slipped in and explored. And God, his mouth was sweet—sweeter than it had been before, for all the roughness, and some part of her understood that she loved this, loved being handled this way. Taken over. Not too many others could have done it—made her head spin and her body go soft and loose with a simple kiss. Maybe no one else in the world.

Only Duff . . .

Holding her closer, he pulled her tightly into his big body, one hand sliding down her spine, his fingers finding their way between the hem of her shirt and the waistband of her jeans and stroking her bare skin.

Desire was a hard, shivering ache in her body, making her legs tremble. As if every tiny spot on her skin where he touched her lit up with electricity. He lifted her off her toes, until her breasts, her hard nipples, were crushed against the massive wall of his chest. Deepening the kiss, he held her head, controlling it with a tight fistful of her hair.

She moaned into his mouth, her body letting go, and letting *him*.

Fucking. Helpless.

Helpless against his touch. Against the things he was making her feel. Against the way he kissed her—as if he were a drowning man who couldn't drink her in enough. She had never been *consumed* this way by any man.

Finally he released her and set her on her feet. "That'll do for now, I suppose."

"I . . . What?" She pushed her hair from her face, trying to regain her balance.

"Think about what I've proposed. Let me know when you have an answer for me, lovely girl." He ran a finger along her jawline, and it took everything she had not to close her eyes and melt into his touch. "Will you do that for me?"

He'd phrased it as a question, but his easy tone demanded an answer.

"Yes."

He smiled, a twinkle in the depths of his hazel eyes, a half-smile on his face. "That's the only word I ever hope to hear from you. Other than 'please.' But that'll come soon enough, lovely. I can promise you that."

She wasn't even sure how to respond. What did one say to a man who had, in one evening, infuriated her, teased her, kissed her, confided in her, tempted her, then rocked her world so hard with one kiss she could barely believe it had actually happened? But it had. Her bruised lips were proof. Crossing her arms over her chest, she looked down at the ground, pressing her lips together.

Fuck.

Don't take too long to respond or he'll know he has you.

Oh, but he already knew, didn't he?

Damn it.

"So, I'll be in touch," she said.

That was so *not brilliant.*

"I do hope you will. Here, hand me your cell and I'll put my number in."

She did so, not even questioning the command.

"Good. But I need your consent to add your number to mine—I can dial myself from your phone. Yes?"

She nodded. "Yes. Sure."

He handed her phone back to her. "Done. Until later, then. Be safe, lovely."

Lifting her hand, he brushed one more searing kiss across it while she watched helplessly.

He got on the big bike, slinging his helmet on, then gave her a nod and a smile before the engine roared to life and he pulled away. She had a small moment of satisfaction when he glanced over his shoulder to take one last look at her.

When he'd disappeared around the corner she shook herself, fumbled for her keys and got into her car. Part of her wanted to call Kitty, but she needed even more to get home. The siren call of her vibrator collection was impossible to resist. There was no way she could have a sensible conversation until she'd worked some of this tension out of her system. Even if it took all damn night.

She blasted music to get herself home, to keep her mind off her evening with Duff. Not that it did much good. The longer she had to wait to get home and find some relief for her aching, needy body, the worse the need became. Lust was like a flame, licking at her, scalding her, setting her body on fire. By the time she parked in the driveway next to her small cottage, she couldn't wait. She hadn't turned her porch light on, and the night was dark. The main house was on the other side of her cottage, and apparently her neighbors either weren't home or hadn't turned on any outside lights. But as she undid the button on her jeans and slid the zipper down, letting her fingers brush the top of her bare mound, she felt a small thrill at the possibility that someone could catch her.

Biting her lip as she shimmied out of her jeans, she pushed them down past her knees so she could open her shaking thighs. She slid her fingers beneath the lace thong she wore, tracing her swollen lips with teasing fingers while pleasure shivered through her system.

Duff.

In her mind's eye she saw him, his impossibly broad shoulders, the gleam in his eye as he moved toward her. The heat of his touch as he slid his hands up under her shirt, finding her braless. Finding her hardening nipples and smoothing his palms over them, then squeezing until it hurt just a little.

"Oh, yes."

Her hips arched, but she wouldn't allow her searching fingers to touch her clitoris. Not yet.

Closing her eyes, she imagined him slipping his shirt over his head, revealing a tight six-pack and a chest carved from granite. And the beautiful tattoos she'd seen on him when he'd worn a white wifebeater at The Bastille, marking his skin in a way that made her wet simply thinking about the hurting little needle working the ink into his skin.

She gasped, arched, let her fingers press on either side of her needy clit.

Not yet.

"Not yet," he would tell her. "Not until I say you can."

"Yes, Sir," she whispered into the dark, her body trembling, on the edge already. If only he would let her come.

* * *

DUFF PARKED THE bike in front of Jamie's place, swung his leg over and ripped the helmet off his head as he moved toward the front door. He fumbled with his key, found the lock, opened the door and slipped through, slamming it behind him. Standing at the bottom of the old wood stairwell, he leaned a hand against one wall, dropping his head, trying to get it to clear. But all he could see was her. Lust burned through him, leaving rage in its place. The raging need to have her. Kneeling at his feet. Sucking his cock with that gorgeous, plush mouth.

His dick pulsed, swelled, pressing against his zipper.

"Fuck . . ."

Reaching down, he dropped his helmet on the floor, unzipped his jeans, pulled his rock-hard erection out and closed a fist over the throbbing head.

He could see it—Layla's dark hair shining in the dim light from the streetlamps through the dormer window above the door as she sank to her knees right *here*.

He'd tear her top off, freeing her succulent breasts—oh, yes, he knew they'd be succulent, that lovely skin, that full swell of flesh.

He ran his hand down the length of his hard shaft, moaning quietly.

"Take it now," he whispered in the darkness of the stairwell, with no one to hear him but the old building. Or maybe the neighbors who lived downstairs, but he didn't care. Layla was too much in his head. In his blood. In his hard, aching cock. No—not in it. Surrounding his swollen flesh with her mouth.

"Suck it hard," he ordered, making a ring of his fingers and teasing the head of his dick.

He paused, sucking his fingers into his mouth, wetting them, then going back to work on his cock.

"Suck me hard, lovely. Take as much of it as you can. Ah, yeah."

He straightened up, falling back against the wall and using it to support his shaking legs as he began to stroke.

"That's a girl. Harder now. Deeper. Suck me . . . Yeah . . ."

His hips arched into his fisted hand, pleasure roaring through him, making him so damn hard it hurt. He would ravage the girl if he had her there with him. And why didn't he? He was a man who took what he wanted—and he wanted Layla. So badly it was painful, if his poor throbbing dick was any testament.

Layla.

He looked down at his stroking hand and imagined it was her hand grasping the base of his cock, her tongue teasing the head, then sliding down on him as she swallowed him.

"Fuck, yeah."

His balls went tight, sensation causing goose bumps to run up his spine. He gritted his teeth, trying to hold back.

LAYLA'S BREATH CAME out on a long sigh as she slid two fingers into her wet sex.

Duff . . .

"Fuck me, Duff," she murmured, imagining his naked body

held over hers, how he would wrap one arm around her waist and hold her down, helpless while he impaled her.

"Oh!"

She thrust her fingers in hard, her sex clenching around them. Wishing it were him, she began a hard, pounding motion. With her other hand she touched the tip of her clit, and had to swallow a scream as her climax tore through her, a blaze of pleasure that rippled through her entire body, wave after wave. And all the time with his face behind her closed eyes.

"Yes, Duff. Yes, Sir."

"LAYLA . . . THAT'S IT, lovely. Take it deep. I need to fuck your mouth. God, I need to fuck you."

He gripped his cock, stroking savagely—it was the only way to satisfy this burning lust. And with her face, her beautiful mouth, in his mind, he came into his hand, so damn hard he could barely hold himself up as his body shook. Pleasure was a deep rumble in his cock, in his balls, in his belly. It was her mouth, her sweeping tongue, her beautiful body just out of reach, and fuck, he had to have her.

Have to.

"Fuck."

He arched into his fist, over and over, milking it for the last dregs of exquisite pleasure. Finally he was left shivering, his still-hard cock in his hand, a stupid half-smile on his face. But he felt little relief, and knew he wouldn't until he could get his hands on her. His mouth. His cock inside her while he spanked that delectable, fine ass. While he took a cane to her fine flesh, nipple clamps on her sweet nipples. While he grazed her skin with his violet wand, the light arcing, ozone crackling in the air.

Oh, yeah, electrical play with Layla . . .

He was going hard again.

"Goddamn it."

He slammed his free hand against the front door, the pain helping to center him. Shaking his head, he tore his T-shirt over his head and used it to wipe up. He didn't bother to tuck his dick back into his jeans as he took the stairs two at a time.

If he needed to spend the rest of his evening wanking into his palm with Layla on his mind, then so be it. But he would damn well have the girl.

LAYLA SAT PANTING in her car, her fingers still deep inside her, her tight clit still pulsing. She could not believe she'd called him—called anyone!—"Sir," even if it had only been a stroke fantasy. But she had to admit Duff brought something out in her. Something that scared her and turned her on like crazy.

She was still trembling as she slipped her fingers from her body and zipped up her jeans. Letting her head fall back against the headrest, she bit her lip. This kind of thing could not go on. Not that it wasn't hot as hell to bring herself to a shattering orgasm in her driveway. But if this was what the man could do to her by simply talking over dinner, with a good-night kiss, a brush of his hand on her naked skin . . .

As she groaned, her body lit up with need once more. And knew she could barely wait to get in her house and pull out every damn sex toy she owned so she could stroke and fuck her way into satiation. Until she worked Duff Stewart out of her system.

But even as she got out of her car, let herself into the house and made her way to her bedroom in the dark, she knew her toys would only do so much. No, it was Duff she wanted—Duff she *needed*—for some reason she couldn't begin to understand. This kind of chemistry was electric. Impossible. Undeniable. And she was in big, big trouble, with this big, big man.

She flopped down on her stomach on the bed and opened the antique sea chest on the floor next to it that held her vibrators and dildos, her lube and condoms. And one pair of shining nipple clamps. She tossed them aside and went for the biggest dildo she owned, a large pink phallus made of fleshlike silicone.

"I'll bet this isn't even half your size, Duff Stewart," she said quietly, her hand curling around the wide girth of the toy.

With a moan she kicked her way out of her jeans and tore her thong down over her legs. Leaning back against the pile of white lace-edged pillows, she spread her thighs, her knees bent, and reached down to find herself wet and ready. She pulled her knees up and worked the tip of the enormous dildo into the entrance to her sex, her body clenching at it already.

"Fuck me, Duff," she murmured, sliding it in farther.

It was big enough to hurt a little, but she welcomed the pain, and the pain itself made her wetter, allowing her body to open more. She spread her legs wider, pulling her knees higher, and slid the big toy in deep, then pulled it out slowly.

"But *you* would make it fast and hard," she murmured.

She thrust it inside her, desire a hungry animal demanding to be fed—as demanding as he would be. She pulled the dildo most of the way out, then rammed it in deep. Did it again, and again and again, her body bowing to take it all. To take the size of the toy. To take the pleasure rippling over her skin, making her clit swell with the need to be touched, but she wanted to come from the inside. She wanted to come the way she knew she would with him.

"Harder, Sir," she begged, fucking herself with the phallus, deep and fast.

She was panting, writhing, arching up to meet the plunging toy, on the edge of climax in moments.

But Duff would give her pain with her pleasure.

She reached under her top and pinched her nipple as hard as she could. Her back arched, her body rising off the bed, and she cried out as sensation shot through her—pain and pleasure melding in her hard nipple as she let her nails dig in, through her needy pussy as she thrust the giant phallus viciously. Pleasure layered on pleasure, shafting deep inside her. She shivered with it, her body rocking, writhing on the bed. She was coming and coming, the spasms rocketing through her system, making her cry out.

"Duff! Yes!"

When her mind came down from the lofty, spiraling ecstasy of orgasm, she slipped the big dildo from her sex. Her legs splayed on the bed, limp and weak. Her breath still came in rasping pants. And in her head spun images of Duff Stewart. His sharp hazel eyes. His strong, broad shoulders. What she imagined his cock would look like. And just like that, even though her body was too spent to move, desire was like a flare going off in her system, her sex clenching. Wanting.

Her cell phone rang, and she saw it had spilled from her purse when she'd dropped it on the bed. Reaching for it, she saw Duff's name on the screen.

Without thinking, she touched the screen. "Hello?"

"Layla, you sound breathless, pretty girl. What did I catch you in the middle of?"

Fuck. Really?

"Nothing." But even the sound of his baritone voice was making her toes curl.

His tone lowered even more. "It doesn't sound like 'nothing.' Perhaps you're doing some heavy lifting? I know I have been, ever since we said good night. Oh, yes, I know that's more than most people want to know. But we're not 'most people,' are we? Especially not together. No, together we could make a fucking bonfire with the chemistry between us. Tell me it's not true and I'll stop."

Fuck.

Just do it. Or don't.

She bit her lip. Goddamn it—why had she picked up the

phone? Why was he saying these things to her *now*, when her body was still thrumming with climax? When she felt helpless to say no to him? But maybe it was time she stopped running scared. Maybe it was time she said yes to the one man—he'd been right about that—she couldn't say no to.

She blew out a long breath, trying to center herself. It didn't help much. "Okay. But, Duff . . . Look, I am telling you again I'm not one of your little slave girls who'll come kneeling at your feet and following your directives without question."

"I understand that. I don't expect you to be a slave, mine or anyone else's. But if we move forward, you *will* follow my directives without question during play, unless I violate our negotiated terms or you come up against an unexpected trigger or you need to safe-word. You know you would expect the same from anyone who submitted to you."

"Yes. True."

"Yes, you agree to what I just said, or yes, you agree to my earlier proposal?"

She had to grin. "It's more a proposition than a proposal."

He chuckled. "Excellent point, my lovely. So, which is it? Or do we need to talk more?"

She took her lower lip between her teeth once more, then released it—and released some of the tight control she always held over every aspect of her life, and none more than kink. "You promise to stay within any negotiated boundaries?"

"If you don't trust me to do so, then we really don't have any more to discuss here."

"You're right. I'm sorry. I'm not used to being on this end of things anymore. It's been a very long time."

"You can tell me about that when you're ready, other than as it pertains to any triggers. What is your answer, then? You know I need to hear it in plain words."

A small, nervous laugh slipped out. "I'm probably a little crazy for saying this, but yes. Let's do this. I will bottom for you. Submit to you, as much as I'm able. I think . . . I think it's time I worked through some of my issues, and maybe this is the time. Maybe you're the man to do this with."

"Oh, darlin', I can guarantee I am the man to do this with. Now—when can we meet to go over negotiations? Are you available one evening this week?"

God, she was really doing this! She had to buy some time, a minute to breathe.

"How about Friday after you're done with work?"

"Good," he agreed. "Let's meet for coffee at six thirty. You name the place."

She nodded to the empty room. "There's a little place in my neighborhood called Swamp Water. I'll text you the address."

"Excellent. And, Layla? Just in case you had any doubt, I'm very, very glad you've agreed to this."

"To be honest, I'm not entirely certain I am."

"Ah, sure you are, lovely. You're far too strong and decisive a woman to have it any other way."

She found her cheeks heating in a blush, and not because she was still lying half naked, spread-eagled and postorgasm on her bed. She was pleased to know he thought of her that way. Pleased and flattered.

You are behaving like an infatuated teenager.

She cleared her throat. "I'm glad you see me for who I am."

"Oh, trust me—I do."

"Why does everything you say sound suggestive?"

"Probably because beneath everything I say, I'm suggesting something. And you know exactly what it is."

Laughing, she let one hand trail over her breast. Her nipple hardened. "At least you're honest."

"I am that. Until Friday, then. Sweet dreams, Layla. I know mine will be."

Before she could say anything, he'd hung up.

She shook her head. If it had been anyone else talking to her this way she'd have been totally pissed off. But she understood quite well that this was a power play. And she liked it.

Tossing her cell phone on the bed, she sat up and ran a hand through her hair.

"What. The. *Fuck* am I doing?"

Flopping back onto the bed, she pressed her fisted hands against her eyes, but it did nothing but bring the image of Duff's too-handsome face to mind.

"Ugh!"

She almost wanted to call Kitty, but she was still too breathless from coming so damn hard. And a part of her wanted to keep this bit of information all to herself for the moment. Which meant there was nothing else to do but work.

Getting up from the bed, she grabbed from her closet the old faded black sundress she wore when she was working and slipped into it, then her beat-up steel-toed work boots. She gathered her hair and put it up in a clip as she moved into the living room. There she took her studio key from the old lamp it hung on by a long leather cord and stepped outside, crossing the driveway to the big garage she rented from her landlords.

Unlocking the door, she flipped on the lights and took a breath, inhaling the scents of clay and dust, her body already relaxing. Pulling her heavy canvas apron from a row of hooks on the wall, she slid it over her head and tied it in the back, then flexed her hands.

Her converted studio space was a bit primitive, but it suited her. The walls were the old plaster and lath original to the main house, without the benefit of drywall, but she loved the rawness of it. The ceilings were high, with a loft area around three sides and a wide staircase leading up. Colorful Chinese lanterns hung from the rafters, and at one end of the studio was a tattered chaise longue from the 1920s she hadn't had the heart to reupholster. Instead she'd laid embroidered shawls over it and piled it with pillows for her comfort when she needed a place to recline and dream. Since she usually did figurative pieces—people, animals—she had photographs hung everywhere with images of her subjects, as well as images that inspired her work: dogs and cheetahs, house cats and elephants, hawks and alligators. Beautiful photos of human faces from all over the world. Graceful nude figures. And tucked in here and there were bits of vintage fabrics and ribbons, especially the old silk she used for her metal-and-textile insects. They were wildly different from her usual work, from the pieces she'd made a career out of. These small pieces were what had inspired her to learn to weld. But she hadn't shown them to anyone yet. They weren't ready. Or *she* wasn't ready.

She turned to the large shelves that lined most of one wall, holding her supplies and tools—and her insects draped in canvas. But she didn't want them tonight. Her gaze was pulled to the enormous wooden table in the center of the room her friend Martin, who owned the community artists' foundry she used to cast her pieces, had built for her. Her latest project sat there, and she almost felt as if it were taunting her, but she didn't want to work on it tonight, either. Wiping her hands on her apron, she blew out a breath. She had no idea what she wanted to work on—all she knew was she'd feel better once she had her hands in the clay.

Moving to the shelves, she cut a fresh slab of the red clay she kept on hand and carried it to the table, where she set it down, then pulled her wooden work stool closer and perched on the edge. Reaching for the shelf below the table's surface, she grabbed the wire she used to make armature, her wire shears, a bottle of water. Pouring some of the water into the ceramic bowl she kept on the table, she took in another long breath as she looked over her materials, waiting for something to come to her. But all she could see was his face. His hands. The breadth of his muscular shoulders. Him in that black kilt she'd first seen him in. His mouth . . .

Duff.

"Fuck."

She got up abruptly, moving back to the shelves, where she turned on her iPod speakers. The sweet, moody tones of Édith Piaf made her shoulders drop, and she closed her eyes, losing herself for a moment in the music. But the French chanteuse's sultry voice brought her mind back to Duff, making her remember the fantasy swimming through her mind, her body, as she'd brought herself to orgasm earlier.

"It seems there will be no escaping you," she muttered. "So . . . I won't."

Turning decisively back to the table, she took her seat and began to mold the wire. In only a few minutes she had the basic shape, and began to lay the clay over it, sculpting the musculature, which was her usual process, then the flesh, which would bring out the detail, the personality of the piece. Her shoulders loosened as she worked the clay, as the music shifted from Édith Piaf to Lana Del Rey and then to Janis Joplin. She loved the feel of the clay between her fingers, working without tools—only her bare hands. It was a sensual experience, and she *needed* it to be tonight. Getting up from her stool and shoving it back in order to gain a different perspective on the piece, she smoothed her palm over the awakening shape, stroking it, working more texture into the form.

"Oh, yes, that's it," she murmured, in the groove now as Etta James, another powerful, strong female singer, filled her studio with music.

Outside, thunder rolled, and soon she heard rain pattering on the roof, felt the damp in the air. It was one of the many things she loved about New Orleans—the sound of thunderstorms, the way it changed the texture of the air. And it always made her studio feel even more like a cocoon.

She had no idea how late it was when she was done. Her hands had the lovely, familiar buzz from working the clay, and she had to forcibly pull her head out of the creative space it had floated in for hours. Staring at the detailed phallus on the table, she wondered how closely it might resemble Duff's. But she didn't mind if it represented nothing more than the heat burning through her body, a heat inspired by him. This piece was erotic—erotica—in visual form, telling her the story she knew deep in her bones, and that was all she needed to know.

Smiling to herself, she wiped her hands on a towel. And knew she had to get back in the house and find her toys once more. Twice more. Because the heat filling her system like smoke on flame needed release. There was no denying what the man was doing to her, mind and body. And getting herself off until she managed to exhaust herself was going to be a full-time occupation until she saw him again. Until she had him. Or, more accurately, under these circumstances, until *he* had *her*.

She traced one fingertip over the clay phallus, feeling every ridge, every vein. "Oh, yes, Duff Stewart. You've definitely won this round."

FRIDAY EVENING DUFF was just about to lock up the shop when Jamie stepped through the door that joined their side-by-side offices.

"Hey, you want to grab some dinner with Summer Grace and me?" his cousin asked.

"Can't tonight."

"No? What do you have going on? You going to The Bastille? We might end up there later."

He shrugged. Why didn't he want to tell Jamie what his plans were? It wasn't the kind of thing he'd ever kept private from his cousin before. "Actually, I'm seeing Layla."

Jamie's brows arched. "Are you? You two kiss and make up?"

"Something like that."

Jamie stepped forward and leaned over Duff's big desk. "You're awfully closemouthed when I'd have figured you'd be crowing from the rooftops about your victory."

Duff rubbed a hand over his stubbled head. "I wouldn't call it a victory just yet. I'll know more after we talk tonight."

"Talk? You're not usually the talking kind. No offense, cousin."

"Oh, I know what I am, and no offense taken. But this girl . . . Well, fuck, Jamie, this girl is a whole different thing."

Jamie straightened, grinning at him. "We told you she would be."

"Yeah. But maybe not quite in the way you warned me about. She's tough enough, and all that. But . . ."

"But what?" Jamie waited a beat, then leaned in again. "You're smitten, cousin."

"What? Fuck off, Jamie."

"You are! Jesus. Never thought I'd see the day. You were never like this over Bess. Not even that crazy chick Eileen. How many years has it been?"

"Yeah, well, really fuck the hell off, cousin, and thanks for mentioning them."

"I will fuck the hell off. Just as soon as you tell me why your panties are in such a wad."

Duff rubbed at his head again, blowing out a long breath. "Stupid American saying, that," he grumbled. "Particularly since I always go commando."

"It is stupid. I have more of them, if you like. Or you can choose to fess up."

"Fine. Fuck. Whatever." He paused, tapping his fingers on the edge of the desk. "So, I'm meeting her for a coffee and we're negotiating."

"What? Seriously?"

"Serious as death and taxes."

"Tell me again why you getting exactly what you wanted is turning you into such a dick?"

Duff pounded both fists on the desk, making the pens he had scattered there jump. "Goddamn it if I know. Ridiculous, right? Right. Fuck."

"You're nervous. Wow. You're nervous because you like her."

"Maybe I am. We can stop the grand goddamn inquisition anytime now, cousin," he growled.

Jamie raised both hands in surrender. "Okay. I'll stop giving you a hard time. I guess I'll just have to wait until you show up at the club to see how things went. Or maybe you'll stop being so weird and talk to me like you always do."

"Yeah. Maybe. Look, I don't know what my problem is. I need to see her. Then maybe I can work it out in my head. And then maybe—*maybe*—we'll talk. Sorry for being such an arse." Duff glanced at the clock high on the wall and got to his feet. "Gotta go, cousin. Lock up for me?"

"Sure," his cousin agreed.

Jamie gave him a hard pat on the back as Duff moved past him toward the front door. By the time he was on his bike and gunning the engine around the corner, he wanted to kick himself a bit for his behavior. But he knew Jamie understood that he needed to work through this himself. His cousin was right—getting to play Layla was exactly what he wanted. And he'd been through dozens of negotiations—hell, maybe hundreds—with gorgeous girls. It wasn't as if this was anything new. But still . . . there was one new factor, and that was Layla herself. And he had to admit he'd never wanted a woman the way he wanted her—so deep in his belly it made his gut ache to think about her. So badly he'd wanked off a good six or eight times a day since the first time they'd spoken—twice in the bathroom at the damn shop in the middle of the day. His dick was sore as hell, but it didn't matter. He couldn't seem to stop. Even porn wasn't doing it for him these days, which was saying a hell of a lot.

He followed the GPS on his bike and pulled up across the street from the Swamp Water Café on St. Claude Avenue, glancing over to see if he could spot her. And sure enough, there she was, standing on the sidewalk in the shade of a tree. She was wearing a short red dress and sandals, her hair up in a tumble of dark curls on top of her head and tied with a floral print scarf, the ends of it stirring in the faint breeze, brushing her shoulder. How she managed to look so fresh and so exotic at the same time was beyond him. And sexy. As fucking sexy fully dressed as any other woman was naked.

Layla naked.

He growled, shifting against the growing hard-on beneath his blue jeans, silently cursing at it to go down so he could get off his bike. A few moments later he was able to draw in a breath and swing his leg over, taking his helmet off and clipping it to the bike seat before striding across the street.

But the closer he got, the more his dick hardened again, and he had to give himself a good internal cussing to get it under control.

"Goddamn fucking ridiculous, this," he muttered, pulling off his leather jacket to hold in front of his growing crotch. "What are ya, a twelve-year-old lad? Fucking. *Control.*"

Luckily he was done grumbling by the time she looked up to see him, and when she did his chest went tight at the light in her eyes, eyes like emeralds in the gleam of the setting sun. She smiled and his dick stiffened even more, his chest doing that tightening thing at the same time, leaving him fucking confused and his brain entirely drained of blood.

Get a grip, man.

Ach, he'd like to grip, all right. On his hard dick. On her body. And the things he would do to her once he had her under his hands were too scandalous to contemplate in a public place.

"Save it for later. Because there damn well *will* be a later," he grumbled under his breath.

He cleared his throat as he approached her. And to get his head back on straight—and to make sure hers was straight, too—he strode up to her, wrapped a hand around the back of her neck and kissed her hard. Harder than was strictly necessary, and his grip was rough, too. But he needed it—to feel her, taste her. He didn't care that they were standing on the sidewalk in front of a café with other people milling about.

When she opened her lips for him and moaned softly, he slid his other arm around her waist and pulled her in close, knowing she could feel his erection. Fuck it. Let her feel it. But it was far too good, and unless he planned to take her down right there on the sidewalk, he had to stop.

He pulled his body back, tore his mouth from hers and whispered against her lush, pretty lips, "Well, hello there, lovely."

She laughed. "You are . . . Jesus, Duff, you are an original."

He loved hearing the desire rough in her voice—every part of him, not just his ever-hard cock.

"I am that. But so are you, sweet Layla. Shall we go in and have some tea and talk?"

"Tea and talk with the incorrigible Duff Stewart?" she asked with a teasing light in her eyes. "Isn't that rather like having tea with the Devil? But yes, let's. I sort of like the idea of having tea with the Devil."

"Adding a mark to the ledger, princess. Your ass may have to pay for that later. If we're able to come to agreement, that is."

"If I agree to let you take it out on my ass? Hmm . . . maybe. But I do like the title of 'princess.' Or you may refer to me as 'Your Highness.'"

"You are really asking for it, aren't you?"

Her smile was saucy—as saucy as she was. "Depends on how this talk goes."

He shook his head as he opened the door of the funky café, with its barn-wood walls and iron-and-wood tables, the alligator and deer bones mounted everywhere. He liked the place. He also liked how damn good this girl made him feel. That she seemed to have gotten to a space where she was simply accepting his dominance, without appearing any less strong herself.

At the counter they ordered iced coffee for her, iced tea for him. He paid, despite her protests, and carried both drinks to a table in the back. Luckily there was enough room, with the tables close by being empty, that he could fit his big body into the chair and stretch his legs out. He was just as glad there would be no one else nearby to overhear their conversation.

"Cheers," he said, clinking glasses with her.

"Cheers," she answered, taking a sip of her coffee. "So, how are things going at the new shop?"

"Quite well. Thank you for asking. But is that what you really wanted to know?"

"What? Of course. I mean, why wouldn't I?"

"Because I can see from the way your pulse is beating at the base of your throat that what you really want to know is when we're going to get down to the business at hand."

She arched one elegant brow, but he could tell from the pink flush rising on her cheeks that he'd hit it on the mark.

"Not even any small talk first?"

"All right, then. How was your day, Layla? How is your work coming along?"

She really did blush then, the pink turning to scarlet under her creamy brown skin. She glanced away momentarily, and he wondered what sore spot he'd happened upon by chance.

"Okay. Let's skip the damn small talk," she said.

He sat back in his chair, took a slug of his iced tea. "Ah, that's more like it. I knew you'd see things my way." He finished by sending her a cocky wink and a grin.

"You really are incorrigible."

"I'm a lot of things." He set his glass down and leaned in, taking her hand in his with just the tips of his fingers. Keeping his voice low, he said, "I am, Layla. I am a Dominant. A sadist. A creative player. An intuitive player, or so I'm told, and it's something I aim for. I'm a wicked, wicked man who has only the most evil intentions when it comes to you. And I believe those are the very things you like about me. But I am also utterly responsible in my kink practice. So shall we bypass all this other nonsense and begin our negotiations? Tea with the Devil?"

He watched her swallow hard. All of the feisty humor seemed to have gone out of her for the moment. She blinked a few times, and he waited to see if she'd pull her hand away—he had only the gentlest of holds on it. But she didn't move.

She said in a small voice, "Yes. Let's get started."

Smiling, he caressed her fingertips with his and watched as her shoulders relaxed. "Right, then. This is how we'll go about it. I'm going to ask you a series of questions, and for each one you will tell me if you've ever tried it as a bottom or as a Top, and how you felt about it from either end. Then tell me if it's a yes, no or maybe. Easy, yes?"

"We'll see."

Keeping his hand over hers to help read her, he said, "We'll start easy enough, get some of the basics out of the way. Rope bondage?"

"I don't tie well, so I usually use leather or metal cuffs as a Top. I've been tied a few times, but really more as a practice exercise. It doesn't do a lot for me. But I suppose it's a maybe." She shrugged. "Maybe one of these days I'll understand the thrill other people get out of it. I think it's not enough sensation for it to really register with me. And since my experiences with rope were more about letting friends practice their knots, there wasn't much of a power exchange. I suppose I don't know how I'd respond if that element were a part of it, but the idea has never been one I've lingered on."

"Answered very thoroughly," he commented.

Her gaze was direct, a little challenging. "I've been through negotiations a time or two, you know."

"I do know. I am not underestimating your experience as a Top, as a Dominant. But I'm much less clear on what bottoming was like for you. Along with your limits and desires, I'll need to know more about your experiences as a bottom and as a submissive—the submissive headspace you reached, as well as any sensation play you've done, which as you know can be two separate things."

She glanced away, looked back at him. "There may be a few things I don't want to discuss with you."

"The submissive part? Yes? All the more reason why that discussion will be necessary, princess. But let's get back to other matters for now. What are your feelings about and experiences with impact play?"

"I've done a lot of it, as a Top and a bottom. I'm fairly good with a flogger—"

"I'd say better than good," he interrupted. "I've seen you Florentine. Your double-handed rhythm is flawless."

"Okay, better than good—I'll take the compliment. I can also crack a singletail, and have a small collection of whips. As a Top I've used paddles, slappers, canes, English tawse. As a bottom I've experienced most of those things."

"And?"

"And I like stingy sensation more than thud."

"Hmm."

"Hmm, what?"

"In the UK, anyway, they say sting is a more sophisticated taste than thud."

"They say it here, too, but I'm not so sure about that. It's simply what my body responds to."

He leaned in once more. "And how is that, exactly, Layla? Does it make goose bumps rise on your flesh? Your heart pound?

Does your body twitch as it resists anticipating each strike? Does it release all those lovely brain chemicals—endorphins, dopamine, serotonin, oxytocin—that make you fly?"

She swallowed, blinked once, color rising again in her smooth cheeks. "Yes. All of that. Or it did at one time."

"So, are these things a yes, a no or a maybe?"

"Yes to all of it," she said without hesitation, making him smile.

"Excellent. Now what about electrical play? Be sure you answer honestly."

"I don't use it as a Top, and never as a bottom. It . . . it scares me, to be honest."

"Honesty is what I want of you. But are you telling me no?"

She swallowed again, bit her lip. "I don't know."

He watched as the pulse ticked in her throat. Her pupils were enormous, and she'd crossed her arms over her chest.

"The electrical really scares you," he said.

"Yes. It does."

"But it's a maybe—is that it?"

She nodded. "If I'm going to do this, then I may as well face some of my fears."

"I think doing this at all is facing your fears."

Her green eyes went dark and stormy. "Damn right it is. And while we're talking about some of my hard limits, I will not bottom at the club. I'm known as a Top there now, and I prefer to keep it that way. I am absolutely not going there and bottoming in front of other people."

"Agreed. It's one of my favorite things, you know— electrical play. But I understand it's not for everyone."

"I've seen you with a violet wand at the club. With Tasers. I really don't like the fucking Tasers. That is *not* happening."

"I'll make note of it."

She nodded.

"You're beautiful when you're angry," he told her. It was true, with her flushed cheeks and her green eyes blazing, the square set of her shoulders. But then, she was always beautiful. Beyond beautiful, this woman.

"Is that a distraction technique?" she asked, still huffing.

"Merely making an observation," he answered, only half a lie. "Tell me about your limits."

"Aside from the usual—scat, anything nonconsensual, anything involving minors, risky cross-contamination—my hard limits are humiliation, age play, anything that leaves a permanent mark, marks that can't be hidden with clothing, foot worship, needles, and I will not sleep with you just because we play."

He ignored her comment about sex. For the time being. "I notice you didn't mention knife play."

"That's because knives are not a hard limit."

"Interesting. Fear play with a blade? Scratching? Actual cutting?"

"Scratching is fine. And fear play. I'm not really afraid of much, and I sort of like the idea of pushing that boundary."

He grinned. "I'm sure we can find something for you to be afraid of."

"And I'm sure you know saying that to me will mess with my head."

"Of course. But don't you find that negotiations are really the beginning of play? That even discussing what we will and won't do is a little thrilling? That it all really begins here?"

He sat back in his chair, and without waiting for her to answer he said, "Tell me about your triggers."

"Why did you wait until after negotiating specific toys and acts to ask me about triggers?"

"Because sometimes your response to a question—your body language—tells me more than you can with words. Most people hold the real truth about their triggers back, or aren't aware of them enough to verbalize clearly. But you're a Domme—and a good one, from what I hear, and from what I've seen at The Bastille, so you must already know that."

She nodded. "I do. I wanted to see if you did."

He arched an eyebrow. "Testing me, are you?"

"Maybe a little."

Leaning forward, he caught her gaze with his. Hers looked a little haunted. A little wary. He kept his tone low. "You have to trust me, Layla, or this is not going to work."

"I trust you as much as I can any man," she answered with a small shrug.

He sat back. "Ah, there it is. But you can, you know. I take the responsibilities of dominance and play very seriously. It's the only way I can do it. It's part of the reason why."

"Is it? Why is that?"

Blowing out a breath, he scrubbed a hand over his head. "We all have our pasts, don't we? Let's just say being a Dominant fills up a part of me that needs it—needs to *feel* responsible, to be behaving responsibly, if that makes sense."

"It does. I'd still like to know what it's about. That sort of real need to be responsible? That kind of hyperresponsibility? It's not a bad thing, not at all, but there has to be something in your history that's made you feel that way."

"You're too used to interviewing your subbies, aren't you? But I'll tell you a bit about it, if only because I don't believe there can be a power exchange without the 'exchange' part." He leaned back in his chair, playing with a paper napkin on the small table, rolling it between his fingers. "I suppose I've let people down in the past. Too many people. And they've paid a price for it. So have I. This is my redemption, of sorts. But what is kink if it doesn't redeem us? Aren't we all looking for the structure and the pain and the release to cleanse our souls in some way?"

"Wow."

"What?"

"I guess—and don't take this the wrong way—I just didn't expect anything so profound to come out of your mouth."

"I'm a big lug. I know it. And believe me, it was more than I expected to say, as well. But I do have a deep thought now and then, in between visions of Harleys, sandwiches and sex, not necessarily in that order."

She smiled, and he was reminded why her gorgeous mouth made him hard. "Yes, you do."

"Does knowing I have my vulnerabilities make you more comfortable with me?" he asked. "With the idea of us playing together?"

She stared at her glass for a few moments, stroking her fingers over the side, wiping drops of condensation away with her thumb. And even though negotiations were serious business, he couldn't help but imagine it was his cock she was stroking.

Focus, damn it!

"We all have our vulnerabilities," she said with a small

shrug. "I've found that's a big part of what makes up the kink dynamic. But maybe it does make me a little more comfortable." When she glanced back up at him, her gaze had gone a bit hard. "Maybe I feel like I have some sort of control still, if you have a chink in your armor. It evens the playing field a little."

Ah, he could see the admission of her own vulnerability was making her feel just that. Well, it did him, too. But this conversation was necessary—more with her than with anyone else he'd played with before. He didn't want to look at it, though. No, better that he keep forging ahead. There would be time for a dark night of self-reflection if he really must go that route. Not his usual style, but things with Layla were different already. He had a feeling there was more of that ahead. Which made this woman feel dangerous to him—not something he was used to; that was certain. Apparently it was something he liked.

"I can assure you I have many chinks, as we all do, just as you said. Why do you feel the need to retain control as a bottom?"

"For the same reasons the whole concept of bottoming freaks me out."

"Fair enough, my mysterious, clever beauty. For now." Reaching across the table, he stroked her cheek, was pleased to see her lashes flutter, to see her full lips part in surprise. To feel the slight leaning of her face against his hand. "I'll let the rest go for the moment. But I know you understand that bottoming is, in some sense, at least, about being broken down. It will be my job to do just that. My job and my great pleasure. I want to see what makes you tick, princess. I want to discover what turns you on, what frightens you, and what's behind it all. Oh, I know you don't want to tell me. But you will. In your own words, in your body's response. You won't be able to help it."

She looked up at him, a small fire back in her eyes. "Is that a challenge?"

"It's a promise. Do you know what else I can promise?"

"What?"

"That you'll like it. No. That you'll love it."

She simply stared at him, her pupils going wide. Then she shook her head, her shoulders dropping. "Fuck," she muttered.

"What is it?"

"I just have to stop fighting it. I know that. But it's going to be a hell of a struggle for me. I don't fucking like this part."

"I understand that. I'll also enjoy every second of it."

Layla rolled her eyes. "Of course you will."

He chuckled. He couldn't help himself. He was too delighted with her. Layla Chouset was going to be a goddamn wildcat, and he fully expected to get scratched. But he'd like it. No. He'd love it.

He grinned at her, then sent her a saucy wink, making her roll her eyes again. Oh, yes, he had this woman exactly where he wanted her. And it was going to be so damn good he could hardly stand to wait.

"S O, WHEN ARE you going to take me for a ride in your Mustang?"

Layla smiled at the sudden change in subject. This man liked to do everything he could to keep her off-balance, and for once she wasn't entirely certain she was up to the challenge he presented—to the many challenges he presented. But this fact in itself was intriguing. Provocative, in every sense of the word. That and his lethal dimples combined with his bad bad-boy giantness and the dominance that seeped from every pore were more than she could resist. She'd given herself over to that fact when they'd talked the other night and she'd agreed to meet him here. But that didn't mean she wasn't still going down without a fight. As much as she could manage to muster in the face of this man. *This* man.

She sighed.

Just handle it. Be your badass self.

"Are you done with your tea, Duff? Because we can go for a drive right now."

Yes. Get behind the wheel. Grab for some last scrap of control.

Jesus, she'd really lost it.

Duff took one final swallow, then got to his feet, offering her his big hand. "Let's go."

She had to admit she loved the way he kept his hand at the small of her back as he guided her through the crush of tables and out the door, then down the sidewalk until they reached her red convertible Mustang, where it was parked beneath a streetlamp.

Duff let out a low whistle. "She really is a beauty." Glancing up, he said, "Just like her owner."

To fight off the blush heating her cheeks, she said, "You don't have to try to seduce me, Duff. I've already agreed to play with you."

"Oh, there will still be seduction, princess. But I don't pay empty compliments. No need to. And this ride is fucking something." He walked around the back of the car. "Dual tailpipes. Nicely chromed. Good chrome rims, too. Quality stuff." Moving around to the driver's side, he took her keys from her hand and opened the door, holding it for her. "Shall we?"

She slid onto the black leather seat, took her keys from his offered hand and started the engine up.

"Love that low rumble," he remarked as he got in on the passenger side. "Two eighty-nine V8 in the '66, yes? Yeah. I'd bet there's a lifter cam to get more power, from the sound of 'er. Very slick car. I like the Fastback, too, but this model gives me more headroom with the top up. But I'm glad you've got it down. It's a beautiful night. Let's take her out and feel the wind in our hair."

Layla grinned. "Duff, I hate to tell you this, but you have no hair."

"I have a little scruff on the old dome. And I have quite the eyebrows, I'm told."

"You want to feel the wind in your eyebrows?"

He smoothed a hand over his head. "You work with what you've got. And I've got other qualities. Too much charm in one man could be lethal, hence the shaved head. Balances the world out a bit."

She laughed as she shifted, then signaled and pulled onto the street. As she headed down St. Claude they were both quiet, enjoying the ride as the rich, sultry tones of Jill Scott played from her iPhone hooked through the car speakers. Eventually she hung a right on St. Bernard and caught the 10 south, heading toward the center of the city. She opened the engine up, and the familiar roar purred through her body.

"Ah, there she is," Duff said so softly she could barely hear him.

He said it as if he were talking to a lover with approval, coaxing her, seducing her, and she didn't know if that low tone was aimed at her or her car. But it almost didn't matter. It had the same effect either way. Suddenly she was acutely aware of the powerful engine rumbling beneath her, making the seat vibrate—making her vibrate in all the right places. Between her thighs. In the steering wheel beneath her hands.

Deep in her belly. And it was a huge turn-on—the power of the car, and controlling that power, next to the man she was going to hand her power over to. She had to bite back a groan.

Focus on the road, woman.

When the 10 turned into the Pontchartrain Expressway she pressed down on the gas, and the wind whipped around her head, her curls bouncing against her cheeks.

"Beautiful," he murmured, and once more a shiver of lust went through her.

Turning to him, she marveled at how finely carved his profile was, silhouetted against the amber lights from the highway as they flashed by: the square jaw, fine jawline, high cheekbones. Handsomest damn man she'd ever seen. She had to force her eyes back to the road.

"Layla."

"Hmm?"

"The speedometer only goes up to one-forty. Can this baby go any faster?"

"Yeah, it can. But we'd have to wait until at least midnight before I'd dare race on the highway."

"Another time, then," he said.

It warmed her up inside for some inexplicable reason—that there would be another time. That he wanted there to be.

"Come on. Let's see a little taste of what your girl can do."

Laughing, she hit the gas and felt the world rush by. Duff let out a hard chuckle, and she knew he was feeling that same deep pleasure at the power of the car, at the freedom of speed.

"You're a bad influence—you know that, don't you?" she yelled over the roar and the wind, easing up on the pedal a bit.

"I try."

She turned to glance at him once more, found his gaze on her and a grin on his face.

Oh, Lord, those dimples.

As she turned back to the road, she felt a wet drop on her cheek. "Damn it, it's starting to rain."

"Pull off here."

She got off at the next exit, and Duff got out to put the top up while she wiped down her leather seats with a towel she kept on the backseat.

He got back in the car. "Hey—how far is this City Park I keep hearing about?"

"The park? Not far. You want to go to City Park at eight o'clock at night? You can see a lot more during the day."

"All of New Orleans is better at night, or so it seems to me. Or maybe that's the morbid Scotsman in me. But I also may have heard that the café there is open twenty-four hours. Something about the best beignets in the city. Why don't we go wait out the rain there?"

"You're right. New Orleans *is* better at night—I've always thought so, too. Well, not better. Maybe simply more suited to me. I can feel the old magic of the city after dark, you know?"

He nodded, smiling just enough for one devastating dimple to crease his cheek. "We are on the same page, my lovely. Take me there."

It was a request as much as it was a command, but she didn't mind the command part—that was the part that made her all soft and shivery. She started the car and turned around, driving back toward the city.

"Who did you hear about the beignets from?"

"Jamie. Well, his girl, Summer, actually. Do you know her?"

"A bit. We've run into each other at the club, and chatted a few times. I like her."

"I'd have thought you might. She's a spitfire, that one."

"So she is," Layla agreed.

"So are you."

"You don't even know the half of it," she told him, grinning as she maneuvered the car over the wet streets.

"Not yet. But I've seen enough of a preview to understand you're no pushover. Don't ever think I'm that delusional. And I'm not interested in a pushover. Not since I met you."

"Am I supposed to swoon at your feet now? Imagine that I'm the first woman you've said something like that to?"

He was quiet a moment. "You are, in fact."

"Wh—" She had to stop herself. She didn't know how to respond. He couldn't have meant that. And yet, apparently he did. She bit her lip.

"Are you surprised?" he asked. "Well, so am I, to be honest, but there it is. Ah, I see the place."

Glad not to have to explain herself—or for him to have to explain any further—she pulled into a spot in front of the Morning Call café. Through the rain the red-and-blue neon sign seemed washed in color, and she had to squint to make out the shape of the giant coffee cup with the words "Open 24 Hours" beneath it.

Shutting off the engine, she turned to him. "Ready for a good soaking?"

"No one in this town seems to carry an umbrella, no matter that it rains without a moment's notice on a regular basis."

"A little rain never hurt anyone."

"Watch it, princess—you're speaking to a Scotsman. *We* know rain."

"Well, I'm no Southern belle who will melt in the rain, either. I'm a Creole woman, and we're a whole different kind of South. And does this really have to be a competition?"

Duff arched one dark eyebrow. "Apparently it does. But again, marks on the ledger, missy."

She shook her head to hide her pinking cheeks. "Okay. Fine. Whatever."

Before he had a chance to realize what she was doing, she clicked out of her seat belt and bolted from the car, her keys grasped in her hand. The rain was a hard pelt against her skin as she ran, laughing—then laughing even harder when Duff caught her around the waist, lifting her off her feet and hauling her to the covered patio of the café before setting her down.

"Oh my God—you're such a damn caveman."

Duff was wiping the rain from his eyes with the back of his hand. "I like to think of myself more as a noble knight responding to a damsel in distress."

"Is that why you call me 'princess'?"

"Nope."

She shook the rain from her hair. "Why, then?"

He moved in close, then closer, until he had his hands around her waist and was whispering in her ear. "Because I plan to treat you like a princess. To play you like a princess, the way you need to be played. And then I plan to fuck you like a princess. Like the dirtiest princess ever born. Like it was a fucking royal proclamation. Because in my mind, it is."

"Jesus, Duff."

She didn't know if she was mad or madly turned on. But

when he leaned in and kissed her, all question was erased from her mind. All she knew was their lips cool with rain, warming up so fast her mouth tingled with the heat. Then her body followed suit as he pulled her in, his arms tight around her. And nothing had ever seemed this sexy—no memory. No moment. No man.

He kept one hand on her waist—that was all he needed to span her lower back—and with the other he smoothed his palm over her shoulder, sliding it into her hair and clasping the back of her neck. And all the while his mouth was working magic on her—lips and tongue and even his teeth as he nibbled here and there.

Sighing, she let her body sort of fall against his. And sighed again as her breasts came into contact with a wall of solid muscle, as her hips pressed against the growing erection under his rough jeans—then moaned when he yanked her in hard, growling into her mouth. She swore she could feel it in her throat, that primal growl. Knew the animal hunger that was *him*. Feeding her hunger. Feeding *her*—something inside her she hadn't known was there. And she didn't care how foolish it was to think these things. She shut her brain down and simply *felt*, fell into the moment while the cool rain fell all around them.

He groaned and pushed her back, one step at a time, until she was up against one of the pale brick pillars. And then he started to pinch her. One small pinch on the outside of her thigh. Another at the curve of her waist. Another on the inside of her forearm. It didn't even hurt much, but it made her understand on some nearly cellular level his authority over her, that this was exactly who he was. No put-on. No grandstanding.

The man who was kissing her like a demon was truly the most dominant human being she'd ever met. And every inch of flesh, everything in her, wanted him. Craved him. Was nearly screaming for him.

Her thighs shook as need washed over her, stinging in her sex, her nipples.

Fucking want him. Now. Now, now, now.

The doors to the café swung open and a young couple walked out.

"Oh, pardon us."

Duff pulled his mouth from hers, flashing them a grin over his shoulder. His hard-on was still pressed tightly against her. "Sure, no problem, friends."

The couple hurried away, and despite the sharp arousal rattling her system—or maybe because of it—Layla had to laugh.

"I like how you assured them you weren't bothered by them walking out of the café, like they'd done something wrong."

He grunted. "They interrupted us, lovely."

Reaching up, she patted his cheek. "Poor Duff."

He smacked her ass. "Poor *you*, if you keep up with the smart mouth, princess."

"I'm sure I can handle whatever you dish out."

He pulled back and arched one dark brow, his hazel eyes glinting in the light from the café. "Are you, now? We'll have to see about that. Your stamina and tolerance as a bottom have yet to be tested. Not by me, at any rate. Come to mind, we've yet to discuss when our first playdate will be."

"Given the last few minutes I sort of thought it had already started."

"Mere warm-up. Why don't we have that talk inside? I smell beignets and my belly wants some."

She had to shake her head again. Duff could certainly amuse her. Amuse her, confuse her, make her body rage with desire. If only he would stay right there and go back to kissing her and pinching her and making her *feel* like a bottom.

"I suppose I'd better feed you. I imagine a man of your size needs plenty of fuel."

"That's right. I eat bears for breakfast and pretty girls like you for supper."

She reached up and gave his shoulder a small, playful shove. "You going to start beating your chest now?"

"I just might." He stepped back and grabbed her hand. "Better not risk it," he said with a wink, pulling her inside.

They stepped through the inner glass-paned double doors and into the café, the scents of sugar and chicory coffee wafting on the warm air.

"I love that this place never changes," she said.

"That seems to be true of many places in this city."

"It is. We try to preserve the old architecture and the feel of the city wherever we can. Our history is important. Maybe even more so since Katrina, in some ways."

"You're proud of New Orleans," he commented.

"Yes. I think that's true of anyone from New Orleans, but being Creole, being part of a group of people that's so specific to this city, maybe I feel it even more deeply. I don't know— perhaps that's not true. I just know how fully I feel it. Pride, and a sense of connection. It's a very special place. I've been to Paris and Venice and Madrid, but there's nothing like this city anywhere on earth."

"'Tis true. Although I do like Paris. But I wouldn't live there—not for more than a month or two at most."

"So you're in New Orleans to stay?" she asked, wondering at the hope blossoming in her chest.

"I am. I'm opening a business here and I don't plan to abandon it. Jamie and I will make a good go of it. I'm aiming for success. I'm good at what I do—restoring vintage bikes and building Harleys. Between that and Jamie's head for business, we'll do well. Why would I want to leave?"

She pushed her damp hair from her suddenly hot cheeks. Whatever was wrong with her? "Oh, you know . . . People like change sometimes."

"Is that what you've found with men in general, or only with the men you've dated?"

"I . . . What?"

"Forgive my bluntness. But it seems to me there was more beneath that observation than mere observation."

She glanced down at the floor, took a breath, then looked back up to find his concerned gaze on her. "Um, both? And can we change the subject?"

He looked into her eyes, his going a little dark for a moment. "Of course. Shall we order?"

"Yes, let's."

He took her hand and led her to the order window, where he asked the white-uniformed attendant, who was wearing the traditional black bowtie and white cap with "Morning Call" printed in red script on the side, for two coffees and three orders of beignets. Then they found an empty table, and Duff pulled out one of the bentwood chairs and held it for her, then seated himself.

"You said the place never changes. I take that to mean you've been coming here for a long while," he said.

She nodded. "I used to come as a kid with my family after church sometimes. We'd have our beignets out on the patio. Then we'd walk through the park. There's a beautiful carousel down the road from here. My father used to take me . . . He'd let me ride it over and over when I was little. That seems like a million years ago now. But I've always loved this park. I love the bridges and the huge weeping trees, and I'm totally in love with the Peristyle."

"The what?"

"Did you see that long, sort of Greek-style open pavilion with all the columns when we drove in? Look out the window— it's right there on the edge of the water. Can you see it?"

He turned around for a moment. "It's a bit dark out there, but I can see the outline of it."

"It was built in 1907, specifically for parties. The architect Paul Andry designed it so it would be large enough to dance there. Sometimes we'd come to the park, my family and I, and there would be a wedding going on, the whole place decked out in flowers . . . Anyway, it was a fairy-tale place for a little girl. My brother and I used to play on the stone lions next to the stairs, imagining they were real. He'd challenge me to roaring contests, which he always won, of course. Sort of like he did everything else. He was a top athlete, ran track in high school, won awards. And he was a straight-A student. He used to help me with my math homework."

"But you and he aren't close anymore?"

She shook her head. "We went in such different directions. Charles always knew he would be a preacher, like my dad, and I always wanted to be an artist. I really never wanted anything else. He's always been so straitlaced, and frankly a little uptight. Well, more than a little. And I got a bit wild in high school, which was pretty much the last straw for our relationship."

Duff laid a hand over his heart, recoiling in mock horror. "No! You? I'd have never imagined."

She grinned at him as a waiter slid their coffees and the steaming, fragrant pastries onto the table. "Thank you," she said to the waiter before turning back to Duff. "No more wild than you, I'm pretty sure."

"Oh, I had my days, no doubt about it. Sometimes being the biggest kid in school can be a problem. Everyone wants to pick a fight. All that early testosterone running through a boy's veins and they think they have to challenge everything and everyone in their path. Problem was, I was just a teenage boy, too, so I let them get to me. Hurt a few of 'em. Didn't know my own size and strength in those days. Didn't learn until I'd been in a few pub brawls and went to jail twice."

"Are you waiting for me to fall over in shock?"

He shrugged, but she could see he was ready for it.

"Perhaps a bit. Some people do."

"I've known other guys your size. Well, almost your size. I've seen them go through the same issues. Did you hurt anyone badly?"

He paused to sip the hot coffee, set the cup down carefully. It looked tiny in his enormous hand. "Yeah, unfortunately, I did."

"I'm sorry. I shouldn't have asked. That was an intrusive question."

"Eh, it's all right, and a fair enough question, given that you're spending time with me, turning over a certain amount of trust to me. Too much drink and too many of 'em getting in my face were a bad combination, and I was young and foolish, as young people tend to be, and me more than most, perhaps. Both times I ended up in jail it was a few blokes at once ganging up on me, and I was defending myself. But I still wasn't happy I'd allowed them to push me that far. There's no excuse for it. Which is why I don't drink anymore. A man my size, as you said, can't afford to take the risk. Haven't had a drink since the last time I was locked up."

"How long ago has it been?"

"Shortly before I turned twenty. I had a very short legal drinking career."

She added cream to her coffee, stirring it thoughtfully for a few moments. "It hasn't been so easy being you, has it?" she asked.

"What? I suppose not. But is it easy being anyone? Has it been easy being you?"

She glanced down at her cup, at the dark liquid swirling there. "In some ways, no. In other ways I count myself very lucky."

"Tell me about the lucky part," he suggested.

When she looked up, he was watching her closely—watching as if he were really interested in what she had to say. And in doing a quick review of the conversations they'd had, she realized either he was doing a very good job of faking it so he could get in her pants, or he actually *was* interested, which was a novel idea. Her experience with men hadn't led her to believe that any man who wanted in her pants had any other interest in her. Which, she realized in that moment for the first time, was a pretty fucked-up scenario, and it was past time that things changed. But she felt pretty certain his interest was sincere. Not that he didn't want to get in her pants, but she was damn happy about that part.

"Hmm . . . okay. Well, I have some pretty amazing friends, especially my best friend, Kitty."

"What's she like?"

"Really? You want to know about my friend?"

"Yeah, I do. And no, I don't want to have a three-way, if that's what you're thinking. Not my thing—too damn much to keep track of. I much prefer to give one woman my undivided attention."

Shivering, she silently filed that remark away for future reference. "Kitty is sassy as hell. Really smart—smart enough to have started one of the best hair salons in town and make a great success of it. She's funny. Kind. I can tell her anything, and I know she'll never judge me. And she's always there, no matter what. She's one of those friends who would help you hide a dead body."

"Good qualities to have in a friend. My cousin Jamie is the same for me. Well, he calls me an asshole on a regular basis, but you know, he's probably right about that."

Layla laughed. "Men have such . . . *interesting* friendships."

Duff grinned, dimples creasing his cheeks, and she went breathless at the sight of them. That and the glittering hazel of his eyes fringed in thick, dark lashes. She had to bite her lip to keep from sighing. She loved that they could sit here having a meaningful conversation, yet at the same time, the chemistry never stopped sizzling. She squeezed her thighs together to ease the pressure suddenly building there.

Clearing her throat, she took a sip of her coffee and tried to clear her head. "What about you? What are your 'lucky parts'?"

"Getting to do what I love for a living, which I know you understand, maybe even better than I do. Getting to come to the U.S.—to be able to stay, to work here."

"That's right—you have dual citizenship, don't you?"

"Yeah, Jamie's mother, my aunt Carrie, is my father's sister—the American side of the family. Good luck for us, since we both love it here. I always have, and Jamie and I have always been close. It was his idea to open the motorcycle division of SGR Motors—he's been at me about it for a while now. I suppose I just needed reason enough to come. To leave Scotland."

"So, you came for the business?"

He ran a hand over his head, looking out the window for several long, silent moments.

"Duff? Did I just step in something here? If there's some part of this you'd rather not talk about . . ."

"It's old news anyway. But, yeah, I did feel as if I needed a fresh start. And I'd been wanting to come—that's every bit as true. I finally saved enough money to contribute enough to the business, and the space next to SGR Motors became available. So, here I am, and glad I made the decision. Sitting here with you isn't hurting any, either."

She smiled, felt the smile spread like blossoming heat. And God, she was as besotted as a girl with her first crush! But the truth was, this *was* her first crush in a very long time. It was something she hadn't allowed herself. Not until Duff came along and she simply couldn't help herself.

Trouble.

Oh, she was in major trouble—the big economy size. Why did it surprise her that it only made him more appealing, knowing how perilous he could be for her? How he made her lose control, whether he was trying or not?

"These beignets smell good enough to eat," Duff said, stuffing one into his mouth, the powdered sugar falling onto his square chin, onto the table. He wiped his chin and picked up another.

"Hey! Leave one for me."

He winked at her. "One if you're quick enough, princess."

They made fast work of the beignets, washing them down with the lovely chicory coffee. Duff laid a tip on the table and stood, taking her hand and helping her to her feet.

"Shall we? It's stopped raining and I want to see this Peristyle of yours."

"Right now?"

"Why not?"

She led the way out of the café and they wandered the winding pathway through the park. The cicadas were singing, and although the rain had stopped, the air smelled of it, clean and fresh and touched with the ever-present scent of flowers that was so common in New Orleans. The Peristyle was a hulking silhouette, lit by the nearly full moon and the lights from the café reflecting on the water of the Bayou Metairie. They moved up the shallow steps and into the beautiful structure, where tall Grecian columns supported the vaulted ceiling.

He led her by the hand to the very center, where he stopped to lean his head back and looked up. "This place is impressive. Enough to make me feel small, which is no simple task. And every bit as beautiful as you said it was." He leaned down and took her earlobe between his teeth as he slid his big arms around her waist. His voice was a low, purring growl. "This is the perfect place. That combination of dangerous openness, yet we're still half-hidden by the dark. The perfect place to let a bit of our darkness out, yes, lovely?"

She took in a gasping breath, but before she could answer, he continued.

"Shh. Don't say a word. This is where I take over. This is where you let me. Just as I said you would."

He bit down hard on the shell of her ear, and she gasped once more. His arms tightened around her, crushing her to him, lifting her onto her toes. She wanted to struggle, felt on some level that she should.

This is not happening.

It was like some dark dream—one she hadn't allowed herself to indulge in for too long. When he slid a hand down over her ass and gave a hard spank, then another, and another, her body went loose, surrendering even before her mind was made up. But no, that wasn't true—her mind had been made up that day in his shop, when she'd seen him up close for the first time. Which was maybe the first real truth she'd told herself about kink and connection in years.

"Breathe, my lovely," he commanded.

She pulled in a breath, exhaled as he grabbed the curve of her ass through her dress *hard*.

"Fuck, Duff."

"Now, princess? But we're in a public place," he murmured, his voice low and rough. He started moving her backward, murmuring to her, "I'm going to be thinking about that, particularly since it's off the table. For now. But there are still plenty of other things I can do to you while still respecting the boundaries you've put in place. Oh, yes, I can be very creative when the need arises. And things are rising right now, my lovely girl, which makes me a very formidable man."

Suddenly her back was up against one of the tall pillars and he was pressing his hips into her, the hard ridge of his arousal a solid shaft grinding against her. And she went soft all over, damp between her thighs. Some part of her thought she should protest. But why? She wanted this man in a way she hadn't wanted anyone in forever. *Truly* forever. She'd never felt desire like this before—as if her body would go up in flames if she didn't do something to bank the embers before they engulfed her. Then Duff leaned in and kissed her neck, sucking and biting, his tongue making slow, sensual patterns on her tender flesh, and all she could do was sigh. Sigh. And surrender.

He pulled back to whisper against her throat, his Scottish brogue thick, "I hear your breath. I can feel it, you know. The rough, warm exhale. The way your body softened under my hands, under my mouth. When I kissed the pulse beat at your neck, it was racing. As fast as my own blood is, Layla. You do something to me. I'll admit it. I'll admit it's all I can do to hold on to some control. But I've got it. I've got *you*. Don't worry about that. Now be a very good girl and do as you're told."

She gasped as he spun her in his arms, then pressed down

on the back of her neck until she was forced to lean forward. And despite the alarm bells clanging in her brain, she let him do it, didn't argue. Didn't want to.

"Good girl. Hang on to that column. Hang on tight. Because I'm about to spank the hell out of you, right here on the edge of this lovely lake, with nothing but the moon to see. Maybe nothing but the moon. But that's a chance we'll just have to take. Because I'm not waiting. And because I know you'll like it, this little bit of risk. Oh, yeah."

She could not believe she was doing this, but she was. Bracing her hands on the cool stone pillar, she bent at the waist as he pulled her hips back. He kept one strong thigh against hers as he stood a little to one side of her. Stroking the back of her bare thigh, he inched the hem of her dress up, higher and higher, until it was bunched around her waist.

"Black lace. Very nice." He smoothed the edge of her panties up a little more, baring her ass, then ran his palms over the exposed flesh. "Ah, your skin is amazing. As soft and silky as I knew it would be."

He smacked her ass, just hard enough to sting, and she wanted to lean into his hand. To ask for more. Was this really *her* doing these things?

But all conscious thought fled from her mind when he began to whale on her, the blows coming hard and fast, taking her out of her head. It was all she could do to process the sensation—sensation that turned very quickly into pain. And just as quickly into pleasure. His big hand came down on her again and again, and her breath was coming in short, sharp pants. The pain was beginning to overwhelm her, and just as she realized she would have to call "yellow," he stopped, running his smooth palm over the soreness.

"Duff . . ." She nearly choked trying to say his name, a small knot forming in her throat.

His voice was right next to her ear. "What is it, princess?"

"I don't know. I don't . . ." She had to pause, trying to figure out what she needed to say, what she was feeling. "It's so much all at once." It was the best she could do.

"Too much? Too hard?"

"No. I . . . No. That's not it."

He pulled her upright, holding her close, so that her shoulders were against his chest. "Can you tell me what's going on?"

She shook her head, but the words came anyway. Words she maybe didn't want to say, rather than not knowing what they were. "I haven't felt anything like this in . . . I've never felt this. This instant sinking into subspace. This instant need for more, when I thought—I *knew*—I'd fight it for a while. When I wasn't sure I'd be able to go there, to be taken there ever again. But all you have to do is touch me, and it simply happens. And I don't like it." She shook her head hard. "I don't like it," she repeated, then said very quietly, "except that I do."

"Ah, princess. Don't you know this is exactly how it's supposed to happen? If it wasn't meant to we'd still be back at my shop arguing, yeah? Yeah, I think it's so. Your body knows it. So does mine. Let me do my job here. All you have to do is give yourself. Give yourself to me. I will take care of everything. Try to quiet the demons arguing inside your beautiful head, telling you to struggle against what you clearly want. All you have to do is *be*."

He stroked her cheek, and she leaned her head back against his muscular chest, relief flooding her system.

"All you have to do is be."

When had any man ever said those words to her? When had anyone ever had that intention? She wanted to fall into the very idea of it. With *Duff*. Because she knew he meant every word he said, and it made it safe. He was the real thing. The kind of Dominant all the others should have been and never were.

Duff.

She sighed, let her body sink against his, because she knew she *could*. His arms held her, so, so strong, wrapping her up. His scent was all around her. Pure sex. But also pure man, pure dominance. Pressing back into him, she reveled in the hardness of his cock against her back, loved knowing she'd caused it. And her sex went wet—soaking wet—in an instant. She ground her ass against him. He moaned and pulled back, spun her until she faced him, holding her at arm's length.

"This is going to get very dangerous very fast, my lovely girl, if you keep that up."

"What if I want it to?" she challenged.

He ground his jaw tight for a moment. "Then it's my responsibility to see nothing happens."

She shook her head. It wasn't computing. "Nothing?"

"Not with you in subspace. It was damned idiotic of me not to initiate negotiations around sexual contact." He yanked her in close, his breath warm against her cheek as he murmured, "Because as badly as I need to throw you up against this pillar and fuck you until you scream into the night, I need to make you come even more. Oh, yeah. Make you come over and over. Until your knees buckle. Until you're limp and sobbing my name. Until you can't even beg me for more."

"Mmm." She bit her lip, her body absorbing his words even more than her brain, and all of it was scorching hot. Making her *need* with a white-hot fury. Making her tremble all over.

"Duff . . . please."

"You see, there's the idiocy in this. Because experienced Dom that I am, I'm also the stupid arse who didn't even think of discussing it once you said you wouldn't sleep with me. So now I do the noble fucking thing and take you home, then spend the rest of the night stroking off while I think of your gorgeous skin and the sound of your panting breath as I cuss myself into the dirt." He paused, his grip on her arms clenching and unclenching. "Then, tomorrow, if you're still talking to me, we start a new part of the negotiations, with you having a clear head and me being so damn horny for you I won't be seeing straight."

As bereft as she was, her body buzzing with desire, she couldn't help but laugh at his self-deprecation.

"Ach, I'm funny, am I, princess? I'm a sad, sad case, I tell you. Have you no pity for my plight?" He clucked his tongue. "Tsk, tsk. Another check on the ledger for you, my lovely."

"You are *not* the only one suffering, you know."

"I know. But that makes it even worse. I haven't done my job with you, and for that I must apologize."

"Wow."

The dim moonlight lit his face just enough that she could see him arch his dark brows.

"Wow, what?"

"A true gentleman Dom. I was beginning to think you were nothing more than a myth."

"Yeah, us and the Loch Ness Monster." His small grin faded as his face sobered, and he touched her shoulders with gentle hands, making her heart swell in a way she didn't quite understand. "It really is unforgivable of me. I need to make sure you come out of every scene satisfied, fulfilled. Feeling good. It's what I've charged myself to do, beyond any Safe, Sane and Consensual code of ethics. It gets me off, to be honest, but it's also the only way I'll feel good about myself. And I want that for *you*. I want this to be good for you. I understand how fragile you are going into this, given whatever your negative history has been. I don't take that lightly, despite my joking around. Right now, with us—this timing—it can either make or break you. And while I want to break you down in order for you to reach the heights of submission you're meant for, I have no desire to break *you*. Or I do. But only in the way that will serve your needs. And you do need it. I saw it from the start—that side you keep hidden because it makes you too vulnerable. That need to be broken in exactly the right way."

Her chest went tight. She couldn't believe he was saying these things to her.

"How do you get me so well?" she asked.

He pulled a breath in, paused, blew it out slowly. "We all have some damage, the detritus of our pasts, yes? Yeah. We've all been broken in some way. We're all of us seeking some sort of rebirth through kink. Even my big, ugly self. Me maybe more than you." Pausing, he cleared his throat, his hands going gentle on her. "Now, my lovely, I think we ought to get you home."

She nodded, even though she didn't want the evening to end. But she also had enough experience in kink to know she was a little out of her head, and it was best that he was the one making the decisions tonight.

Give it over to him. He really will take care of everything.

The idea almost made her want to cry, but she wasn't much of a crier. Still, she had to swallow past a lump in her throat.

He took her hand and led her back to her car, where he took her keys and put her into the passenger seat, then went around to the driver's side and let himself in.

"Thank you for trusting me with your car," he said. "You know I'll treat her as the precious thing she is."

"I do know that," she answered as he started the engine. "I know a lot of things about you after tonight."

"Do you, now?"

"Yes," she answered, her head too light to allow her to really filter what she was saying, which was what she'd have normally done. But there was nothing "normal" about being with Duff. Not for her. "I know you're what I think of as a 'true Dom,' the kind who takes the great responsibility that comes with great power very seriously. I know . . . that I can trust you. That I can give myself over into your hands in a way I frankly thought was highly unlikely, at best. And that you believe in my ability to reach that scary, ethereal place that is submission, even when I can't believe it myself. I'm still not sure how far I can go."

She could see from the dimple in his cheek that he was grinning. "Could be mere ego on my part."

"Yes. It could be. Except that it's not."

He turned and flashed a quick smile at her, and something in his expression made her go warm all over—with desire and pleasure and that sensation of just having had a momentary meeting of the minds. She liked it, despite herself. And had to admit it was happening a lot.

"How am I getting to your house?" he asked.

"I'll show you the way."

He turned to glance at her for a moment, his face sober despite the small smile still lingering there. "Yeah. I think you will, at that."

She absorbed the words, cuddled into the leather seat and held them to her. She had no idea why she felt so warmly pleased. So . . . happy.

She hadn't been happy for far too long.

When they pulled into her driveway, she had a flashback of the orgasm she'd had in that very spot so recently. Her body heated, but she fought it down as she unbuckled her seat belt and grabbed for the door handle.

"Ah, now that I won't have, princess. Wait there while I come round."

She was too confused to do anything but follow his directive. In a moment he'd opened the car door and was helping her out. He walked her up the shallow stairs to her front door, where he slid an arm around her waist and looked into her eyes.

"How are you doing?" he asked.

"Me? I'm fine."

"Flying at all? Do you need aftercare?"

"Oh. No. I'm . . . I feel a little light-headed, but I had a pretty good endorphin rush. I seem to be coming down nicely. And I can call Kitty if I need aftercare."

"You can call *me* if you need aftercare. Although if you need it right now, I'll have to find a way to do it while keeping this raging hard-on as far away from your luscious body as possible so I won't ravage you inappropriately."

She grinned. "Is there any other way to ravage?"

"I suppose not. Perhaps one of the most promising features of a good ravage."

She shook her head. "I'm really fine, Duff. I promise. I'm going to have a hot bath, then go to bed."

He cleared his throat. "All of which creates some lovely imagery that, alas, is not helping my current situation. But go on—into your bath. Expect a call from me sometime tomorrow. And I'd like to see you tomorrow night."

"I'm not sure if that was phrased as a request or an order."

He winked at her, his wide mouth spreading in a grin, the dimples creasing his cheeks as he handed her keys back to her. "Neither am I. Now get inside before I have my way with you on your front porch."

She put the key in the lock while he stood just behind her, and even with her back to him she could feel his presence, the heat radiating from his big body. Once the door was open she turned to face him once more.

He had one hand braced over her head on the doorframe, his head bent, his eyes full of shadows and questions and the same lust she felt, as if it were mirrored there. He stared down at her for what felt like a very long time while her body filled with anticipation and a stark hunger that gnawed at her belly. No, it wasn't her belly that begged to be fed.

Finally, he said, "Know that I want to kiss you, princess. But if I do, I can't be held responsible for my actions."

She blinked once, knowing damn well she was playing with fire. "Do it anyway."

CHAPTER

Five

D UFF HEARD THE challenge in her tone. The stark need.
And felt it reverberate like an echo in his system. He
took one step closer.

You are losing your shit, man.

Another step closer, and she tilted her chin, clearly waiting—
wanting—to be kissed. Could he simply kiss her and leave it
at that?

Fuck no.

He was doing it anyway.

He grabbed her slim waist and yanked her in hard, a small
growl escaping his tortured throat as he ground his hard-on
against her sweet body, pressing against her curves. One hand
went into her hair, grabbing on tight, pulling her head back
and back. And then he went for her throat. Went for it like

the hungry wolf he was, teeth and tongue, lapping and biting, drinking her in, then moving up to her jaw, lingering there, nipping and kissing before he found her mouth.

And oh, sweet Christ, her mouth was nothing short of perfection, her lips full and succulent beneath his. He licked them, sucked them, heard her quiet moan. Then he opened her lips with his tongue—*had* to—and some part of him knew it was all over. He was drowning in this woman.

Pressing her back a step, then another, he kicked the front door shut behind him. When she backed a step away from him, her green eyes glittering in the dim light of a single hanging lamp, he saw the question there. Her small palms rested on his chest—small, yet he felt the enormous power of the woman she was in them. The woman who was challenging his control—hell, the woman who had torn it down like a brick wall crumbling under the slam of a wrecking ball. He tried to catch his breath as he waited for her to tell him to get out.

Fuck.

She shook her head the tiniest bit, but his cock only throbbed harder.

"This is a pretty kind of hell I'm in, princess. But I can't help but like it."

"Duff . . . ?"

"Lovely Layla," he murmured, reaching out to stroke his thumb over her cheek.

"We should not be doing this. I know that. And I can't . . . I can't promise you I'm clearheaded enough to make a decision right now. But I want this. Now. *Right now.* Don't make me wait."

"Jesus, woman. As if I could after you telling me this."

Her nails dug into his chest then, through the fabric of his

T-shirt. And he swore as he tore it over his head, then advanced on her, heat rushing through his system, coiled like a serpent waiting to escape in his belly, his balls. He grabbed her, kissed her mouth hard, released her to unzip her dress, pushing her farther back into the living room the whole time. He pulled the straps down over her shoulders, then her red bra straps as he spun her around, then tore the pretty scarf from her hair and slipped it over her eyes.

"Duff, no."

She pulled the makeshift blindfold from her face and spun around, question in her eyes. Fear, maybe. But it only drove the need higher.

"This won't be gentle. It won't be easy. This is the time, Layla, and I'm sure you know what I mean. Give yourself over. Or tell me to go."

Her lips parted, formed a small O of surprise. But then her features slowly settled even as a blush rose in her cheeks, and she gave a small nod. He couldn't help his grin, and he was certain it looked as wicked as he felt.

Taking the scarf from her, he tied it over her eyes, her silky curls falling all over his hands. He wanted to feel her hair on his skin. On his hard cock. But first things first.

Yanking her dress down, he paused a moment to admire the pretty red lace lingerie underneath it, and the small lotus inked in what looked like the delicate lines of a henna tattoo over her right hip before reaching behind her and unsnapping her bra. And Lord, her breasts were beautiful—full and round with dark, dusky nipples, which were already hard. Desire was a hot surge in his body. Electric. Sharp. He had to draw in a breath.

Get ahold of yourself.

Then he was on her, taking those gorgeous nipples into his mouth one at a time, licking and sucking, biting and tasting, while she gasped and moaned. When she reached for him he pulled her arms behind her back, holding both slender wrists there with one hand, his grip tight enough to hurt. Her body immediately stilled.

"Ah, yeah, now that's where I want you, princess. Yielding under my touch. I will make you pliant, you know. Pliant. Bending to my will. Bowing under my hands. My mouth. Under the pain. And fuck, but I'll enjoy it."

"I—"

"Shh. No talking now. You know what to do. What I will require of you. Just do it, Layla."

Reaching down, he squeezed one full breast hard, and she gasped in pain, her brows drawing together under the silk blindfold. He filled both his hands, her flesh firm, her nipples two hard points against his palms. He squeezed again, felt her wriggle, and took her down to the floor, putting her on her back. Straddling her, he used his knees to press her legs together, holding her still while he kneaded her tits, pressing and pulling the sweet flesh of her rigid nipples, working her hard. She was panting, but she didn't make a sound, even though he understood he was hurting her. Meant to.

Good. She could really take it. And he needed to hurt her. Needed to let the beast inside him out.

He bent and took one nipple into his mouth again, rubbing the hardened tip with his teeth, then bit down.

"Oh!"

He chuckled. "Now, that I don't mind you saying, lovely."

Grinning, he bent and did it again, sucking that reddening tip in between the edges of his teeth. And smiled to himself when he felt her hips trying to undulate. "Do you need something, princess? I think you do."

Shifting, he shoved her thighs apart, pushed them wider as he settled his knees in between them, pausing to take in the sight of the sheer black lace against her lush pussy lips. His cock gave a hard jump.

No.

He tucked his fingers under the edge of the lace and tore them off.

"Ah!"

"I'll replace them, not to worry," he told her. Then his voice stuttered in his throat as he looked at her lovely shaved pussy.

So damn beautiful. So damn hot. The lips were plump, a little duskier than her gorgeous caramel skin. And between them the flesh was pink and wet, so wet he had to bend down and taste her.

He stroked her with his tongue, drinking her in, then pushed his tongue inside her as her body shook. And nearly came.

He sat up, wiped his mouth with the back of one hand while pressing down on his rigid, pulsing dick with the other.

Jesus. Fucking. God.

He shook his head, trying to clear it.

"You test me, woman," he told her. "We're both going to pay."

Grabbing one of her thighs, he pressed down, putting some of his weight behind it, his nails digging into her skin. She struggled against him, but he only held on tighter, dug his nails deeper.

When she couldn't seem to stop squirming he used his other hand to pry her pussy lips apart, and shoved two fingers into her all at once. And had to bite the inside of his mouth to hold his orgasm back.

Figure this shit out, man.

He started a hard, punishing stroke, pressing deeper and deeper inside her, watching her clit swell. Silently cussing at himself.

Don't you fucking do it. Hold it together. For her. Do what you're supposed to.

But soon she was grinding her hips against his hand and he couldn't help himself—he bent and put his mouth on her once more, sucking on that hard little clit, using his tongue, then his teeth. And she was groaning and panting and writhing and his poor, tortured cock was going to explode. He bit her clit hard, if only to keep himself from coming, to shift his focus.

"Ah, fuck!" she yelled.

Iron. Fucking. Control.

He sucked harder, thrusting his fingers into her. She was shivering, her hands clenching and unclenching at her sides. His cock was pressing so hard against the front of his jeans he couldn't take the friction.

"Fuck," he muttered as he flipped her over onto her stomach, pulling her over his knees. He started to spank her gorgeous ass right away, and when she struggled, her legs kicking, he grabbed a handful of hair and pulled tight, pulled until her back was arched, her throat elongated. He had never seen anything more beautiful.

Not helping.

In frustration he picked her up as he got to his feet, tossed her roughly onto the big white suede couch, knocking the piles of brightly colored throw pillows onto the floor.

"Stay," he ordered, keeping his gaze on her lovely little body as he told himself he wasn't going to fuck her even as he started to pull his zipper down.

She pulled in a sharp breath. Was she excited? Was she afraid? He was good either way, and hoped for both.

He looked around the room, decorated in Bohemian style, all brilliantly colored silks and brass lanterns, candles on an old steamer trunk, the windows draped in red velvet and ivory lace. And a tall vase in a corner filled with slender bamboo poles.

"Stay," he ordered again, getting up and taking a handful of bamboo from the vase.

"Duff, I . . ." She stopped, biting her lip.

"Thought better of it, did you, my lovely? This is not the time to question me. But I'm sure you know exactly what this is." He snapped one of the canes against his thigh. It stung even through the heavy denim, but the pain helped to center him.

Her hands were working nervously, her fingers in a tight grip on the blanket draped over the sofa cushions. He paused, breathed her in, the scents of her perfume and her desire blending like some intoxicating cocktail.

"Spread for me, Layla." When she hesitated, he added harshly, "*Now.*"

When she didn't move quickly enough for him, he reached down and did it for her, until he could see her luscious pink flesh once more. She tried to draw her thighs back together, but he used one booted heel to hold her down. Her body calmed, and he was aware that him taking total physical command of her body was what seemed to help her.

He raised the bamboo cane, pausing for several moments, allowing her body, her mind, to fill with anticipation. Then he struck.

"Fuck!"

Smiling to himself, he leaned down to run his fingertips over the red welt rising on her inner thigh. "Not yet, lovely. We haven't allowed ourselves that yet."

But even as he said it he knew it was probably a lie. He didn't know how he could prevent himself.

Just hurt her. Bring her pain. Bring yourself back to that place of control.

An impossible task, perhaps. But he could do what he needed to for her, at any rate. And he knew she liked the pain. Oh yeah, that he could deliver.

He struck the top of her thigh, waited a half-second while she breathed through the pain, then did it again. He struck the other thigh, then made a regular, steady strike zone of her inner thighs until her cries were a strangled sob in her throat. He stopped and dropped the cane, ran a hand between her gorgeously welted thighs, found her soaking wet.

"Ah, you do like it, lovely girl. The harder I hit you, the wetter you become. It's a beautiful thing." He pushed his thumb inside her, and she was so slippery inside, her hips arching. His dick throbbed, hot and needy. "Yeah, a beautiful thing," he murmured. "Time to reward you, and m'self, too. I can't fuck you, but I can have this. And I want you to watch."

* * *

HE STRIPPED THE blindfold off her, and Layla blinked as Duff paused to pull his hard cock from his jeans, gripping himself in his hand. God, he was huge. Huge and beautifully formed, the shaft so thick, the head so dark and swollen it made her sex ache with the need to have him inside her. Her mouth was actually watering. She licked her lips, and spread her thighs wider.

He chuckled. "Oh, you tempt me. Bad, bad girl, Layla. But tonight bad girls get rewarded."

When he stroked the seam of her damp pussy lips with his fingertips, her whole body filled with pleasure—even more when he squeezed his cock in his fist, the head going darker. She'd always loved to watch a man handle himself. And now, when her brain was in that light, floaty space, she loved it even more. Loved it *all* even more—being spread out for him, wanton, wanting. Loved his touch, which was making her crazy, making her need to come. Loved the wicked gleam in his hazel eyes.

"Oh, yeah. If I can't fuck you, princess, I will fuck you with my hand. And I'll stroke my hard cock—hard for you— and imagine it's your sweet, tight pussy." He pressed his fingers inside her, spread them, opening her up. "But I'll bet it's even better to be inside you. So, so much better."

He gave a few hard thrusts, making her gasp.

"Oh!"

"You like it, do you? Tell me."

"I . . . I like it. Oh . . ."

He gave his stiff cock one slow stroke, his big fingers feathering over the head. "I can see that you do, but I love to hear you say it. Tell me what you feel. Tell me what you want."

She licked her lips once more, and for several moments she was frozen, struggling against his command, some part of her feeling that Duff ordering her to say these things was too submissive an act for a woman like her. But she'd never had a problem talking to her lovers. Why should this be any different? And she liked to say the words, liked to talk a little dirty.

"Mmm . . . I'm so, so close to coming I can barely stand for you to touch me. But don't stop. Please don't stop. I want you to fuck me with your hand. I want you to tease my clit, but I want to come with your hand inside me. Hell, I want to come with your cock inside me, but I know, I *know* . . . we have to talk about that another time. Damn it. Because . . ." She had to stop and draw in another gasping breath. "Because watching you touch yourself is so damn hot. And I want to suck your cock so badly. I want to feel you in my mouth, in my throat."

"Jesus fucking Christ, woman." He gave his cock a few savage strokes, his dark brows drawing together, his mouth going loose with pleasure. "You are going to be the death of me."

His words reverberated like a shaft of desire deep in her body, in her brain, making her spread her legs wider.

Letting out a hard, rasping chuckle, he told her, "Oh, no you don't. You're not making me come before you do."

He started a hard, punishing stroke, his fingers plunging inside her, working her G-spot so hard that pleasure and pain were one sensation—she could find no dividing line between the two. And as he worked her, he worked his cock just as mercilessly. As her climax bore down on her, as heavy as a thundercloud and just as powerful, she saw his throbbing cock go absolutely rigid in his hand, then his face twisting in pleasure as a raw scream tore at her throat and sensation knifed into her, rending her with pleasure.

"Ah, God! Duff!"

"Fuck, Layla . . . fuuuuuuck!"

His hot come spewed onto her stomach, her breasts, and his pleasure drove hers on as his plunging fingers took her to new heights. And she was coming again, or still—she couldn't tell. Even as the last waves rippled through her system and his hand slowed to a sweet, even stroking, then to a whispering touch, she wanted more.

He drew his booted foot from her thigh, but she grabbed at it, her fingers clumsy.

"Duff, please don't."

"I'm not going anywhere, lovely," he said, his voice a low rasp.

She ran her tongue over her lips. "Duff? Please don't stop."

He grinned, released his softening cock and leaned over her, then bent and buried his face between her thighs. His tongue was soft against her, lapping at her clitoris, and it swelled instantly.

"Mmm . . ."

He began to lick faster, flattening his tongue and pressing hard against her clit, and at the same time he pinched the lips of her sex with his fingers.

"Ah, God, that hurts!"

"Mmm," he rumbled against her, the vibration of his voice going through her.

Pushing his fingers inside, he surged gently into her while he licked her, knowing somehow to keep just the right tempo and pressure on her sore, used flesh. Very quickly the pressure built, and at that lovely moment when her body was ready to fly, to spiral into the eye of the storm, he pinched her again, the pain driving her over that keen edge, and she was falling and flying all at once. She called out his name, pleasure shimmering over her skin, deep into her belly, into her sex.

"Duff!"

When it was over he rolled onto his side on the wide sofa next to her. They were both panting. Her muscles were warm and loose, and her mind was still trying to rebel against her own yielding, but it was too damn late for that. She'd done it. And loved it.

"Well," she said finally, "at least you didn't come on my face."

He let out a guffaw. "Ah, I do like you, princess. Princess with a filthy mouth."

"It's probably a good thing you like a filthy mouth or this would never work out."

He stroked one finger through the come drying on her stomach. "Dirty girl, too."

"Whose fault is that?"

"I'd say it's yours."

She rolled her eyes. "Of course you would."

"It wouldn't have happened without you being here."

"Hmm. Good point. Maybe."

"Maybe?"

"I'd argue the point that if you were at home you still might have left this lovely mess *somewhere*," she said, "but I'm too exhausted."

"Now, that's definitely your own fault, since you begged me for that last orgasm."

"I did *not* beg," she protested. "I simply asked."

"Sassy wench, too." He lifted her hand and bit the palm.

"Hey!"

"Quiet, wench. I'm about to be nice to you."

"I'm not so sure I can take any more of your 'nice' tonight."

"Ha!"

He got up and disappeared, and she really was too tired to do anything more than lie back and enjoy the postclimax buzzing in her body and the view of his retreating denim-clad ass, which really was superb. He returned a few moments later with a damp washcloth in his hand, and to her surprise he used it to gently wipe the come from her body. She looked up at him as he ran the warm cloth over her skin, amazed at his tender touch. At the way he focused so closely on his task, as if it were the most important thing on earth at that moment.

Don't get too used to it.

She wouldn't have thought she'd want to. This was nothing more than an experiment, wasn't it? Well, wasn't it?

That's sort of how it had started. That's what she'd been telling herself, anyway—or trying to. But the fact was, she *liked* him. Not the way a sixteen-year-old liked a boy at school, even if that was sort of what it felt like when she looked into his eyes and saw the shades of gray and gold and green there. No, this was a much more grown-up thing. More grown-up than maybe any interaction she'd had with a man in her life.

He was a really good guy. A good man. Kind and responsible, smart and funny. And if tonight was any indication, a great player. And he'd be killer in bed.

Am I going to bed with him?

Damn right I am.

She would have right then and there if it hadn't been beyond the scope of their negotiations.

Duff stroked her cheek with his fingertips. "What's going on in there, lovely?"

"Hmm? Oh, I was just thinking about sex."

He chuckled, a deep rumble in his chest. "Excellent."

She turned to grin up at him. "I like how you assume it was all good thoughts. No insecurities in you, Duff."

"Eh? I think someone would have told me by now. Anyway, I've always believed sex is something one should make a study of. What kind of man would I be if I didn't know my way around a woman's body? Or at least make a damn good effort to learn."

"I totally agree. I don't understand women who feel they have to pretend not to like sex, but do it anyway, usually using alcohol as an excuse. I feel like it's nothing more than a way to get around having to admit they like it, God forbid, or a reason to be lazy."

"Right?" he agreed. "Men, too. Like charts of the female anatomy aren't readily available, never mind videos on how to make a woman come sixteen different ways. There's too much information for men to rely on porn for lessons in how to please a woman."

"Because we all know how accurate porn is."

"Even I know, big lug that I am. No excuse for a *really* smart fellow not to know."

She searched his face, unsure about how serious he was. Reaching up, she traced a finger over his collarbone. "You're plenty smart, Duff."

"Eh? Maybe. Not smart enough to be a good example to anyone, but smart enough to get by."

"Who were you not a good example to?" she asked, then wished she hadn't pressed him. "Never mind. You can tell me some other time, if you want."

He nodded, then bent and brushed a quick kiss across her cheek. "Hey, how're you doing?"

"From play, you mean? My thighs are sore as hell, but I'm good. Perfect."

He smiled down at her, making her heart thump in her chest. "Yeah, you are."

She smiled back at him, their gazes meeting, and she swore she saw sincerity in his beautifully gleaming eyes, in his face. It made her feel shy, suddenly, and she glanced away, looking instead at the tattoos that had been revealed when he'd taken his shirt off. She touched one of the seven ravens on his right shoulder, done in black silhouette.

"Tell me about these?" she asked him.

"The crows? They're a symbol. They represent the darkness we all carry, except that mine is often worn on the outside. No, don't try to argue it. I see it as many things, in many incarnations. The foolishness and violence of my youth. My kink. The sadness we all have somewhere in our personal history, yes? Yeah. And seven is my lucky number, so it's sort of the battle between good and evil—mine, anyway—with a little luck on my side, if that makes any sense."

"It does." She ran her fingers over the tattoo, and as was sometimes the case with heavy black work, she felt where his skin was raised a bit by the ink, which was a huge turn-on for her. "And your back piece? I only glimpsed it. May I see?"

"Sure."

He rolled onto his other side, and she gasped first at the finely cut muscles in his broad shoulders and back, then at the beauty of the tattoo, the fineness of the detail and shading. It covered most of his upper back, a Tree of Life in the most exquisite Celtic style, flanked by a pair of wolves and encircled by intricate knot work.

"It's beautiful. May I . . . ?" But she couldn't wait for him to answer before reaching out to touch it—and smiling when she felt his small shiver. "This is really incredible, Duff."

"I had it done by a master artist in Edinburgh a few years ago."

"It must have taken hours."

"Aye, sixteen, as close as I can count it. Three sessions. The final one, when he did the shading, was a bitch."

"So you can dish it out, but you can't take it?" she teased.

He rolled back over to face her, wrapping her in one big arm and yanking her in close. "Oh, I can take it, mouthy girl. But as soon as you're recovered, and we've had a moment to renegotiate, we'll really see what *you* can take. And that's three ticks on the ledger, by the way."

"I figured."

She couldn't help but grin. He just made her feel so good. Some small part of her mind wanted to run screaming, but she was too comfortable with him. Comfortable, hot for him, needing to explore all he had to offer in terms of dominance.

"Duff?"

"Yeah?"

"I think there's no doubt that my masochistic tendencies were—are—more than tendencies."

He laughed. "You think?"

She nodded. "And I believe this needed to happen. That I needed to explore this part of me. I still don't have to like it. I mean, I do, but I don't."

"Do you think maybe you're flying a little higher than you thought, princess? Because you're not entirely making sense."

"Maybe."

"Well, then, you tell me what you need to help you come back to earth."

She wanted to ask him to simply stay with her and hold her all night. But she couldn't get the words out. She felt far too vulnerable already—she wasn't about to ask him for anything like that. It was too much like the things she'd said to Adrien. Marcel. Vincent. And fucking Jimmy. Things they'd used against her, ultimately—the words, her needs and desires.

He won't do that.

Maybe he wouldn't. But maybe he would.

The fear was back, like some ancient drumbeat in her belly. But she refused to give in to it. Not tonight. Not when he was holding her so tight for the moment, giving her exactly what she wanted, saying all the right things.

They're all so damn smooth.

But maybe, just maybe, this man was for real. She'd like to believe there was at least one out there who was.

"Hey."

She blinked, trying to clear her brain of the old shadows. "Hmm?"

"You falling asleep on me?" Duff asked.

"What? No."

"You can, you know. I'm not going anywhere, if that's all right with you. Actually, I'm staying unless you're really opposed. This is the first time you've bottomed for some time, and I'd rather be here to make sure you're okay." He paused, then said, "Yeah, I'd really rather stay, either way."

Some strange combination of shock and warm pleasure went through her, and it was several seconds before she could find her voice.

"Sure. It's more than all right."

"Good," he said, as if that settled everything. Drawing her in closer, he snuggled into her, burying his face in her hair and taking a deep breath. "Lord, you smell good," he murmured.

So do you.

It was impossible to say the words out loud. She barely wanted to think them. She knew she was getting her hopes up—about what, exactly, she wasn't certain. All she knew was this felt so *right* to her. And simultaneously, as if she were on the edge of disaster.

Just bottoming out a little. Just subdrop.

Tomorrow would be less confusing. Maybe.

Turning her face into his neck, she breathed him in. Oh, yes, he smelled good. He smelled *right*. And breathing him in, over and over, losing herself and her fears in his scent, she drifted off.

* * *

SHE WOKE WITH a stiff neck and a stupid grin on her face. She was already starting to stretch before she remembered why— why the stiff neck, and why the grin. Her head was pillowed on Duff's massive chest, her body still shimmering with the lovely soreness from being played and the aftereffects of repeated orgasms.

Thank you, universe.

Her grin widened. She slapped a hand over her mouth, feeling like an idiot.

Despite the bad angle of her neck, she was far too cozy in the arms of the big man. And damn it—her eyes had been open all of twenty seconds and her body was already burning with need, her sex going slick in response to his warm skin beneath her cheek, the tight line of abs under her right hand. And the way the man smelled was pure sin. She'd never been so turned on by a man's natural scent in her life. And Jesus God, she could drink that in all day long, swallow it down and hold it in her lungs.

Dangerous . . .

Oh, yes, this man was dangerous, and it had little to do with his dominance or even the wicked sadist in him. No, it was more about the way her body responded to him, the way she trusted him, the way he made her smile. The way she wanted to stay right there with her head on his chest, sore neck and all, the entire day.

Damn it.

Better to create a little distance, get her head on straight.

Sliding her hand from his stomach with some reluctance, she sat upright on the sofa, pushed the throw blanket off her legs and started to get to her feet when Duff's hand shot out and grabbed her. He pulled her down on top of him with a growl, and the heat in her body ramped up.

"Where are you going, lovely?"

She let out a short laugh. "What, are you gonna get all stalker-y on me now? Can't a lady go to the bathroom?"

His features shifted and he released his grip on her immediately. "Of course. Didn't mean to scare you."

"What? No, you didn't. Just . . . really full bladder."

"Of course."

She got up, all too aware that she was still naked as she made her way through her bedroom to the bathroom. There she ran the water in the old pedestal sink, searching her gaze in the oval mirror. She still looked the same, other than the small bruises around her nipples. Running her fingertips over them, she winced a little, but they went hard with pleasure all the same. She shook her head at her reflection, then took care of her urgent bladder and washed her hands. Taking her hair pick from the wooden shelf on the wall, she tried to get her hair in order.

"You are fine. Just fine," she told herself quietly. "Just because this man is the hottest human being ever born, just because he plays you the way no man ever has, doesn't mean anything. Lust, maybe. You can deal with lust."

She pulled her short garnet-colored silk robe from the hook on the door, slipped it around her and cinched the belt tight, then stepped back and lifted the hem of the robe to check out her marks in the mirror. Her thighs were crisscrossed with narrow red welts from the makeshift bamboo cane he'd used on her. She didn't want to, but she gloried in her marks. *Hers*. Because Duff had put them there. She allowed herself to gaze at them for another three seconds before dropping the hem of the robe.

"You are one sorry girl," she muttered to herself, pulling open the bathroom door.

When she stepped back into the living room, Duff had propped himself up on a few of the throw pillows, looking like a lazy sultan against the rich jewel tones.

"Come 'ere, lovely," he commanded.

She wanted to—she really did. But she couldn't do it. Not yet.

"How about some coffee first?" she suggested.

"Tea? Say yes and I'll leave the mark off the ledger for disobeying me, princess."

"I have tea," she said over her shoulder, already turning toward the kitchen.

There she busied herself with starting the coffeemaker and the kettle. She poured some milk into her coffee before carrying both mugs back into the living room. How was she going to handle the morning? Her need to run? Her need to climb into his lap, which was just as strong, and infinitely more terrifying? Setting her cup on the coffee table, she handed him his tea, taking a long, steady breath.

"Come sit with me," he said.

She did, keeping as much distance as she could from his big body, which amounted to a few inches. Picking up her coffee, she held it in both hands as if it could protect her from . . . what? From what she felt for him?

He put his mug down on the side table. "Layla, is there something we need to discuss? Are you crashing?"

"What? No. I never . . . Fuck. I don't know. Maybe that's what this is."

He narrowed his gaze. "What *what* is?"

"I thought it was just . . ." She paused, biting her lip. "You know, I really was not going to discuss this with you."

"Bad idea. You know how this works. I need you to check in with me. Are you having some subdrop?"

She nodded, her mind fumbling for what to say. "I woke up this morning a little freaked out."

"Because we played, or because I was still here when you woke up?"

"A little of both, maybe?"

He was quiet a few moments, watching her, his brows drawn. Then he said, his tone soft, "I get it. I do. You've been on your own for a long while. There must be a reason for it, you being the beautiful, enticing woman you are. I'm certain that wouldn't be the case if you had any desire not to be. So, I won't intrude, but I'll assume I'm right."

She nodded slowly.

"And," he continued, "waking up with a strange man can be a bit of a shock."

"I think what was more shocking was how *not* strange it is," she murmured, glancing away. But she couldn't help turning back to him to see what his reaction to her words might be.

He was rubbing a hand over his shaved head. "Yeah. Me, too. Weird, eh?"

For some reason, him admitting to the same feeling allowed

her to laugh, allowed her tight shoulders to drop. "Yeah, really weird."

"All right. So, this is what we do about it: we go along with it, yes? We just let things happen and don't stop to worry over it."

"I think I can do that," she told him, hoping it was true. She wanted it to be true. Wanted not to worry or overanalyze. Maybe if they had an agreement about it, she could manage it.

Maybe.

"Good. Good girl. Now put that coffee down."

She did as he asked without thinking about it, and he pulled her over his lap while she squealed.

"What are you doing, Duff?"

"Sealing it with a spanking."

"Isn't that supposed to be sealed with a kiss?"

"Nah. We're kinky folk. It's always a spanking. Prepare yourself."

She tried to cover her bottom with her hands, but he pulled them behind her back and held them there.

"Duff, wait!"

"Wait? Really, princess? Why should I do that?"

Her brain scrambled for an answer against the crazy push and pull. *Don't do it. Please do it.* "Because we have some more negotiating to do, and you know we can't negotiate once you've spanked me."

"Ah." He ran a palm over her ass.

"Hey," she prompted.

"I'm thinking about it."

She shook her head. "You really are hopeless."

"Another mark on the ledger. But you're right." He released her and let her up. "Negotiate away."

"Why do you have to make this so hard on me? No, never mind. I know the answer to that. So . . . we need to talk about sex."

"My favorite subject."

"And one of mine, as we agreed last night."

"All right, lovely, let's hash it out. I want to do it—you want to do it. I'd say we're done, but I'm too damn responsible a Dom to end it there. Do you still want to?"

That question, the mere suggestion of sex, went through her like a heated touch between her thighs, and suddenly she was soaking wet. She looked into his shining hazel eyes and nodded very slowly.

"Ah, don't look at me like that, Layla," he said, gravel in his tone.

"Like what?"

"With that naked wanting in your beautiful eyes." He wrapped a hand behind her neck, burying his fingers in her hair. "Like you could eat me alive. I know you could. One of the things I like most about you. About *this*. Being with a woman who is as unabashedly sensual—as sexual—as I am. Oh, yeah. Knowing it's harnessed under my hands. Too. Fucking. Hot."

"Duff?"

"Yeah?"

She slipped the robe from her shoulders. "Please?"

CHAPTER

Six

His GAZE WENT wide; then his lush lips came down hard on hers as he threw her onto her back. She wrapped her legs around his waist. He pulled them off and pinned her thighs with his knees, making her body surge with new desire. His tongue opened her mouth up, slipped inside, explored, commanded, drank her in.

She could barely breathe between his demanding mouth and the weight of him on her, but she loved it. His hips ground against her, and she felt the solid ridge of his cock through his jeans. Then, tearing his mouth from hers, he swore, backed off her long enough to unzip and kick his jeans off. She would almost have been sorry not to see what she was certain was his gorgeous cock, except that it was pressed against her mound, just above her aching clitoris. Oh, how she wanted him.

"Duff," she panted. "It *hurts*."

Somehow it wasn't necessary to explain what she meant.

"Yeah, it does, lovely. Hurts me, too. But not for long, now. Finally."

Kicking her thighs apart, he used his hands to spread her wider and knelt between her legs. She felt his hot breath on her sex for one seemingly endless moment—and gasped as he flicked his tongue at her needy flesh.

"Ah!"

When he did it again, over and over, she reached over her head to grab onto the arm of the couch and held on tight as he went to work with his clever tongue. He lapped at her clit, pressing his fingers into her, opening her up. She was so damn wet she took his fingers easily, and would have spread her thighs wider to welcome his every touch if he hadn't already done it for her. And oh, God, he was pumping into her, three fingers, four—filling her, rubbing at her G-spot while his tongue worked her clit just as hard. The aching need really did begin to hurt, and her mind was a blur of searing sensation and drifting thoughts. Was she allowed to come? Could she stop herself?

And then her body went into fifth gear and she was falling, falling, her climax shattering her system, blinding her, and she was screaming and twisting beneath him. It went on and on, until finally the pleasure rolled back and out to sea, leaving her shivering and twitching.

"Christ, princess. You really do know how to come."

"You have no idea," she murmured, half out of her head.

"Don't I, now? Well, then I shall have to make it my mission to find out." Raising himself over her, he reached behind him for his jeans and pulled a condom from a pocket.

"Oh, thank God."

He grinned, an animal hunger in his glittering gaze, in the loose softness of his mouth as he tore the packet with his sharp white teeth and rolled it onto his heavy erection. "You can thank me later," he growled, positioning his thick cock at the entrance to her body, making her sex clench. "After I fuck you senseless. Or maybe I'll be the senseless one. Luckily, it doesn't really matter, does it, lovely?"

"Not at all. I mean, yes, please. I mean . . . I don't know, Duff. Just do it."

Reaching down between them, he pinched her pussy lips between hard, hurting fingers, but it only made her need spiral higher. He used the same fingers to spread her open, and pushed the swollen tip of his cock into her.

"Oh! God . . ."

He was so damn big—beautifully so. She wanted to take him in all at once, but she knew, even wet as she was, that it would take a moment for her body to open for a man of his size.

"Ah, that's it, princess. So. Damn. Good. So tight. Fuck." He pressed a little deeper. "I am gonna fuck you so good and hard," he muttered, taking her face in one big hand and holding her tight. "I am gonna bury myself until my balls are pressed tight up against your lovely . . . hot . . . pussy."

He was forcing her to look at him, and the intensity of his gaze on hers was almost shocking. Electric. She was shaking all over—with scorching pleasure at the first hint of him filling her, with the need to take as much of him in as she could. Shaking with sharp desire and a touch of fear at the restrained beast she saw behind his eyes. She wanted that animal to be let loose, unleashed on her body. She didn't care if it hurt. She wanted it all. Wanted all of *him*.

In one punishing thrust he buried his cock to the hilt, driving the breath from her body. Driving pleasure deep. Then he bent to kiss her mouth, shifted to bite her shoulder, his teeth grinding into her skin. And she loved it all, the *ownership* of his actions. She refused to think about it—she wanted to be in the moment, in the pure pleasure of it as he slung his hips and began to fuck her.

It was a rough, relentless pounding, his teeth sinking deeper, his rigid flesh driving harder into her. And all she could do was hang on to his broad shoulders, her fingernails digging into his skin. He was hitting her G-spot, his pelvis crashing into hers, and the pressure built inside her until it was screaming to get out.

"Need to come . . ." she panted.

"No." He buried a hand in the back of her hair and pulled. "No. Not yet."

With his other hand he held her wrists above her head, bent and bit into the tender flesh on the underside of her arm. When she yelped, he growled, like a lion purring before devouring its prey. And she knew that was what she was at that moment. A part of her wanted to fight back—she loved that primal struggle—but she felt too taken over by him. Letting her hair go, he slid his hand under her buttocks, lifting her hips to meet his as his fingers dug in, pressing into the pressure points there.

"Ah!"

"Does it hurt, lovely?" he ground out, his Scottish accent so heavy she could barely make out the words. His hips slammed into her as pleasure and pain melded in her system. "I want it to. Need it to. Tell me you need it, Layla. *Tell me*."

"Yes." It came out on a sob—a sob of reluctant yielding and overwhelming sensation and the exquisite need to come. "Yes, I need it. I need you not to be careful with me."

"I won't be. I can guarantee you that."

He started to buck harder into her, one stabbing thrust after another, faster and faster. Pleasure was a hammer, then a tight coil, then a fiery heat, the steam needing to be released.

"Duff, goddamn it! Let me come."

"Too damn used to being the boss," he muttered, his fingers digging deeper into the sore flesh of her ass.

"Fucking hell, Duff!"

"Oh, yeah," he ground out, his voice low and guttural. "Beg me. Cuss me out. Let it out, princess. I love it."

Lifting her hips, he knelt up over her, then pulled her up until she was straddling his thighs. And using his enormous strength, his hands on her hips, he raised her up, then slammed her down on his cock so hard it made her teeth rattle. But she loved it—*needed* the savage tempo of it. The beast was out, released from whatever cage he kept it in, and she wanted it all.

"Jesus. God. Fucking you, princess . . . fucking you so. Damn. Hard. Yeah!"

He threw his head back and the beast screamed, unleashed at last. Her body let loose, her orgasm a wild animal meeting his wild beast. She cried out, pleasure searing her, rising up like a fine white light inside her that exploded over and over, like fireworks and stars and a brilliant, blinding sun.

"Ahhhhhhhh!"

Falling on top of her, he kept plunging into her, and she was helpless against it. Helpless when he demanded, "Come again."

Then, still inside her, he turned her onto her side before his hand went to her clit and circled the swollen flesh. His heavy cock was still half-hard, moving inside her. And as hard as she'd come, it was as if her body hadn't had enough. Desire built so quickly, it shocked her. Her pussy began to clench, and he bit her shoulder, his teeth dragging over her skin.

"Oh, fuck!"

"You hold it back this time," he ordered, his voice harsh, threatening. "You hold it until I tell you to come."

She loved that, too—enough that she pulled in a breath and did as he said. She held it back even as he swept the teeth marks on her shoulder with his hot, sweet tongue, as he continued to fuck her, to circle her tight, throbbing clitoris. Her hips were bucking against his hand, against the still-solid shaft inside her. And she was dizzy with the effort it took not to let go.

"Duff," she gasped.

"Not yet."

"Please . . ."

"No, Layla."

She squeezed her eyes shut. "Fuck."

"Look at me," he commanded.

He shifted her body until she was on her back once more, with him still inside her, and she opened her eyes—what else could she do? And his gaze was still full of intensity, the beast still lurking in the light and the shadows.

When he said, "Kiss me," all she could do was tilt her chin and wait for his lips.

His mouth was so, so soft on hers—there was an odd romance to it, despite the rough sex, despite his stern orders. Emotion welled in her chest, but she swallowed it back, along with her climax. He moaned into her mouth and she groaned in answer. It seemed as if time had stopped, suspended in those timeless, keen-edged moments while she waited to be allowed to come.

"Now," he murmured quietly against her lips.

That was all it took—one sharp stab of pleasure tore at her insides; then she was screaming his name, her body convulsing, the fireworks going off in her head once more. She felt torn apart by pleasure, by this man.

This man.

A tear fell from her eye and she couldn't do a damn thing about it.

Can't do a thing.

A small sob escaped her and he crushed her in his arms, crushed her to his big, muscle-packed body.

"It's all right, lovely. You did well. Yes. So good." Stroking her hair, he held her even tighter. "So, so good. I know it was hard on you. You're too used to being in charge. But now you know bone deep that with me, *I* am the one in charge. Always. Soon you won't fight it anymore. And it'll be even better."

She tried to push him away, even though every cell in her body craved his touch, wanted to be enfolded in his arms. But her mind was like a siren, shrieking at her that she'd let this go too far. Her yielding. Her submission to this man on so many levels. She'd allowed herself to want this. To *need* this. And it all spelled danger in bright red capital letters.

He pulled her in closer, her breasts pressed against his chest, until she swore she could feel his heart beating against hers.

"Shh, Layla," he murmured. "Don't crash on me."

"I'm not," she protested, hating that her voice broke.

"No? What, then? Tell me."

"It's just . . . *this*!" Her throat tightened, the words wanting to choke her. "Fuck, Duff. I gave over too much. I can't do that. I can't. This is not good."

He let her push back a few inches, until he could take her chin and tilt her face so she had to look at him. His dark brows were drawn, and for some reason she noticed every sharp line of his bone structure—his carved cheekbones, his sculpted jaw. He was too beautiful. But it did nothing to calm her mind, which felt as if it were going off in sixteen directions at once.

"Layla. You *are* crashing. Look, I know this was a lot for you, but this is the only way it can be with me. I am thoroughly dominant, whether it's sex or real kink, and there's a very thin dividing line between the two for me. I'm a primal, and it seems you are, too, yes? The biting and scratching and rough sex. Taking you down. Yeah?"

She nodded, her throat still tight. "Yes."

"Does it not feel natural to you?"

She nodded once more. "It did. It does."

"I felt it from the start. Trust me, we wouldn't be here otherwise. But something in you responds to that wild creature in me. Ah, I know he's a rough one. I keep it under control— to an extent. There's that dark part of me . . . I'll never be able to dial it back entirely. I don't want to. And once I start fucking, there's only so much I can do aside from simply being who and what I am. Which is why negotiations are so important. I'm saying this so we know we understand one another."

"I know." She shoved her hair back from her heated cheeks. "I know. I'm not saying you did anything you shouldn't have, or that I didn't agree to. But, Duff, it's been a long time since I've been with anyone—the few men I've slept with or the women I've played with—where *I* haven't been the aggressor. Not since my last relationship."

"Tell me about him."

"What? Now?" She gave a small, helpless, spurting laugh. "You're still inside me."

He shrugged, a grin lifting one corner of his mouth. "Call it pillow talk."

"Shouldn't at least one of us have our head on a pillow?"

"Taken care of easily enough," he said, leaning down to grab a throw pillow from the floor and shoving it under her head. Slipping out of her, he slipped the condom off, twisting the end of it and setting it on the floor before sliding an arm under her shoulders and settling in beside her.

She shook her head, but she was calming down between his straightforward manner and his good humor. That didn't make it any easier to talk about *him*—the straw that broke the camel's back. Fucking Jimmy. But she also knew Duff wouldn't let her get away with making any excuses.

Pulling a long breath into her lungs, she took in the scents of sex and the sandalwood candles she kept all over her house and a touch of the soft New Orleans air. Exhaling slowly, she decided to simply start talking, rather than planning what she was going to say. It was too much to figure out, with her brain still fuzzy and her body still hypersensitized from the sex. And she knew how easily she could start overanalyzing.

"Jimmy and I broke up fifteen months ago. He was another damn cheater. He cheated on me with everything that walked. He's a musician and he tours a lot, and I should have known better than to think I could date another musician and have him *not* cheat on me. Crazy, right? But he was a Dom, and claimed to be operating under the Safe, Sane and Consensual credo, and he had me fooled into thinking he was someone who took that seriously. But there was nothing safe or sane and certainly nothing consensual about him sleeping around. I heard rumors, but I didn't want to believe it. Not again. Then one night . . ."

She had to stop for a moment, swallowing hard, and it hurt, but not the way it used to. Thank God. "One night I just sort of *got* it, finally, and I started searching, and I came up with a ridiculous ton of photos online. Girls who took pictures of him in their beds, for God's sake. At a couple of dungeons. On his tour bus. In hot tubs. He had no shame. It was as if he wanted to be busted, and looking back I think he really did—or he simply liked to challenge himself with it, and maybe me. Testing me to see if I'd put up with it. And like an idiot, I hid my head in the sand for a while and I *did* put up with it. I had myself convinced that I believed all the crap he spouted about being a true, responsible Dominant. When I confronted him, he said I'd always known who he was, and all this shit about him being the boss, or had I forgotten that part?"

"Such bollocks," Duff muttered. "'Being the boss' is not

what a Dom/sub dynamic is about. That crap cheapens it. Bastard."

When she glanced up she found his jaw clenched tight. And something in that moment in which she felt his protectiveness made her body relax the tiniest bit, made her feel as if he really did give a damn. As if he truly was different.

Maybe.

She blew out another long breath before continuing. "So, I took all his crap he'd left at my place while he was on the road and I dumped it out on the curb, and it was all gone a few days later—his clothes and his favorite boots and one of his guitars, and I don't even know what else. Oh, he was pissed." She had to smile a little at that.

"Good riddance. So, why not date another musician? Just because he was an asshole, surely that can't condemn them all."

"Oh, no—they're all bad news. I'd been there before and it always ended the same way. They've all been cheaters, or they party too much, or think it's cool to get speeding tickets they never pay. And it's always about *them*—they have to be the star of the show. All the bad boys—musicians and guys with motorcycles, guys in leather jackets. All the men I've always been most attracted to. Bartenders are maybe the worst of the man-whores. I'd finally given up the bad boys after Jimmy— well, I'd kind of given up on *men* for the last year. Until you came along."

"Ah, well, the damn, despicable bad boys. The musicians, and the ones who ride motorcycles."

He was grinning outright now, and she sort of wanted to smack him, but he was right—he'd always be the one in charge.

With her. In any situation, probably. And while she could sass him, this wasn't the time.

"Duff? Can I ask you some things now?"

"I'm feeling generous," he joked. "Why not?"

"What about you? Last relationship, I mean."

"Ah." She felt him tense for a moment, but then it melted away. "Jamie is the only person I've spoken to about this. My brother, Leith, and my friends back in Edinburgh knew her, but after it ended, I wasn't up for having a discussion with anyone else."

"What was her name?"

"Bess."

HE COULD HARDLY believe he'd said her name out loud, never mind that he was going to tell Layla about her. But perhaps it was time he worked some of it out of his system. His very reluctance to talk about her told him he was still carrying the memory around like old baggage, and he didn't like it.

"Yeah, Bess was her name. She was an English girl, come to Edinburgh for school. Then she stayed for work. Then she stayed for me, which was . . . a mistake."

"A mistake? Why was it a mistake?"

He glanced down. Did he really want to answer the question? Sure as hell not. But he'd said she could ask.

It's time.

"Duff?" she prompted.

He looked back at her. "Yeah. Well. We stayed together for two years, and it's the longest run I've had with a girl, which maybe says something about me. And I was rough on her—I can see it now. I spent a lot of time working on my bikes, and everyone else's, as well. I love my work, but I should have loved my woman more, right? Right." He gave a sharp nod for emphasis. He'd never been able to really love her, and if he couldn't fall in love with a good girl like Bess, then he was a hopeless case, wasn't he?

After a moment, he went on. "She was a bit kinky—a little spanking, and she'd put up with me blindfolding her. 'Bedroom' kink. Not really enough for me, and I know she felt the pressure. And perhaps it wasn't fair of me. No, I know it wasn't. She was a good girl, and she deserved more. Sweet and even-tempered and probably more docile than was healthy for her in dealing with a man like me. But Lord knows that relationship was better than the one before her. Eileen was mad— totally out of her head. I loved her passion, and she was kinky as fuck, which is a better fit for me, but oi! She was trouble, that one. Jealous as hell. She caused scenes at the pubs, at the dungeon a few times. Slashed the tires on my Harley when I broke off with her. Could have been worse. I was three years between the two of them, and you'd think I'd have learned more. Well."

He stopped, cleared his throat. Why the hell had he just dumped all this on Layla? It was more than he'd meant to say.

"And vanilla relationships?" she asked.

"Oh, yeah—that never ends well. They're not for me. I tried, with Bess, who was mostly vanilla, but I couldn't dial it back much. Well, I did, but it was a strain. It was always an issue that I wasn't getting what I wanted, and to be honest, neither was she. Kink wasn't what she was about, but it's too much a part of who I am to give it up."

"I get that. It's the same for me."

"Is it, now?" He looked at her, into those lovely green eyes. His dick was getting hard again, despite the difficult conversation, which he was secretly rather proud of.

"Yes, absolutely. Vanilla relationships have been a disaster—almost as disastrous as the kink relationships. I've come to the conclusion that maybe it's the 'relationship' part that doesn't work for me."

"Ah, me, as well."

"Yes, but I've removed the sex part, too. Until now."

"Now, that I can't claim to have done."

She smiled, her eyes twinkling. "I wouldn't have thought so."

His dick was still hard—too hard to ignore, with an armful of warm, fragrant, beautiful woman.

"Princess."

"Yes?"

"How did you know that's exactly what I wanted to hear you say?"

She laughed. "I'm sure it was. What am I agreeing to, exactly?"

"This."

He picked her up and wrapped her legs around his waist, then carried her through the French doors and into her bedroom, where he tossed her down on the bed, which was a mattress on the floor, swagged in what looked to be Indian saris. It suited her, this room. He quickly took in an old armoire with chipping white paint on one wall, two windows hung with more colorful saris. But what he liked most was the long mirrors on the doors of the armoire—he could see the bed reflected there. The bed and the incredibly gorgeous woman lying naked on it. Waiting for him.

Oh, yeah.

He had to stand there a moment, looking at her—taking in her sleek skin, the luscious curve of her breasts, the nipples going hard, darkening. The small indentations where he'd bitten her.

"Lord, but you must have the most delicious-looking tits I've ever seen. I have to get my mouth on 'em again. I have to fuck you there, between your tits, with all that beautiful flesh wrapped around my cock until I come on your face. Oh, yeah, don't look so shocked. You knew I was the kind of guy who'd want to come on your lovely face."

"Jesus, Duff."

She started to sit up, but he pushed her down onto her back, catching her gaze. There was fire there. He didn't mind. Not one bit.

"We're going to have a struggle, are we? You going to fight it out with me? Come on, then, princess. Let's see what you've got."

She lunged at him and had her nails in his shoulders before he had a chance to do more than laugh. He was both amused and wanting to egg her on.

"You are a goddamn beast!"

"That I am," he agreed. "Can you take the beast down, Layla? Give it a try."

She backed off and met his gaze with hers, her eyes flashing dangerously. Then she lunged at him again, and he was shocked when her shoulder slammed into his midsection. He rolled onto his side, grabbing her around the waist and taking her with him onto the floor. He was on his back, holding her on top of him, and her sleek, naked little pussy was hot against his stomach, making his hard cock jump.

Nice.

"How much bigger am I than you, little Layla? Could be you're getting yourself into trouble here."

"Big enough to go down hard," she said before lunging again and sinking her teeth into his left pectoral muscle.

"My, what sharp teeth you have," he teased as he held her off, pain a small lance in his flesh.

"I'll show you how sharp," she muttered before slipping under his hands, somehow, and taking the steel bar piercing his left nipple between her teeth.

"Hey, now—careful."

She gave it a good, hard tug and murmured around it, "You still want to wrestle me?"

"Sure I do. My left nipple, not so much."

"Ha!"

He grabbed her at that moment, when she was crowing over her victory, and turned her roughly onto her back under him. Using the weight of his body, he held her down on the wood floor, and the morning sun coming through the jewel-colored curtains lit the blaze in her green eyes, tipped her dark hair in gold and red. Beautiful.

"I'm gonna fuck you now, princess. And I'll call you 'princess' while I do it. And maybe I'll take your ass, too, while I'm at it, right here on the floor in full daylight. Oh, yeah. And when I let you up we're going to talk about playing with my violet wand at The Bastille."

Her lips parted, but no sound came out. He could tell from

the way her nipples had gone instantly hard when he'd told her what he was about to do, then harder still at the mention of electrical play, that she was into it all. Oh, yeah, she was the girl for him.

For now.

"Condoms, lovely?" he asked.

"In the sea chest right behind my head. But check the expiration date."

He grinned. "Handy." Straddling her chest, he knelt up and lifted the lid of the antique trunk. "Nice collection you have here," he told her, sifting through the vibrators and floggers, paddles and cuffs.

Cuffs. Oh, yeah.

He pulled out the pair of soft leather cuffs and quickly buckled them around her wrists.

"Hey! Those are *not* condoms."

"No, but they'll certainly keep me safe, my little wildcat. Hands over your head, that's a good girl."

She grumbled even as she did as he asked, but he couldn't make out what she was saying.

"What was that?" he asked. When she clenched her jaw tighter, he took her face in one hand and demanded, "Tell me."

"I said you're a fucking gorilla and I can hardly hope to do any damage to you."

"Eh? I know that well enough. But I did enjoy seeing you try. Loved it."

"Hmph!"

"Another mark on the ledger, which I also happen to love, lucky for you. Or unlucky." He smiled as he continued to dig through her toy chest. "Ah, a Hitachi."

"*No*, Duff."

He put a hand to his ear and cocked his head. "What was that? Did you tell me no?"

She pouted, her lovely lips so full he had to lean down and kiss her—*had* to—a quick kiss followed by a quick bite.

"Oh!"

"Some nice leather straps in here, as well. An idea is formulating."

He glanced down at her pouting mouth, her tight jaw. But her nipples were still hard as two dark stones. Leaning down, he gave each of them a quick, nibbling kiss and was gratified when she squirmed beneath him. He was maybe even harder than her nipples—hard enough that it was torture to wait—but he couldn't resist what he was about to do.

Taking the beltlike straps he slipped one under and around her waist, then did the same with another across her pelvis, crossing the ends and lacing them under her buttocks, leaving the open ends lying on the floor at her sides. He shifted until he was kneeling between her thighs, then spread them a little wider with his hands and jammed his knees against her inner thighs to hold them wide. When he reached for the Hitachi and switched it on, her eyes went wide.

"Duff . . ."

He raised his brows, and that was enough to silence her. For the moment. He reached inside the trunk and came up with a long purple silk scarf.

"Goddamn it, Duff!"

"Silence is golden, lovely," he said before forcing her lips apart and placing a bit of the silk between them, then tying the makeshift gag behind her head.

She was blinking very fast, as if she couldn't believe he was doing it, which made him smile—and for her sake he let the smile widen into a wicked grin.

"You should enjoy this. I know I will."

He picked up the heavily buzzing Hitachi and pressed it to her clit. She groaned from behind the silk gag. He did it again, this time holding it there firmly, and her hips began to buck immediately.

"That's right. I want you to come, princess. Over and over and over, until you can't take anymore. And then I want you to come again. Again and again. And to ensure that happens— and to leave my hands free for other uses—I'm going to strap this to you with the belts you had in your very handy sea chest."

He did as he said, crossing the leather belts over her pelvis and buckling them tightly against the big vibrator, adjusting the humming Hitachi wand until he was sure he had it seated just right against her clitoris. Then he sat back to watch the color rise in her cheeks, even on her chest, her succulent breasts beneath the gorgeous caramel skin. In moments she began to shake, then twitch, then scream behind the gag as she came. His dick was twitching, too, the pressure building. Taking it in his hand, he started a light, feathering stroke, then reached down and forced the lips of her sex apart with his fingers. She was soaking wet. He slid his fingers in her soft, damp flesh, then pushed two inside her and went for her G-spot, stroking firmly. And instantly she was coming again, that same growling yell rising from deep in her throat as her inner walls clenched around his plunging fingers.

"Again," he ordered, thrusting hard into her, his hand going a little numb from the rumbling vibration of the Hitachi.

She came once more, her body shaking, that low growl turning into a scream that left her panting and left his cock ready to explode.

"You're about to come again for me, princess."

She shook her head, her green eyes glazed, and he saw her fighting it—the impossible task of resisting another orgasm as well as her submission to him. But he would make her do it—*make* her, and have her like it. He wanted her to give herself over. Wanted to see her yield to him, this strong, powerful woman. Oh, yeah, that made it so much better.

Letting his cock go, he stood and pressed down onto the wand with his foot, applying the slightest bit of pressure. Her eyes went wider as she began to climax once more, this time her entire body jerking, her neck and back arching up off the floor, and it was the hottest thing he'd seen in his life. She came and came—it was a full minute or more before it eased off, leaving her panting. Leaving him so hard, needing her so badly, he couldn't wait a moment longer.

He bent and tore the gag from her mouth, yanked the belts from her body and tossed the Hitachi aside. He was almost inside her before he had to stop, biting his lip hard.

"Need a damn condom. God-fucking-damn it."

He fumbled on the floor for the string of condoms he'd pulled from the chest, and it took a few endless moments before he managed to sheathe himself. Then he grabbed her calves, lifted her legs until they were on his shoulders, and plowed into her all at once.

"Oh, yes," she moaned, her soaking-wet pussy taking him easily.

Still, she was so beautifully tight he had to hold still a

moment, commanding his system to calm. But it was all desperate heat with her, every single moment between them. All he could do was fuck her and hope he managed to last more than a minute.

"Yes, lovely," he murmured, fighting the surge of pleasure that jolted his body even as he slowly pulled back, his hard flesh sliding out inch by excruciating inch. "This may hurt," he warned her.

"Make it hurt," she panted. "I want it to."

"You may have just said that to the wrong man."

He arched hard into her, shivering with the pure pleasure of being inside her. He pulled back and did it again, trying to measure out his pace, to hold something back. But it was Layla, and at this point control was impossible.

Not a good thing for a Dom, man.

No. But he was too full of stark, raving need to give that fact more than a passing thought. All he could do was begin a hard, punishing stroke, gliding like stone against silk in and out, faster, faster. All he could do was take in her wide glassy gaze, the fullness of her beautiful mouth as she bit down on her lip, the curve of her slender shoulders. Lord, this woman was full of gorgeous curves: hips, breasts, that incredible ass.

That incredible ass.

He groaned. Forced himself to stop.

"Layla."

"Hmm? Don't stop, Duff. Please."

He bent and ran his teeth along the edge of her jaw, nipping at her earlobe, trying to get his body to calm enough for him to get the words out. But the anticipation was making him feel as if he would burst, his climax already a sharp pulse at the base of his cock.

Finally he was able to mutter, "Time for me to take that sweet ass of yours, princess."

"I . . . Oh."

He slid out of her long enough to wrap his hands around her slender waist and bend her over the side of the bed. He uncuffed her hands, massaged her wrists for a moment, then tossed the cuffs onto the bed.

"You have lube in that sea chest, lovely?"

"Yes."

He leaned over and saw it right away, picked up the bottle and squeezed a little onto one finger. "All right. Breathe in . . . Good." He pressed his lubed fingertip to that small, tight spot between the beautiful curve of her ass cheeks. "Now exhale, nice and slow."

Massaging her hole with his finger, he reached around with his other hand and began to massage her clitoris, which was swollen from the working-over she'd had with the Hitachi.

"Oh, yeah. Still so sensitive, yes, princess? But I like you like that. I like it when it hurts to feel good. And I think you do, too, yes?"

"Yes."

"Tell me."

"I like it when it hurts. I love when the pain and the pleasure meld together. When I can't tell where one ends and the other begins."

He slipped the fingertip in.

"Oh! Oh . . ." She moaned as he began to move just the tip in and out. "God, I love that."

He went deeper, sliding slowly past the tight ring of muscle, and she relaxed instantly, allowing him through, telling him silently that her body knew exactly what to do.

"Ah, you take it well," he murmured, pausing to squeeze some more lube onto another finger, then adding it to the first.

She gasped.

"Just breathe. Good." He slipped his fingers in farther, and her body clenched and unclenched. "Good girl."

She shivered at the words, which made him smile. The girl might claim to have left her submissive years behind her, but that response said it all. Layla was truly submissive—she had that in her—and her ability to dominate didn't make it any less real.

He pumped a few more times, watching her body for every minute reaction, but she was taking it well, opening up for him, her breathing slow and rhythmic and done with intent.

Reaching around, he massaged her hard little clitoris again, and her hips started to move, her pelvis pressing forward against his hand, then arching back, taking his fingers deeper into her ass. And the whole time his dick was hard and throbbing in time with the sinuous motion of her hips. He felt in awe of her ability to wantonly enjoy what he was doing to her. In awe of how lovely this girl was—her body, her desire.

"Layla. Beautiful girl. Jesus fuck, but you're something." He paused, licking his lips. "Have to be inside your ass now, lovely. Have to do it. You ready for me?"

"Yes," she gasped. "I'm ready, Duff. Come on."

He let out a harsh laugh as he reached for a fresh condom, slipping the old one off and rolling the new one on, then coating it in lube. "Trying to hurry me, are you? I can hurry my way right into your sweet flesh, girl." He leaned over her, his erection in his hand, the tip at her tight, tempting entrance. "Do you really want me to plow into your ass? Because I can, and I will. But be very certain you don't want me to be careful with you."

"Just do it. Please, Duff. I can't stand to wait."

He threw back his head and let out a long laugh then—he was so damn delighted with her. "All right, then. Hang on."

He saw her grip the bedcover in both fists, heard her sigh as he eased the tip into her backside. He felt her body tense; then every muscle went loose and he sank inside.

"Ah, fuck," he muttered from between teeth clenched in agony as pleasure surged through him, belly and balls, scorching hot, sharp as a blade. "Never felt anything like it," he ground out. "Never anything so. Damn. Good. Ah . . ."

Wrapping an arm around her waist, he really went to work, pounding into her, loving every panting breath she took, the way the front of her body arched up off the bed. The wood floor was biting into his knees, but he didn't care—couldn't care. Everything felt too good, pleasure building upon pleasure and knifing into his system until he was certain he would bleed his pleasure onto the floor before this was done.

And she was pressing back against him, taking him in, despite how tight she was inside. Pressing against him and groaning and her breath was a harsh, rasping pant, and so was his own.

"Duff! Oh, God . . . Please. Please just . . . yes!"

She was writhing and twisting under him, and even her back was a beautiful thing, the tattoo running down the long arch of her slender neck dancing as she moved. Sensation built, coiled in his system—his cock and his balls, but his spine, too, and his hips, even his mouth. His thighs grew weak, as if there was too much sensation to be contained in one place. Sliding his hand down between her thighs, he found the nub of her clit and began to massage it once more.

"Oh, yes, please . . . Ah . . . Going to come. Duff . . . can I?"

"Come, lovely, yes. Come for me. Come with me in your beautiful, tight ass."

She arched hard into his hand once, twice; then she was groaning, that same hard, rasping sound deep in her throat, and her body spasmed around his swollen flesh inside her. He only pounded into her harder, her orgasm giving him the permission he needed to allow himself to come. And he did, furiously, hard enough to make his bones rattle, to make him yell.

"Ahhhhhhhh! Fucking God, honey!"

Pleasure poured through him, flowed out of his stiff flesh in savage jolts. But he couldn't stop, his hips moving, his body hammering into her so damn hard—too hard, probably, and she'd be sore as hell, but he couldn't help himself; he was too far gone.

"Can't. Fucking. Stop."

"Don't stop." Her voice was a harsh sob, but he understood she meant it.

A few more piercing jabs and his orgasm was finally over, other than the small tremors running through him like electrical arcs. It occurred to him that he'd be feeling those arcs for a while.

"That was amazing," he murmured, still shivering.

"Mmm." Her head was turned to the side, her cheek resting on the coverlet. So damn pretty.

Bending over her, he placed a soft kiss on her spine, then another and another. She smelled like sex. Like woman. He bit into her taut flesh, smiling when she did nothing but moan quietly. He did it again, then licked the pink spot he'd left on her skin. She tasted like sex, too. Sex and woman. Like a woman he'd like to do this with every damn day.

"What the fuck?" he muttered out loud before he could stop himself.

"Duff? Is everything okay?"

He could hear the alarm in her voice and felt like a cad.

"What? Yeah, everything is good. Great. Baby wipes in that magic box of yours?"

"Yes."

Leaning over the side of the sea chest, he found the plastic container, pulled a few wipes out and used them as he slipped out of her, pausing to clean her up before sliding the condom off and wrapping it in the wipes, which he placed on the lid of the box. Then, climbing up onto the bed, he pulled her into his lap, where she nestled, eyes closed, a smile on her lips. And for some reason he couldn't understand, he could do nothing more than pet her hair and her cheek and the slender length of her neck, watching her, absorbing the weary pleasure on her face. The loveliest face he'd ever seen.

He noticed now how thick her black lashes were, curling at the ends. How the flush on her cheeks only brought out the perfectly curving cheekbones even more. How delicate her chin was beneath the plush pout of her pink mouth.

He ran a fingertip over her lips, needing to touch them, to make her smile, and she did. And he smiled. He couldn't help it. He'd never felt so damn pleased with the presence of a woman in his life.

Never before . . .

His chest went tight. Fuck.

But he wouldn't think about the words that had run through his head, unbidden and unwanted, or that he'd never felt this way or thought these things about anyone. Not Eileen. Not Bess. He couldn't think about it. Not now, when he felt so ridiculously good. After all, they'd not promised more than sex and play to each other, and that's all this was. Spectacularly good kinky sex. He hadn't done anything to mislead her, and she was no innocent thing he was leading down the kinky path. It was all fine.

Right?

Then why was his heart slamming against his ribs without him even being out of breath? Why did he feel this need to touch her? Just touch her face and her hair and stare at her, drinking her in, as if he couldn't get enough?

Don't think about all that shit. Nothing more than the aftermath of a killer orgasm. That's. Fucking. It.

That *was* it. Right?

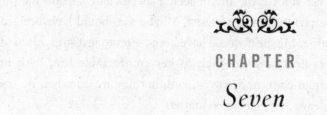

LAYLA WOKE TO the pleasant weight of Duff's big hand on her breast. She turned to look at him, but he was dead asleep. How was it possible that this enormous, wicked man could look so sweet while he was sleeping? But then, he *was* sweet to her, in between all the wickedness. There had been plenty over the weekend, which reminded her that it was Monday morning and he'd have to get up soon and take off for work. Glancing at the clock she saw it was a quarter to seven. All she had with him was another few minutes.

Why did that feel like precious time? She was being ridiculous. She'd only known the man for a week—it had only been eight days since she'd barged into his shop and told him to back off. It wasn't like her to let things progress so fast. It wasn't like her to let things progress at all in the last year. Did that mean she was ready for more? Or was it only because he was the first man she'd wanted to submit to since she'd left her last failed relationship behind? The first man to bring that out in her since then, and in such a spectacular fashion she was completely unable to resist. Maybe she should have been resisting. Maybe it would have been better to just stop this madness now, and go back to her comfortable life, with no dramatic ups and downs, with nothing to scare her, no one to leave her. No one to matter.

Morbid thoughts on a rainy morning.

She usually loved the rain, and this morning it was a light rainfall, just enough to hear through the windows, to cool the air deliciously. Pulling the blanket up around her shoulders, she rolled onto her side, allowing herself to revel in the heat of Duff's big body next to hers. But watching him sleep made her want to touch him, and she knew if she did, seeing him walk out the door would feel even worse.

Blowing out a breath, she flipped onto her back. What in the world was wrong with her? Crossing her arms over her chest, she stared up at the ceiling. And suddenly she couldn't wait for Duff to leave. She was still brooding when the alarm on Duff's cell phone went off. He slapped at it to shut it off, then grabbed her, his eyes still closed, and pulled her into a bear hug.

"Hey. Aren't you going to be late?"

"What? Yeah, probably. But you feel better than riding my bike in the rain will. You feel better than most things."

She started to smile, then stopped herself.

Don't give into it. It doesn't mean anything.

"I can make you some tea, if you want," she offered.

"Nah. I'll stop and get some. What do you have planned today?" he asked, his voice low and gravelly with sleep.

"I have to meet with one of the galleries where I show. We're going over placement for some new pieces. Then a few errands, and tonight I want to start a new piece."

"It's pretty fucking awesome, what you do. Have I told you that?"

"Um . . . maybe?"

"Well, it is." He pulled her in tighter, burying his face in her neck, then kissing her there. She didn't want to shiver in response, but her body had other ideas.

"Hey, lovely? What's up?"

"What do you mean?"

"You just went tight as piano wire all over. You crashing again?"

"No, I . . ." Was she? Or was she simply being reasonable about what was or wasn't happening here. "I don't know. Maybe. I'll take a nice, long shower and have some hot chocolate. I'll be fine."

He dragged her body onto his strong, broad chest, until she had to look down into his face. His dark brows were drawn. "You call me if you need to—you hear me?"

She started to shake her head. "Oh, I really don't think I'll—"

"Layla," he interrupted. "You know the rules. You call me if you find yourself crashing. Now, who else can you talk to if I'm unable to pick up the phone?"

"I can talk to Kitty. Or Rosie."

"She's Finn's girl, yeah? Great girl. Great tattoo artist, too. She did the biomech piece on my forearm soon after I arrived from Scotland. Glad you're friends with her."

"So am I."

"All right. Will you do it? Call one of them if you start to drop and you can't reach me?"

"Are you saying you don't believe me?"

"Not entirely."

She rolled her eyes, partly because she knew he could see right through her. "Okay, I promise."

"Good girl." He grabbed her and kissed her firmly on the mouth. "Gotta get up and head to work."

Placing her on the mattress, he stood up and stretched, his wide, muscled back to her, and she couldn't help but admire with some degree of awe the taut muscles of his ass, his narrow waist, the bunching and flexing of muscle across his shoulders beneath the gorgeous Celtic artwork. She watched quietly as he pulled his clothes on, then his big black boots.

He sat on the edge of the bed. "Come here and give me a kiss, woman," he ordered.

She moved toward him and lifted her chin, expecting a small peck, but he wrapped her up in his arms, and her stomach knotted as he held her tight, then kissed her hard and thoroughly. Her body wanted to melt with heat and desire, but something inside her was warning her to hold back.

Duff pulled back a few inches and looked down at her, and she was struck once more by the utterly masculine beauty of his face, the metallic gleam of his hazel eyes.

"We'll talk later about whatever is going on with you, princess."

"I kind of hate that I can't hide anything from you," she grumbled, glancing down at the bedcover.

"Just doing my job," he joked.

But his words went through her like a punch in the gut and she looked back up at him.

"Shit. Sorry, lovely. You don't think that's what all this is, do you?"

"I really have no idea *what* this is, Duff," she admitted. "And I hate that I'm being such a damn girl about it. Maybe I am crashing. Because this is *not* me."

He stroked her hair with a gentle hand and said quietly, "I like you being a girl. Wouldn't have it any other way. I don't think you're being weak or needy or any of that other crap we men spew at women to keep our distance. I . . ." He paused, shaking his head. "I don't know. Somehow I don't want to keep my distance from you."

"You don't have to say that."

He grabbed her chin and forced her gaze to his. "No. I don't, in fact."

Leaning in, he kissed her, then kissed her again, and again and again until she finally gave in and opened her lips for him. Opened herself. She was still afraid this would end disastrously. But she didn't seem to be able to resist Duff Stewart. And as he turned to leave, she breathed him in as he stepped away from her and out of her house, wondering if she'd ever be able to.

THE DAY HAD dragged, despite Layla doing her best to keep busy. She'd done her grocery shopping, lingering over the produce, catching herself daydreaming about the way Duff kissed her. She'd gone to her gallery appointment, but had found herself distracted by images flitting through her mind—images of the huge phallus she'd sculpted after that first meeting with him, and by images of Duff himself: his eminently kissable mouth, the muscles running through his forearms, his boots. She had a major crush on those boots, but only because of the man who wore them.

She'd dropped by Midnight Ink to see if Rosie was available for lunch, forgetting the tattoo shop was usually closed on Mondays, and when she tried calling her cell, Rosie hadn't picked up. Then she'd taken a long drive, but even that was no help. She swore she could still smell him all over her car, and had finally turned around and headed home. Now she stood in front of her bathroom mirror, searching her face for some sign of the strangeness she was feeling.

I am a mess.

But she felt damn good for being a mess—sore in all the best places, inside and out, and the tiny ripples of pain only made her smile. Had it simply been too long since she'd had a chance to remember what it felt like to be a well-played bottom? Or was it something more?

Oh, yes, there was a glimmer in her green eyes, and her damn cheeks were glowing, despite her lack of sleep—Duff Stewart knew how to keep a girl *up*. But in between, hadn't she slept like a baby in his big, strong arms?

She scowled at her too-giddy reflection in the mirror. "You're talking like you've never seen a man before in your life. Like some schoolgirl who's just lost her virginity to the hottest guy in school."

But she *had* lost her virginity to the hottest guy in school when she was seventeen, and he hadn't made her feel like this.

Not even close. Neither had her long string of poor choices—Adrien, her first musician, whom she'd met the year after she'd graduated from high school. He'd been so damn *pretty* for a bad boy, and insanely charming—and he was her first kink experience. It had been relatively mild—a little spanking, rough sex, some biting—but it had been a sexual epiphany for her. Then there had been Marcel, who was a star New Orleans chef. It had taken her eight months to realize his "dominance" was nothing more than bossiness, a bad attitude and an inflated sense of entitlement. Then it was Vincent, the race car driver, who had expanded her BDSM realm with wax play and nipple clamps and her first flogging, which had really gone to her head. But she'd been a bit wiser that time—six months in she'd caught him cheating and been too pissed to pretend it wasn't happening. Then there was Jimmy. She'd been single for a while, bottoming at the clubs, and had thought somehow that she'd learned better. She should have known better than to date another musician, especially a friend of Adrien's, especially a lead guitarist. But she'd met him at a kink club, and he was known there as a Dom. He was seven years older than her, and she'd made the mistaken assumption that with age came wisdom. She'd thought he was the real thing—real enough that she'd wasted two years of her life with him. Oh, yeah, she'd paid her dues with men—with cheating men—and she didn't quite trust her own judgment any longer.

How much had she learned in her year off from men? Enough? How could she possibly know?

Turning from the mirror with a small huff, she reached for the small window next to the sink and unlatched it, pushing it open. What was on the other side was a little secret, of sorts, something she used to comfort herself. It wasn't really ridiculous, if she didn't allow herself to think too much about it. She reached through to let her fingertips drift over the tiny house made of twigs and bits of copper wire that had turned a lovely aqua shade with oxidization, with a single tiny brass dragonfly on the roof and glass marbles inside—her little faery house. She'd made it soon after she'd moved in, after one of her terrible breakups. It was set in the crook of an old crepe myrtle tree that was just beginning to drop its bright pink blossoms. She pulled at the hinged door, pushing the blue and green marbles nestled inside around with one finger. The tiny structure was always charming, but it had been a while since she'd needed the comfort of it. Duff was messing with her head, and she didn't like it.

Except that she kind of did.

Turning back to the bathroom mirror, she pushed her curls back from her face, blowing out a long breath.

"Okay. Get it together," she murmured.

But all she could think of was his scent, his touch, the vulnerability in his voice when he'd talked to her about his past. The man had opened up to her, and she had a feeling that, like her, it wasn't something he did often, if at all. She loved that he made her laugh, but she also sensed the jokester in him was partially a cover for some not-so-deeply-buried pain. It made her feel for him, and his openness reached out to the pain she carried herself. And it was all a little too overwhelming.

Stalking from the bathroom, she moved through her bedroom, intending to go out to her studio and lose herself in clay.

But she stopped just short of the front door, knowing she was too damned distracted to work. She paced the living room for a few minutes, her hands fisted at her sides as she fought the sensations in her chest—the tightness and flutter that felt so good and so awful at the same time—before giving in and picking up her cell phone to dial Kitty at the salon.

"Allure Salon. This is Kitty."

"Hey, it's me. What time are you out of there tonight?"

"I'm almost done. Why do you sound weird?" her friend asked.

"I do not!"

"Okay. But, yeah, you do. All breathless and stuff."

"Jeez, Kitty. Thanks for not cutting me any slack."

"What kind of friend would I be if I did? So, are you gonna tell me?"

She blew out a breath. "Yes. That's why I called, I guess. Can you meet me after work?"

"Sure. Want me to come over? I can bring chocolate. And booze, 'cause it sounds like it's going to be one of those nights. It's been a hell of a Monday, so I don't mind."

"Crap. I'm sorry, Kitty. You okay?"

"Yeah. Just too many clients who don't understand why I can't take them from their natural brunette to platinum blond in one day without their hair cracking and falling out. The usual. But luckily I'm out of here in a few minutes, so I won't have to kill anyone. How's seven fifteen?"

"Perfect. I'll order some Indian food."

"Oh, goody! I love it when you cook for me."

That made her laugh. "I actually can be domestic. Sometimes."

"I'll believe it when I see it. Meanwhile, Indian is just fine. Be there in a bit, honey."

She felt a bit better after they hung up. She only had to make it through another half hour without driving herself crazy.

By the time she'd dug up the menu to her favorite local Indian delivery and placed their order—tikka masala for her and butter chicken with jasmine rice for Kitty—Kitty was knocking on the door. She opened it and hugged her friend.

"Thanks for coming."

"For you? Anytime, honey—you know that. Let's get a good buzz going while we wait for the food, and you can tell me everything."

They settled on the sofa with the Malibu and pineapple juice Kitty mixed for them in the kitchen, and Layla leaned back into the pile of pillows, her feet curled under her.

"I love Malibu," she said.

"I know you do—that's why I brought it. So, tell Mama Kitty what's made you all weird."

Layla grinned, shaking her head. "You know I love how straight and to the point you are, but tonight I just wish . . . that you could read my mind without me having to say it out loud."

Kitty reached out and patted her arm, her sweet face softening. "You know I would if I could, hon."

"I know." She smiled at her dear friend, then took a breath and simply began. "Okay, be honest with me—is it crazy to think I'm falling for him after only eight days?"

"I don't know. How is the sex?"

"Amazing. Off-the-charts amazing. Fucking fireworks on the Fourth of July. But that's not all it is."

"Well, it never is just the sex, is it? But that can be where it starts."

"This is the thing, Kitty—this man is so big and tough, and I mean really badass. He's so damn dominant, I can't even begin to fight it. I know that's part of the attraction—sort of being sucked under by his natural dominance. But he doesn't lord it over me the way a lot of men do. The way most men seem to feel they have to. He simply *is* that way. But he also doesn't take himself too seriously. He shows me who he is, warts and all. I know there's a lot more to him than what he's told me, but he really has opened himself to me in this short period of time we've had. And I don't think it's an act. I really don't. I know my judgment has been absolute shit when it comes to men, but this last year off has been good for me, and I think I've learned a lot. Some, anyway. I'm much better at protecting myself from the dogs and the Dom wannabes. I think this guy could be the real thing."

Kitty arched one blond brow. "A real man? Or a real Dom?"

"All of it. I think he's being sincere with me, which sort of blows my mind, because after my history, I wasn't certain I could ever trust anyone again. In fact, I've been pretty damn opposed to the idea, but here I am, trusting him, giving myself over to him, and it feels right. Is that crazy? Please tell me if I'm crazy—if I'm losing my mind here."

"Well, to be honest, you are kinda losing it, hon. But only because you obviously *are* falling for him. And yes, it can happen in only a week. Sometimes things just *fit*. And honestly?

Hearing you talk like this? Things are fitting all over the place between you two. I know that's bad English, but it makes sense in my head." Kitty grinned at her.

"No, I get it. It makes sense to me, too. But goddamn it, Kitty, if he's not being real with me, I'll kill him. I really will."

"And I'll be right behind you with a shovel to bury the body."

Layla reached for her, pulling her in for a brief, tight hug. "You're a true friend."

"Always. Ah—there's the door. Food is here. Let's stuff ourselves and get a little drunk and you can tell me about the fireworks in detail."

SATURDAY MORNING LAYLA woke to her cell phone chiming with a text message. She glanced at the time before looking at her phone—it was after ten, much later than she normally woke. But she'd been up late the last few nights giving her toy box a workout. She needed to go buy more lube. And batteries. Lots of batteries.

She rubbed her eyes and looked at her phone—and smiled when she saw the text was from Duff.

Morning, lovely. Hope you've had your beauty sleep. I plan to work you over well and good at my place tonight. Be ready for me at six. Don't worry. I plan to feed you first.

She groaned, her body lighting up in all the right places, and her heart fluttering. She'd almost gotten used to it over the course of the week. Her talk with Kitty the other night had helped. And it had helped—and *not* helped, as far as the constant state of arousal her body had been in—that Duff had kept in touch with her all week, despite some big problems with the shop buildout that had come up, keeping him there late every evening. He'd texted several times a day, every day, and called to say good night. But those good-night calls only led to her need for lube and batteries. He had the sexiest damn voice she'd ever heard in her life.

He hadn't done much of the D/s stuff over the phone her exes had all been prone to—nothing more than a few suggestive, teasing remarks—and she appreciated that he wasn't trying to conduct mind-fuck via text. She'd had enough experience as a Domme herself at this point to understand how dangerous that could be to someone's headspace. And to know how that made her long line of exes—especially Jimmy, who had claimed to be an experienced, knowledgeable Dominant—a bunch of "romper-doms." None of them had really known what the hell they were doing. Sure, they could throw a flogger or a whip, but beyond that? Not one of them had gotten the psychology behind kink, or knew what a healthy power exchange was. Or had even really cared.

Her cell phone chimed once more and she saw Duff's name with a sense of relief and aching anticipation. Enough about her exes—he was giving her better things to think about.

Be sure to pack your toothbrush and an extra pair of panties.
I don't plan to let you go until at least Monday morning.
Scratch that. Forget the panties. You won't need them.

He didn't plan to let her go. That made her smile more than she wanted to. Giving herself a firm shake, she sat up and, throwing the covers back, got out of bed and stretched. She needed to try to be productive, rather than lazing around in a swoony state all day. She'd get into her studio for a few hours, then spend time on her bath, preparing herself for Duff.

She'd always loved the ritual of preparation, even as a Domme, but making herself ready for Duff, the man who was making her feel what it truly was to submit to someone for the first time, was a sort of revelation. She was looking forward to a long soak in the tub. To rubbing scented lotion into her skin. Dressing for him. Presenting herself to him. All of which scared the hell out of her, if she let herself linger too long on the idea. So she wouldn't linger. She'd simply do it, and enjoy it. That was the deal she'd made with herself after talking with Kitty.

Padding on bare feet, she grabbed her phone, carried it into the kitchen and got her coffee started. She was just pulling a mug out of the cupboard when her cell phone rang. Her heart gave a hard thump before she glanced at the screen and saw it was Kitty.

"Hey."

"Hey, yourself, honey. Did I wake you up?"

Layla yawned. "Hmm? No, but I just got out of bed. I'm having a lazy morning, apparently. What's up?"

"Just calling to make sure you were still planning to keep your part of the deal from the other night . . . ?"

"I'm trying really damn hard. I'm seeing him tonight. In fact, I'll probably be there the rest of the weekend, in case you want to reach me, because . . . well, I probably won't be available."

"Good."

"Good? Do you really think so?"

"I'm all for you finding some happiness, Layla. It'd be about time. But just so you know, I still have my shovel ready."

She laughed. "Thanks."

"I wonder if I can start a 401(k) for bail money," Kitty mused.

"Let's hope we won't need it. So far, so good. What are you up to tonight?"

"I have a hot date." Kitty sighed. "Which probably won't be nearly as hot as I'd like it to be. I sure would love to end this slump one of these days. Got a hot Dom you can fix me up with?"

"You're going to have to let me know if you're serious about that."

There was an unusually long pause on the other end. "I . . . might be."

"Really?"

"Well, let's see if we can get you settled first. But yeah. I finally have a great staff and business is good, and I finally feel like I can focus some of my attention on my nonexistent personal life."

"Maybe I'll have to ask Duff if he has any friends."

"Oh, Lord help me. If they all look and act like him, I could be in big trouble."

"You see my dilemma?"

"I do. You going to stop thinking about the 'dilemma' part and enjoy yourself this weekend?"

"Damn right I am," she answered, meaning every word.

"Then my job here is done."

"Okay. But I'll want full date report on Monday."

"You'll have it. Not sure I want the same in return—I don't know that my poor, deprived, single-girl heart could take it."

"Wimp," Layla teased.

"That's right. I'm not the masochist you are. Apparently. And by the way? If this doesn't go well, I might have to get a cat. Just sayin'."

"It's just one more date, Kitty."

"Is that what you're telling yourself about tonight?"

"Nope. But Duff isn't just one more man. Not by a long shot. And God, I still hate to admit that out loud. Is this ever going to get any easier? And what the hell am I going to wear?"

"You'll figure it out. My next client is just walking in— gotta run. Sorry, honey."

"No problem. Talk to you on Monday."

"Talk to you then."

Layla took her coffee back into her bedroom to change. But the sheets she'd left in a tangle on her bed only reminded her of when Duff had been there.

Duff.

No man had ever taken up so much space in her brain, or had such a profound effect on her libido. Her body was burning simply looking down at her bed.

Setting her coffee mug down on the sea chest next to the bed, she pulled off the cotton chemise she'd slept in, catching sight of herself in the mirrors set into the front of the old armoire. It was a nice, warm New Orleans morning, but her nipples were hard—hard with thoughts of Duff. Of what he might do to her tonight. How he might touch her. Hurt her. Kiss her. Fuck her.

"Oh . . ."

She sat on the edge of her bed and, watching herself in the mirror, she spread her thighs, stroking her already-hardening clitoris with her fingertips, biting her lip at the sensitivity of her flesh. Not because she'd spent so much time with her vibrators lately, but because even thinking about him made her so damn excited, she could barely contain herself. Hell, totally unable to contain herself, if she couldn't walk through her bedroom without it starting all over again.

Keeping her gaze glued to her reflection in the mirror, she spread her thighs wider.

"Come on, Duff," she murmured, hearing her own voice rough with need. "Make me come for you. For *you*."

She stroked harder, then thrust her fingers into her waiting sex.

"Oh, yes."

She began a hard pumping rhythm, impatient for release, knowing she would only need more. And more and more and more. With her other hand she pinched one nipple, pulled on it, elongating the swollen nub, twisted it, bringing herself the pain she needed from *him*.

"Come on, Duff," she repeated. "Touch me. Yes, just like that. Oh . . ."

Angling her hand, she pressed on her tight clit with her thumb even as her fingers surged into her body, over and over. Heat crept over her breasts, pressure building between her thighs, signaling her climax. Biting her lip, she held it back, knowing he'd want her to. Would order her to. And she was transfixed by the image of her own hand working herself, at her fingers sinking into her flesh, pulling out, stabbing into her once more. Imagining it was his hand. His seeking tongue.

Oh, yes . . .

"Please, Duff."

Pleasure coiled inside her, making her stomach tighten, and her sex was soaking wet, drenching her fingers as she plunged inside. Harder. Deeper. Harder.

"Duff!"

She spread her legs wide as she came, needing to feel completely wanton. Abandoned to pleasure. For *him*.

"Ah, God!"

She shivered as she came, her hips bucking into her hand, as she cried out his name until her throat hurt. Then, falling back on the bed, her body warm and loose, she drew in a rasping breath. The man made her come so damn hard—all she had to do was think of him. How much more would it be tonight? What would he ask of her? Demand of her? She shivered again. She couldn't wait to find out.

Closing her eyes, she forced herself to do some meditative breathing—it was either that, or spend the entire day in bed getting herself off. She had to leave something for him, didn't she?

Finally, she caught her breath and sat up, pushing her curls from her heated cheeks, then got up to dress in her "work" outfit. Her hands were itching to feel the clay, which was always either a good sign or a bad sign. Today, all was good in her world. She was seeing Duff tonight, and no matter how many stern talks she had with herself, no matter how many orgasms she'd had all week, she wasn't able to swallow down her excitement. Now if she could only manage to sculpt something other than Duff's big, beautiful member and keep away from her toy box, the day would be perfect. She knew her night would be.

* * *

THE AFTERNOON WENT by almost too quickly. Her late start to the morning meant she hadn't had much time to work. But her postorgasmic haze had fueled her creative fire, and she was happy with her progress, even though she'd ended up working on one of her metal insects, weaving the ribbons and bits of old silk through it, using chemicals and heat on the copper to attain different color effects. She often felt as if she were using her time unwisely when she worked on her metal bugs, but today it felt like the right thing to do.

She'd left her studio and taken her time getting ready, lingering over her bath, which she'd dropped her favorite scented oils into, then layered on the same scent with her body lotion, massaging it carefully into her skin. She'd kept her makeup light—a little blush to highlight her cheekbones, a few coats of mascara and her favorite lip gloss. She'd dressed most carefully in a tangerine silk slip dress that set off her toffee-colored skin and her green eyes, then added a simple pair of green glass teardrop earrings. With an understanding of how jewelry could get in the way of play, she wore no other accessories. And no panties, as Duff had—sort of—requested.

Smiling at herself in the armoire mirror, she remembered her earlier session on the end of the bed, naked, thighs parted, and her body gave a sharp surge of desire. If Duff didn't get there soon and take her away, she wouldn't be able to sit down without soaking through her dress.

"Like that won't be a problem once he's right in front of me," she muttered to her reflection. Then, rolling her eyes, she shook her hands out and moved into the living room, checking her bag to make sure she had everything she needed—toothbrush, panties (despite what Duff had said), a pair of shorts and a tank top, her facial cleanser and lotion. It was her briefest overnight kit, and she wasn't sure why it made her nervous to think about spending the weekend at his place. Maybe because it meant she was giving up a little more control over the situation? She'd always preferred to have a play partner or lover—which wasn't always necessarily the same thing—at her place, on her own stomping grounds. But when Duff had suggested—hell, when he'd stated—that she was going to his place tonight, there had been no argument from her, no question in her mind. He seemed to have that effect on her.

She checked her purse once more to make sure her keys were in there, then looked out the window. It was still light out, although the sky was beginning to turn pink and gold with the impending sunset. The street was quiet, empty. She checked her phone. Five minutes to six, and he hadn't called or texted to say he was running late.

"You are being ridiculous," she told herself.

She spent the next five minutes checking email on her cell phone, pretending she felt calmer. But when she finally heard his bike pull up out front, then his heavy footsteps on her front deck, her heart pounded in her chest, and she had to order herself to calm the hell down and *breathe*.

But when she opened the door and he grabbed her by the waist, pulling her in for a long, hot kiss, her breath stuttered and all she could manage to do was melt into him.

CHAPTER

Eight

LORD, THE MAN was all pure masculine power and just the right touch; his hands on her set off shimmering sparks of need all over her skin, in her hair, on her cheeks—everywhere he touched her. It was several moments after he'd pulled back before she realized they were both still fully dressed and standing in her doorway. The scorching heat between them made her feel *naked*—made her want to be.

Licking her lips, she found all of her lip gloss gone.

"You look quite fetching, princess," Duff told her.

She found herself batting her lashes. "Do I?"

"Always," he said, his voice a low, husky rumble in his massive chest. "But never more than tonight, when I'm taking you to my lair to do lewd, wicked things to you."

She laughed. "Oh, it's your 'lair,' is it?"

"Damn right. Otherwise known as Jamie's house, which

he's been kind enough to lend me the use of while I get settled and get the shop opened, since he's always at Summer's place, anyway. But my toy bag is there, so 'lair' is not a bad description."

"Why do I think anywhere you are could fairly be called that?"

He grinned, his cheeks dimpling, and she had to order her knees not to soften and buckle. "Because you're getting to know me. Shall we go, my lovely?"

"Sure. Are we on your bike tonight?"

"We are. I could've borrowed the truck from the shop, but there's something about having your naked legs wrapped around me that I enjoy."

Mmm. Me, too.

"Okay. Let me grab my jacket."

She opened the small hall closet and pulled her black leather jacket out, and was surprised when Duff helped her into it.

"You know," she told him, "it still always surprises me when you're such a gentleman."

"Rather than an oaf? As I believe I've mentioned before, you've obviously been hanging out with far too many oafs."

"That's the truth."

"Maybe sometime you'll tell me more about it. But not now. Let's keep you in this flirtatious headspace."

"Am I being flirtatious?" she asked, batting her lashes at him once more.

"You are, which you know perfectly well, little minx. Not that I'm complaining. I like it when you flirt. With *me*."

Was he teasing, or had she heard a hint of possessiveness

from him? That usually would have set off alarms in her head, but from Duff, she liked it.

He slipped an arm around her waist and they stepped onto the small front deck. Taking her keys from her hand, he locked the front door, then walked her to his motorcycle. His Harley was one fine piece of machinery, as utterly masculine as he was and just as badass. He helped her into her helmet, then slung his on and lifted her onto the back of the bike before mounting it himself and gunning the big engine to life. Then, with her legs tight against his strong thighs, her arms around his waist and the rumbling engine vibrating between her thighs, they made the short drive across town.

His big body felt incredible, his wide back pressed up against her, her breasts crushed to the solid muscle there, where she could feel every ripple and flex as he shifted the bike. By the time they pulled up in front of Jamie's building on Kerlerec Street in the Seventh Ward, her system was trembling with need.

Jamie's place was in one of the areas hit hard by Katrina, but the neighborhood was bouncing back nicely. His beautiful Victorian had obviously been newly repainted in contrasting shades of green, with the trim done in ivory and a rich brick red. It had a masculine sensibility to it, despite some of the more ornate woodwork. Masculine and homey.

Inside and up the stairs to the third floor flat and it was even more homey.

"Wow, Jamie's done a gorgeous job here," she said when she was standing inside the door of the flat.

"Yeah, he has, eh? Well, his brother Allister did most of the remodel, but Jamie's too much of a control freak not to have had his hand in things. I'm fairly certain he made the coffee table himself from reclaimed wood."

"Huh. That's what my coffee table is made of." She glanced around the inviting room, taking in the modern furnishings set against the old ornate crown moldings and the curved archways, along with a collection of vintage hubcaps on one wall. "Definitely a guy's house."

"Wouldn't you be disappointed if you'd come here to find it filled with lacy doilies and . . . what are those called? Hummel figurines?"

She smiled. "I'd be shocked. Neither you nor Jamie are the lace-doily types. Far from it. *I'm* not the lace doily type."

"No, just the lace-underwear type, which I happen to like. But"—he narrowed his eyes at her—"you weren't supposed to wear any tonight. Did you?"

"You'll just have to find out."

He moved in and pulled her in tight, grabbing her ass through her silk dress.

"Hmm. Nope. Can't say I feel a thing. Good girl."

She couldn't help the way her body went soft and liquid at the words, at the rough touch of his big hands, but he let her go and took a step back.

"Now, off to the kitchen with you, wench, and watch the master at work."

"You're a master chef, are you?"

"Nah. I just like to brag. But it sounded good, didn't it?"

That made her giggle and shake her head as she sat on the stool he held out for her at the counter dividing the living room from the kitchen. It was a very male-looking space, too, with gray slate counters and pewter finishes. She liked it. There was a certain art to its simplicity.

Duff immediately began to move around the kitchen, pulling cookware from beneath a counter, olive oil and cooking wine from a wood tray next to the stove, which faced where she was perched on her stool. He grabbed a jar of crushed garlic from the refrigerator, as well as a bunch of fresh, fragrant basil, a container of heavy cream and a covered bowl, then opened a bottle of sparkling water, pouring two glasses and setting one in front of her. She knew there would be no wine with dinner—like most respected players in the kink community, there was no drinking before play.

"I hope you like pasta?" he asked.

"Everyone likes pasta. And I'm not one of those girls who doesn't eat."

"One more thing to like about you. What about spicy sausage?" He waggled a brow at her.

"Was that thinly veiled sexual innuendo?" she asked, leaning forward, her chin in her hand.

"Always with me, princess. But more specifically, it was a question about your taste in food."

"I like pretty much everything. Except okra."

"Haven't I mentioned it's a bad idea to tell a sadist what you don't like?"

"No. No way. I'm calling a hard limit on okra."

He mock-sighed. "If you insist. But I'll hold it aside for later negotiations."

She smiled at him, and he gave her a wink and went to work slicing the sausage, then sautéing it in the pan while setting a big pot of water to boil for the pasta. She liked watching him work, seeing how deft he was with his hands, and realized not only had he not been kidding about knowing his way around a kitchen, but wow, did the man have great hands! He was so sure of himself on every level—even in the way he chopped the basil or flipped the pan to keep the sausage from scorching.

"The secret," he said, keeping his gaze on the stove, "is to keep all the ingredients moving. You don't want the basil to brown, but to wilt the tiniest bit to release the flavor. And once I get the Alfredo sauce going, you can never let it rest, or it gets stiff."

"Sounds like more innuendo."

He glanced up. "Touché, lovely girl. But I like to think you hope so."

"I do."

He lowered the flame on the stove and moved around the counter, taking her chin in his hand and raising her face for a quick kiss. "You know, you set my blood on fire with your fire and sass. I like you, Layla." He paused, looking down at her while her own blood heated and she had to cross her legs against the pressure building there. "Yeah, I do like you." He gave her another brief, tantalizing brush of his lips before turning to move back into the kitchen and dropping some finely chopped garlic into the olive oil warming in a pan to start the sauce. He moved the garlic around with a wooden spoon, his brows drawn in concentration.

Hmm . . . wooden spoon. Maybe he'll spank me with it later.

Something in her was loosening up. It was a process that

had been happening since their first meeting. Maybe it was his good sense of humor, how he shifted from teasing to serious to pure, searing heat in seconds. Moments. He kept her head spinning, her gears shifting. And maybe it was calculated on his part, or maybe that was simply him, but it was working. Maybe a little too well.

The alarms in her head started to shriek distantly.

"Duff? Where's the restroom?"

"Eh? Down that hall."

She got up, trying to suppress the faint panic that had suddenly flooded her system as she made her way into the bathroom and closed the door behind her. The small room was as cozy as the rest of the house—small because most of the space was taken up by a big glassed-in shower stall done in green slate tiles. Standing in front of the mirror, she braced her hands against the edge of the sink.

"What is wrong with you?" she asked herself quietly.

The evening was going well, and each time she saw Duff she felt closer to him, the chemistry burning hotter and hotter. And maybe that was the problem.

Was she running scared? Because there was plenty to run from. The guy seemed sincere, despite his playboy reputation. But more than that, she *wanted* him to be. Not simply so she could turn herself over to him and give herself completely to the power dynamic, but because she was definitely falling for the guy.

"Oh, God," she groaned. "I really *am* falling for him. Already fallen. Totally fallen. Shit."

Pressing her hands to her cheeks, she tried to swallow that admission. To take it in so she could either deal with it or reject it. But she knew damn well there was no denying what she felt. She really was falling for this amazing man, and she was freaking out because when a person fell, where did they inevitably fall *to*? And why was she reduced to a teenager under these circumstances? She wished she'd taken her purse into the bathroom with her so she could call Kitty. But that was absurd. She was a grown-ass woman who could handle any situation on her own. Wasn't she?

"Goddamn it," she grumbled, turning the faucet on and washing her hands simply to have something to do, to calm herself down. "No need to freak out. Everything is fine. You're here with one of the hottest men in existence. He's into you, you're into him. In reality, that's as far as it's really gone, right? You trust him. He's an amazing Dom. And he's cooking a lovely meal for you, so stop being such a drama queen."

She took a deep breath, patted her curls into place, squared her shoulders and opened the door, moving back to her stool at the counter.

Duff was just setting their food down on the countertop, which he'd set with place mats and cloth napkins.

"Fancy," she said, trying to maintain a casual demeanor as she ran her fingers over the gray-and-white-patterned cloth.

"They're Jamie's, but I do like them. Ready to eat?"

"Yes. I'm starving, actually," she said, realizing only then it was true.

Duff placed a small bowl of grated Parmesan between their plates, then settled onto the stool next to hers, his big frame barely fitting—he had to turn to the side to find room for his long legs. But she didn't mind—it kept him turned toward her.

He still made her nervous. Or, more correctly, her own

feelings about him made her nervous. But if she focused on Duff she always felt better.

"So," he began, "tell me more about your friend Kitty."

"About Kitty?"

"Yeah. You can tell a lot about a person by who their friends are, don't you agree?"

"Sure."

"But first, take a bite and let me know what you think."

She did as he asked, swirling the creamy pasta onto her fork, making sure she caught a piece of sausage and a bit of basil.

"Oh my God. This is amazing," she said as soon as she'd had a chance to chew and swallow. "I'm impressed."

He dusted his knuckles on his chest. "Knew you would be."

She rolled her eyes. "Your ego never ceases to amaze me. But you really can cook, Duff."

He grinned at her, his dimples creasing his cheeks. "I know a few dishes. I'd like to learn more, if I can ever find the time."

"You could be practicing your cooking instead of having me here taking up your evening," she suggested, teasing him, then glanced away when she realized how needy she'd sounded.

He caught her chin in his fingers—something he seemed quite practiced at—and forced her gaze to his. His hazel eyes were glittering. "No. I couldn't."

There was that damn melting sensation again. She would have found it impossible to tear her gaze from his if his features hadn't softened as he released her chin.

"Eat up, my lovely. You'll need your energy tonight." He took a sip from his glass. "So, about Kitty?"

She busied herself with another mouthful of her dinner,

giving herself a moment to recover from his heated gaze and the intensity of his words before answering. "What haven't I mentioned already? She owns a successful salon. She's worked so hard at it, and her business is really taking off. Recently she's hired some new staff, and the marketing she's done has really paid off. She's a very savvy businesswoman. I have so much respect and admiration for her."

"I can see that. It's good to have a friend you feel that way about. Good for her, as well. What about your other friend? Rosie? I've come to know her a bit myself, by the way—she did the tattoo on my forearm, which I think I've mentioned. And I've hung out with her and Finn a time or two. He's a mate of mine, being that we're the only giant foreigners at The Bastille. We get each other."

"Life has to be . . . I don't know . . . different, being as big as the two of you are."

"Yeah. That whole thing where other guys feel some need to challenge us. To see if they can take us down. It gets old, but you learn to deal with it. We've both had to."

"I think it takes a pretty insecure man to behave that way."

"Agreed. Unfortunately, that doesn't make it happen any less often. But back to Rosie. She seems like a pretty cool girl."

Layla finished her bite of food, took a sip of her sparkling water. "She is. We've been closer the last few months. I think we connected initially because of kink, then because we're both artists. We can relate to each other in a way that's maybe hard for other people to understand, even Kitty, as much as she loves me."

"I get it. No one friend can give you everything. No one

partner, for that matter, which is something I've had to learn the hard way."

"What do you mean?"

There was a long pause while he took a bite of his pasta, chewed and swallowed, then took another bite before setting his fork down and wiping his mouth. He cleared his throat. "Well. There was my ex, you know? I always felt she was too needy with me, wrapping her entire life up in mine, giving up her own interests and even her friends. And she really *did* do that—it wasn't only my perception of the situation. But after things broke off, I saw that I'd been doing the same with her—putting too many expectations on her. It wasn't fair of me. Particularly expecting her not to do what I was doing myself, yeah?"

"My exes always made me wonder if I was doing that, but to be perfectly honest—and this is what I found after doing a lot of soul-searching—I *was* doing it, to some degree, because that's what they wanted of me. Which is why I refuse to date any more musicians. They're such narcissists, most of them. They want a woman whose entire life is them. They want us to sit around waiting for them to want us, or to need a meal, or sex, or to be soothed after a stressful day. There was nothing left over for me. And in the end even the sex was bad—awful, really, because that was all about them, too. And my stupid submissive side wanted so much to please them, wanted to make them happy, and I gave up too damn much of myself, until I had nothing left to give. Less and less in each relationship, which in the end wasn't fair even to them, narcissists or not."

She stopped herself, her chest so tight she could barely breathe, and realized how much she'd said. "God, I'm sorry, Duff. You must think I'm out of my head."

He shook his head, his eyes narrowing, focusing hard on her face. Stroking her hair from her cheek, he said quietly, "No. Not at all. What I think is that you've just gotten real with me—vulnerable—in a way you haven't before. No, don't look like that. It's a good thing. I understand more about you now. I needed to. For the sake of a clean connection within the power dynamic, but also just because . . . just because I needed to, lovely girl."

He leaned in, an inch at a time, a storm brewing in his hazel eyes. She felt that same storm. It was made up of need that was as much mental and emotional as it was physical. And she felt something going loose inside her. Breaking apart, some sort of emotional detritus falling away. It was freeing and terrifying at the same time.

"Duff," she started, not even knowing what she needed to say.

"Yeah," he murmured, moving closer. "I've got you, lovely."

Then he kissed her, and her mind went quiet as she lost herself in his soft lips, his sweet, silky tongue, his hands on her face. He kept kissing her, and her mind emptied out as he used his touch and his big body to take her over, bit by bit. It was the way his hand pressed against the side of her face, then her shoulder, his fingers stroking her skin, moving up and pressing the tiniest bit into her collarbone. The way his lips became more and more demanding, controlling the kiss, forcing her to follow his lead. The way his energy shifted, leaving her no doubt that somehow it was time to transition into the roles the kink between them required. Dominant and submissive. And there was no question about who was dominant here—nor would there ever be with him. The idea came as a relief.

She had no idea how long they'd been there, with him kissing her and quietly manhandling her, but when he pulled back her head was buzzing, and she knew she was already going down into the ethereal plane of subspace.

"Dinner is over, princess. It's time to sate my other hunger." He stood and held a hand out to her, and she took it as he helped her off the stool. "Come into my lair, lovely girl. It's time for me to really see what you can take. Come and be mine for the night."

He led her down the hallway, and she thought he was taking her into the master bedroom, but instead he led her into the room next to it. She wasn't really surprised to see it was a dungeon of sorts, with a spanking bench padded in black leather and a hard point mounted in the ceiling, with chains hung from it that ended in a spreader bar with padded leather suspension cuffs attached. There were a long padded table with eyebolts and wrist and ankle cuffs for restraint and a sleek modern wood armoire hung with floggers and whips, canes and paddles. And his violet wand and various attachments were laid out on a table. Candles burned in wall sconces around the room, and on a high dresser, lending soft, flickering lighting and a subtle scent to the room. It was a sensual den of decadence—a true lair. She had one fleeting moment to imagine how many other women he'd brought there. But she also knew none of that mattered, because now it was *her* there, in this place where he had gone to some trouble to set up a gorgeous seduction. And despite the strong woman she was—or maybe because of it, she realized in a small flash—she was giving in to that seduction. Enjoying it. She would revel in it tonight, be in the moment. With *him*.

When he led her to the center of the room and began to undress her, she stood quietly, shivering at every touch of his hands, at the slip and slide of her silk dress as he drew it over her head.

"Ah, that's perfect. You're perfect," he told her, running his hands over her bare body. "So delectably naked under your pretty dress. Even more naked, knowing there was only this thin layer of silk between us over dinner. While you were behind me on my bike. Fucking delicious."

"I know how to follow instructions," she said through the languid haze settling over her.

"Mmm, yes, you do."

He smoothed his palms over her naked breasts, and she closed her eyes, surging into his touch as desire rippled over her skin, then down deep into her belly, her sex.

"Good girl. So good. So responsive when you allow yourself to be. I need you to allow yourself tonight, Layla. No, look at me."

She opened her eyes and his dark gaze met hers. There was simmering heat there. Stark command. Gears shifted in her head once more, and a part of her was a little afraid, but it was blanketed deep beneath the absolute *need* to cross over into complete submission.

Did he really see the struggle she'd been going through with herself? Did he know how quickly she was losing that battle tonight?

Except tonight it doesn't matter.

As he stared into her eyes a small smile crossed his handsome face—so damn handsome. Jesus God, had there ever been a man who looked like him?

"Yes," he cooed, "there you are, my lovely. Right there. Right *here*, with me. Yeah."

He ran his hands over her shoulders, his touch gentle, then down over her sides, grasping her waist, then grabbing hard, his fingers biting into her flesh until she had to suck a breath in between her teeth.

"Oh, yeah, princess. Lord, I love to see that. Just let it go. You'll have to, you know. Because I'm going to strap you to that table and there won't be a damn thing you can do about it. We're going to play with my wand. It's going to hurt. This is your last chance to get out of it. Unless you call 'red,' of course."

"I don't want to, Duff," she said, with no need to consider it. He was right—she was right there with him, and nothing in her wanted to run anymore. Not now. Now, in this moment, she would be his. And she would glory in it.

With his hands on her shoulders, pressing just hard enough for her to feel his absolute authority over her, he guided her to the padded table, then helped her up onto it, pressing her back until she was lying flat. With his fierce gaze on hers, he drew one arm over her head, leaned in to place a soft kiss on her wrist, then buckled it into the leather cuff. Straightening up, he watched her for what seemed like a long while before he moved around the table, cuffing her other wrist, then drawing her ankles to the edges of the table to fasten them into the leather shackles. She was shaking a little all over, but it was mostly excitement, the keen edge of exquisite desire and the anticipation of what was to come.

Standing over her, he looked down at her once more, and placing his big hand in the center of her chest, he exerted the slightest pressure, his sharp gaze boring into hers. His expression was both shadow and light, meltingly soft and edged in glittering glass, gold and silver and the black of his heavy lashes. She didn't know what to make of what might be going on in his head. But she felt drawn in, drowning in the unexplained intensity. There was something so primal in his eyes, she should have been afraid. And she was—except that nothing within her wanted to escape. Instead, she *wanted* the fear, craved it.

"Are you ready, princess? We'll start out easy, until I have a chance to read how you respond to the wand. I need to make sure I can read you. Then it will be my great pleasure to bring you pain—such beautiful pain. We'll both love it, won't we?"

She opened her mouth to answer, but nothing came out. She felt paralyzed, but in the most wonderful, excruciating way.

"I have to turn my back to you to get the equipment going, but I'm right here, lovely girl."

He moved away then, and she turned her head and saw him fit a slender glass tube with a flat, disk-shaped tip into the end of the violet wand, which really did look a bit wandlike—it was a thick plastic shaft that was perhaps eight or ten inches long, with the cord coming out of one end, and the glass tube protruding from the other. He switched it on, and she heard the low buzz, saw the glass tube gleam with a narrow beam of purple light. As he moved it toward her, she couldn't help that her breath caught in her throat, tight with nerves.

"Does it scare you? Yes? I like that it does. Here, see how gentle it can be." He touched the flat end of the glass tube to her arm and she jumped, then realized it only tickled.

"It's not bad, right? Right. For now. But truthfully, it's turned down quite low at the moment." He ran the glass up her arm, then over her stomach, which tickled even more, and she let out a small gasp. "But we have a long way to go tonight. Oh, yes, a very long way."

Did he know what these subtle threats did to her head? Of course he did. So did she, when she was topping. But she could barely think about that. She had slipped all too easily into bottom mode, and there was no climbing back out of it. Not now. Never with him.

He paused to turn the power up, and she steeled herself, but the tickle only turned into a bright humming against her flesh.

"See? It doesn't hurt at all, does it? Unless I hold the tube the slightest distance from your skin so the current can arc."

"Oh!"

"Hurts a bit, yeah? Tell me what it feels like to you."

"It's sort of like . . . being flicked with a rubber band."

He turned up the power a little more before touching the wand to her arm again. "And now?"

"Ah . . . it stings."

"But you like sting, or so you told me."

"I do. Oh, I can smell . . . What is it?"

"Ozone. I do love that smell. When we're done you'll be able to smell it all over your skin, and so will I. But let's try something else."

He switched the wand off and pulled the glass tube out, exchanging it for one with a pointed tip. "This one will focus the sensation over a much smaller area, so the current, and therefore the sting, will be more concentrated."

He turned the wand on and swept a hand over her stomach, making her shiver. Then he touched the glass tip there, and she yelped.

"Ah!"

He grinned, his dimples flashing, and pleasure washed over her—even more when he bent and kissed the spot where the wand had stung her skin.

"Oh, you like that. Your nipples are hard, and I can see it in your eyes. Let's see if we can really get you a good rush of endorphins, shall we?"

Before she had a chance to think, he touched the wand to the tip of one nipple, and pain lanced through her.

"Fuck, Duff!"

Immediately he had his hand there, cupping her breast, his touch bringing her pleasure in the wake of the pain.

"Soon enough, lovely girl. Soon enough. But I need to hurt you a bit more first. You need it, too. Yeah, don't worry about a thing. I know what you need, and I'll give it to you. That is my first concern. You're in my hands now. All you have to do is lie there, princess. Lie there and take it."

She watched in a combination of fascination and dread as he turned up the dial on the humming instrument. Then he began to sort of tap her skin with it, drawing it back before quickly touching her again. And it created a breathless sort of zapping, like a series of tiny bee stings, punctuated by a sweep of his smooth palm over her skin that had her system pinging back and forth between pain and pleasure, until the pain *was* pleasure.

She knew this was how it worked, but it seemed like an epiphany to her—that this could happen to *her*. That she could trust him so implicitly, yet still be afraid. Oh, it was a beautiful mind-fuck—one she wanted more of.

He paused to lean in close, to whisper against her mouth, "How are we doing? Are you good?"

"Yes," she answered, her voice a breathy pant. "Yes, I'm good."

"Yeah, you are. You're fucking gorgeous. Responsive as hell. It's like you're dancing on the table. Dancing in your bonds. You have no idea how much I love to see it. How hard it makes me." He slipped a hand between her spread thighs, and his fingers slipped in her juices. "It makes you hot, too. Oh, yeah, that's the really good part."

He started to stroke her there, and even though she was afraid he'd stick the damn wand between her legs—which she couldn't believe a part of her actually wanted—her body responded like crazy, her hips arching into his touch.

"Do you need me to get you off, princess? It feels like you do. And I could almost be happy to stand here and stroke your hot little pussy all night, you feel so damn good. *Almost.* But I have work to do yet, don't I?"

When he pulled his hand away, a small sob escaped her, but it only made him smile.

"Goddamn it, Duff," she muttered between teeth clenched against pleasure and helplessness.

He chuckled. "It's nice to be wanted," he teased before dropping his tone. "Do you want me, Layla?"

She ground her jaw tight, trying to defy him, but he only grabbed her face in a hard, punishing grip.

"Do you want me?" he demanded, his tone stern.

Her body melted, her defiance diffusing beneath his command.

"How do you always know exactly what I need?" she asked, her voice low, raspy with desire.

"That's my job, isn't it? I happen to very good at my job."

He bent and kissed her, and she was only vaguely aware of the low buzzing of the wand as his lips and tongue explored her mouth, making her thighs tighten up, fighting her bonds, needing to press them together to relieve the ache between them.

"Now," he murmured against her lips, "let's see what else I can find to amuse myself with."

Straightening up, he switched the instrument off, and she watched as he pulled the glass tube out and replaced it with a heavy cord, one end with a metal tube that he plugged into the wand. The other end was a flat rectangle of metal, which he tucked into the waistband of his jeans.

"This is a contact pad," he explained. "And *I* am now the conductor of the electrical current. Which means I'll feel it, too, as it runs through my fingers, but I don't mind."

Switching the wand on once more, he ran his fingertips over her stomach, and it tickled and hurt at the same time. She swore she saw sparks flying from his fingers. When he reached up to run his fingers through her hair, her whole scalp tingled—it was titillating and oddly relaxing at the same time, and she couldn't help but squirm. He turned the intensity up and the tickling sensation and the release of endorphins made her giggle.

"Are you finding electricity funny, princess?"

"No. Well, not funny, but . . . Hey!" She yelped and laughed when he feathered his fingers through her hair again. "I don't mean to giggle like this, and I feel like a fool, but it's an amazing feeling. I can't help it."

"Have you never laughed while playing before? Such a shame. Know you can laugh with me, Layla. And a fool isn't necessarily a bad thing. It was Jonathan Swift who said, 'I wonder what fool it was that first invented kissing.' A fine fool, indeed, yes? Yes."

He grinned at her as he took one finger and let it dance down the center of her chest, so the sparks flew and sensation was a series of tiny snapping shocks. Then he let his fingers flutter over the curve of her breast and she groaned, knowing from the desire and amusement on his face that her nipple was next. He drew his hand back, then extended one finger and moved in slowly while she held her breath. When he touched his fingertip to her nipple, the shock was sharp, and she yelped again.

"Fuck!"

He laughed. "What's wrong, princess? It doesn't tickle anymore?"

"It does but . . . God, Duff, you are *so* mean."

"Aw. That hurts my feelings—it really does. I think I'll have to punish you for that cruel remark."

She held her breath as he started to torture her nipples with his dancing, electrified fingertips. Quick, sharp jolts of pain poured through her, along with desire. When her brain released more of the lovely chemicals in response to the pain, it was in a flooding rush, and her entire body went slack.

He backed off, letting her ride it out, then leaned in to kiss her once more. She didn't realize he'd switched off the wand and set it down until his hand was between her thighs, his fingers pressing inside her. He was pumping into her, catching her G-spot. Pleasure rose in mere seconds, and she was on the verge of climax, panting into his mouth.

When he reached up with his free hand to pinch her nipple, she couldn't hold back—she came in a dizzying torrent, her body arching up off the table, her mouth latching onto his as pleasure knifed into her in sharp waves that seemed to carry some leftover sensation of sparking, electric tingles.

Her orgasm began to subside, but he wasn't having it. He kept working her with his hand, and pressure built once more, quickly taking her up and over the edge as she came so hard her face went numb. And before the sensation had a chance to fade, he started in again.

"Duff," she panted. "I don't think . . . I can't."

"You can. And you will," he said, his tone low and threatening in the most lovely way, heavy with the Scottish accent.

"Oh . . ."

Pressure built, twined with pleasure, and it was like a snake weaving its way through her system. She thought she was too worn-out, too overstimulated. But it was *Duff*, and she wanted to come for him again, wanted to be rendered helpless in this way. And soon pleasure spiraled and dove, and she dove with it, crashing through the clouds of sensation that threatened to envelop her. Even as she was coming she knew she was completely out of her head. But all she could do was groan, then yell.

"Ah, Jesus fuck! Dufffffff!"

"Again," he ordered.

She let out a sob, but he was relentless, his hand pumping into her, his warm, wet mouth going to her nipple, bringing new sensation. And something about the sweet liquid heat allowed her body to release whatever tenuous threads held it back, and suddenly she was coming again. Or still. All she could do was shiver under his touch, drink him in as he kissed her hard. And come until *he* decided it was enough.

DUFF PUMPED HIS hand into her. He couldn't get enough—enough of her cries as she came, the sensation of her hot pussy clenching around his fingers, how she drenched his hand over and over. He couldn't get enough of her gorgeously glazed eyes, the flush in her cheeks, the way her body moved so sinuously within the restraints. He was hard as iron, hot and eager to be inside her. He just needed to make her come a few dozen times—or as many times as he could stand before climbing on top of her and pushing his way in. Lord, she was beautiful. Her face. Her curving body. Her submission. Even more beautiful knowing how hard-won it was, how difficult for her to go there. It felt like the gift he knew it was.

"Come on, my lovely girl. You're going to come for me again, as many times as I want you to. Until you're so sore the coming itself hurts. Until you scream your throat raw. Then I'm going to be inside you, and you're going to come again for me, around my cock. Oh, yeah. Come on, Layla."

He thrust into her, his curved fingers stroking at her G-spot, and she was so thoroughly wet inside he could barely keep his aim straight. Using his other hand, he spread the lips of her sex wide, and began a rhythmic tapping on her swollen clit. She was pink and glistening and, good Lord, simply looking at her made his cock twitch. He jabbed harder, deeper, and when she tried to close her eyes, her face awash with languid pleasure, he ordered her, "No, princess. You look at me. See my face when you come. Know it's *me* that makes you come so hard."

Her lashes fluttered; then she focused on his face, her green eyes enormous, glossy. She bit her lip as the contractions started inside her once more, and he had to fight down his own spiraling desire. A low groan started in her throat, then rose in tone and volume, until she was crying out, yelling, then screaming as he continued to work her mercilessly. But the moment was as much without mercy for him—it was all he could do to keep his fingers buried deep inside her when he wanted—*needed* unbearably—to bury his dick inside her to the hilt.

She was still trembling when he pulled his hand from her, her hips undulating on the table as he yanked his shirt off, his jeans down. They caught on his boots and he swore as he kicked them off. Grabbing a condom from the table, he sheathed his swollen cock and climbed onto the table on top of her. He paused for one excruciating moment, watching as she writhed in her cuffs, at the wanton, hungry expression on her lovely face, before he opened her with his hand and plowed into her.

He groaned. "Ah . . ."

"Oh! Yes, Duff."

He could feel that she was still coming, and it was nearly his undoing. He had to pause, to force a long breath into his lungs.

"Do you have any idea what you do to me?" he asked her through gritted teeth, not really needing an answer. "How you challenge my self-control? Like no other woman. Christ, you're like no other woman I've known." Angling his hips, he thrust into her, making her gasp. "No other woman makes me feel like this—harder than I've ever been in my life. Like I need to devour you. Fucking *need* to. So badly it makes my teeth ache not to bite into your skin."

He thrust again, then again and again, and he couldn't have uttered another sensible word if his life had depended on it. No, he was nothing but sensation. Aching, soaring, shattering sensation. He had to reach down and squeeze the base of his cock to keep from coming too soon. He needed to wait, had to have some time to kiss her while he was inside her body.

He attacked her lovely mouth—there was no other word for it. He was too damn hungry for her. And she was all soft, honeyed flesh beneath him, surrounding his throbbing, rigid shaft. She was a *part* of him at that moment, and he didn't know what the fuck was happening. But it was far too good to stop.

When he pulled his mouth away—only because he was about to come—she sighed quietly, her breath warm on his face as she whispered his name.

"Duff. Oh, yes. Yes, yes . . . yes . . ."

Her hips were rising to join his, despite being bound, and her sleek little pussy felt so good. He ramped up the pace, pounding into her. As his climax blasted through him he felt her coming, too, her pussy clenching him so hard it was painful. But he welcomed it. His body emptied into her as his brain emptied of all thought—empty of everything but her name.

Layla.

"Ah, Christ, woman."

His body shook—pleasure was an earthquake that tore through him, threatening to tear him apart. And as soon as it started to ease off, it began again as her body clenched his hard flesh.

"Ah! Fuck! Layla . . . Yeah!"

He couldn't stop surging into her, and he had to kiss her again. *Had* to.

He lowered his mouth to hers. Fisted a hand in her hair, and he felt something release in her body, as if some final boundary had been crossed. And knew that for him, it had.

Something is different with her. Has been from the start. But now . . .

But now what? But Lord, he couldn't think. Her little body was so baby soft beneath him, her skin like silk against his. And the gorgeous flesh of her full breasts against his chest might make him come all over again.

In fact, he was growing hard once more. But he'd need another condom. He kissed her again, then tore himself away, somehow managed to climb off her, off the table, and, discarding the used condom, he unbuckled her less carefully than he should.

"Duff?"

"Shh, lovely girl. I just need to take you to bed. I need to fuck you again. Here."

He picked her up in his arms. She weighed nothing. And her arms went around his neck, her head resting against his shoulder, which made more than his cock jump—there was a quick little stab in his chest. He didn't know what it was.

You do know, damn it.

But he didn't want to stop and dissect it. Not now, when he had her in his arms, and was about to have her in his bed.

He managed to grab another condom before carrying her into the bedroom and laying her down on the bed. He rolled the latex sheath over his hard shaft, looking down at her.

"I don't think I'll ever tire of this view—you all worn from coming and play, glassy-eyed with subspace. It's a beautiful thing. *You're* a beautiful thing."

Had he ever said such things to a woman? Maybe he should have. But all that mattered was that he was saying it now to her.

As he parted her thighs and pushed into her, she sighed, wrapping her legs around him. He pushed on her knees, until they were almost flat against her shoulders, opening her wide. Then he was in, buried to the hilt, his balls pressed tight against the curve of her lovely ass.

"Fuuuuuuuck."

He began to move and, freed now, she moved with him, her hips arching up against him, her mound crashing into him, the muscles in her body working.

"Duff," she rasped, "I need to . . . God, I think I need to come again."

"Yes, do it. Come for me, my lovely girl."

It started as a small tremor in her limbs; then he felt it as her insides squeezed, then squeezed again. Her nails dug into his hips as she drew him deeper. And very quickly it was too much to take. He had one moment to raise himself up so he could watch her face as she came. He had to—*had* to see her gleaming green eyes and beautiful, plush mouth. Their gazes locked as his orgasm hit him, and this time it was like flying, soaring to heights he'd never reached before. Like dark earth and night sky and the fucking moon. Sensation poured through him, blinding him, out of control.

"Ahhhhh! Ah, good Lord, Layla. Feels. So. Good." Then he was whispering, "So good, darlin' girl. Ah, Christ. You don't know what you do to me. You don't know."

He found himself cradling her head, his bowed against her hair as he drew in one gasping breath after another, trying to recover from the climax that had just rocked his body.

"You are a most dangerous woman," he whispered against her cheek, uncertain if she heard him.

He hadn't meant to say the words aloud. But there was a lot going on between them that wasn't what he'd intended— with her, or ever. Oh, yeah, she was dangerous for him. Because he knew this was more than sex, maybe for the first time in his life. And that changed everything.

CHAPTER

Nine

I T WAS A weekend unlike the other time they'd had together. On Sunday they took a steamboat brunch tour along the Mississippi River, with Layla pointing out the sites. He couldn't remember whose idea it had been, but it didn't really matter. All that mattered was how impossibly good it felt to have her in his arms, the breeze blowing through her hair, seeing how the sunlight reflected in her eyes. He loved watching the way her mouth moved when she talked, and couldn't resist stealing kiss after kiss—although, to be fair, it couldn't exactly be called "stealing" since she didn't fight it one bit. She was full of the usual fire at times, but once he was touching her she simply melted against him. The Dominant in him was pleased as hell. It made the man in him . . . well, it made him smile, inside and out. And what man wouldn't smile, with this gorgeous girl—gorgeous *woman*—giving herself into his hands?

Putting up with him forcing her to come six times the night before and twice more that morning? He could count himself as lucky, and he damn well did.

After Layla proclaimed the food served on the boat was "tourist crap," they got off at the end of the tour and went to the infamous Court of Two Sisters, where they sat in the brick-walled terrace and loaded up on a rich shrimp étouffée and spicy andouille sausage gumbo. The green-jacketed waiters brought her a glass of cold beer while he drank glass after glass of iced tea. Finally they were both stuffed, lounging in their chairs while the three-tiered fountain in the center of the courtyard splashed against the low tones of a live jazz trio.

"You know," Layla said, her eyes sparkling, "the great pirate Jean Lafitte is said to have killed three men in three separate duels in a single night in this very courtyard."

"Badass. Sounds like my kind of pirate."

"You may be a sadist, but I don't believe you'd kill a man, Duff."

He sat back in his chair and crossed his arms. "Ah, but the day is young yet." She laughed, and he felt inexplicably pleased with himself. "What else? This city is so rich with history—one of the few places in the U.S. as filled with history as Europe—and I like that you know all the stories."

"Oh, not all of them—not by a long shot. But I will tell you, the voodoo queen Marie Laveau lived only a few blocks from here. Legend has it she practiced voodoo rites in the wishing well right here in this courtyard. Its real name is the Devil's Wishing Well, and no one knows if the name came first, or if it was named for her practice of the dark arts."

"Why do you look so happy about that?"

"She fascinates me. A strong, powerful, fearless woman who held her own in a man's world? That's the kind of woman I want to know about."

"It's the kind of woman you are," he said.

She paused, watching his face for several long moments. Then she shook her head. "No. I'm afraid of a lot of things."

"Like what, lovely?" he asked softly, not wanting to frighten her off. He didn't understand why he felt he needed to know. Perhaps for the same reason she felt compelled to know about the infamous voodoo queen.

She bit her lip. "Well, like June bugs. Goddamn exoskeletal creatures from hell. They always fly into my hair." She shivered. "Seriously. The world would be a better place without them. I need a giant exterminator to come along and wipe them from the face of the earth."

He chuckled. "What else?"

"I'm . . . a little afraid of you."

"As you should be."

"No. Not like that. I don't mean the kink. That's the good kind of fear. I mean that I'm . . ." She trailed off, looking down at the table and twisting her cloth napkin between her fingers. Without looking up, she said softly, "I'm afraid because I *want* you to dominate me. And that's something I haven't wanted for a very long time—something I was certain I'd never want again." She raised her chin and met his gaze then. "It frankly scares the shit out of me—that I've let you so far in, you know? And I like it all a little too much. The kink. *This*."

"Yeah, I know what you mean, lovely girl. I do. I'm kind of going through the same thing myself. It's weird, eh? You and me. But it's not really, when you stop and think about it.

We have a lot in common. Granted, some of it is the bad stuff, but still, it's common ground."

"Like what?"

"Like feeling as if we're outcasts in our own families. And our shitty relationship histories. Except, of course, in my case, it was my own doing."

"It was in my case, too, though, Duff. I chose badly."

"And so you mean to not choose at all now—is that it?"

"What?"

He saw the storm in her expression, and knew immediately he'd said the wrong thing. Reaching across the table, he tried to take her hand, but she yanked it back, green eyes blazing.

"Oh, I like your fire, darlin' girl, but I truly didn't mean to offend or to imply I know your mind. Except I believe I do. Because I'm of the same mind." He leaned in closer and took her hand again, and this time she let him hold on to it. "We are birds of a feather, you and I."

"Maybe."

"You know we are. We are the black sheep, you and I, yes? Yeah. But I'm coming to figure out, on an intellectual level, at least, that we simply walk to the beat of our own drummers, rather than those set down by our parents. You know, my folks are convinced that those bar brawls were my own fault. They don't believe me when I tell them how many blokes come at me because of my size. My da, especially. He thinks I've done something to provoke it. But I swear, I mind my own business, never hit on anyone's girl. When you're my size, you can't afford to throw your weight around, unless you're truly dedicated to becoming a hoodlum. And my brother, Leith . . . all right, so maybe he looked up to me and I did have something to do with him wanting to be a musician, and I'm fairly certain his fascination with fast bikes is my fault. But he's male. We like fast things, and let's face it: playing guitar gets a guy laid, although he's pretty enough that he doesn't need to be in a band for that. But I didn't turn him on to kink— that's something he came to on his own, not that my parents know about that part, with him or me. There has to be some genetic factor, or something. And fuck, that came out in a pretty flood, didn't it? Sorry."

"No, don't be sorry, Duff. This is probably the most open you've been with me."

He ran a hand over his smooth head. "Yeah. Yeah, I guess it is. I just don't want anyone to feel sorry for me, right? I have a good life. I'm a damn happy man, as I should be. Not complaining, really. I was trying to point out that we have some history in common."

"You're right—we do. I can't tell you how many times I got the 'you should be more like your brother' speech. My brother the preacher! In our church, women aren't even allowed to preach, which is even more alienating. But I don't have that in me—to be pious and follow someone's rules without question. I never have. My mother has that mind-set—other than her one big fuckup—and she's paid for that her whole life. Sometimes I think she shouldn't have stayed with my father, despite us kids."

"Do you want to tell me what happened, this 'fuckup'? Or is it too much your family's business?"

"No, I'll tell you." She pulled in a breath, exhaled, took a slow sip of her beer, then set the glass down before answering. "When I was a kid my mother got caught cheating on my dad.

I wish they'd kept it from us, but there was yelling . . . and kids hear more than parents give them credit for. I heard every ugly accusation, every ugly, angry word. And the thing is, I can't blame him, because I knew he was hurt by it. Of course he was. My mother was so contrite, but he's never really forgiven her. And now, as an adult, I've come to realize that there's as much concern about him being judged by his congregation as there is pain—maybe more so. But still, it's been really hard for me to let it go, to forgive her. In my head I understand how awful it must have been for her living in a largely loveless relationship. My mother is so sweet and loving. God, thinking about it now, I feel like I've let her down, because I've sort of held my affection back from her. But after all the cheating men I've been with, I think I allowed it to harden me a bit. Or maybe a lot. And that's a really hard thing to admit." She looked up at him, her eyes big and round. "Does that make me a terrible person? Because right now, saying this stuff out loud, I'm kind of feeling that way."

"Nah, I think it just makes you human." He lowered his tone, trying to be gentle with her. "And I know you're feeling a lot right now, but I like to see this in you—to see how deeply you feel things. To know you'll let yourself go there with me."

Her gaze narrowed, and she bit her lip. "Do you, Duff? Why?"

Sitting back in his chair, he felt a bit as if he'd been punched in the gut. Because he damn well knew the answer to her question. He wasn't ready to say it all. He wasn't ready to face it. But he said what he could. "Because I like you, Layla. I like who you are. You're a good woman and probably more than I deserve."

"Because you're such a bad seed?"

He wiped his hands on his jeans. "Maybe."

"If you are, then I am, too."

He cracked a smile. "A perfect match, then."

Her face went perfectly still, and he realized what he'd said. But it was the truth. Grasping her small hand in his, he gave it a squeeze, his chest going tight. This woman touched something in him he knew he'd never felt before. Not with Bess, not with Eileen. He understood now, with a sharp and undeniable clarity, that Eileen had been nothing more than a dizzying lust—lust that didn't even begin to match the chemistry he felt with Layla. And Bess had been more about trying to do the right thing than anything he'd truly felt for her, and shame on him for doing that to the girl. No, this was the real thing. For the first time. And sometimes he felt like a goddamn giddy schoolboy.

Some big, strong Dom you are.

Yeah, he didn't like that part. But the rest of it was so good, he was caring less and less about the part that told him he was being weak. Being foolish.

Maybe he'd talk to Jamie in the morning, see if his cousin could help him get his head on straight—and damn if he wasn't about to become one of those guys who had deep, emotional talks with people. But that's what she did to him, how off-balance she had him. Meanwhile, he had Layla right in front of him, and she'd never been more beautiful.

"Woolgathering, Duff?" she asked.

"Yeah. Thinking about all the things I could be doing to you right now if I had you back at my place. The spanking bench. My violet wand."

She smiled, batting her long, dark lashes. "Let's go, then."

He knew they were both avoiding a subject neither one was comfortable with. But it was easy enough to let his need to touch her override everything else, and it seemed she was relieved to be back on surer footing herself. Kink and sex were their comfort zone.

You are one fucked-up dude.

Yeah. But he was willing to let that go for the time being. As long as he could be with Layla, and thank Christ the girl was willing. He could happily lose the giddiness and the overthinking in the lush curves of her gorgeous body, in doing lovely, wicked things to her. Well, the overthinking, anyway. The giddiness, he feared, was there to stay.

He slapped some cash down on the table and stood to hold her chair. "Let's go, darlin' girl. Despite this wonderful meal, I could eat *you* alive about now."

IT WAS THURSDAY afternoon before things calmed down enough at the shop for Duff to have a quiet minute or two with Jamie. Lunch was po'boy sandwiches at Duff's desk, but it was the first quiet moment they'd been able to find all week, and it suited him just fine. They'd sent the work crew to lunch and it was just the two of them in the nearly finished shop.

"Work's going well," Jamie remarked, unwrapping his sandwich, his feet propped up on the opposite side of the big desk.

"Yeah, seems to be on track."

"We should be able to get the mural started by Monday. I have the artist on standby"

"Yeah, good, that."

"You could show a little more enthusiasm, cousin."

"Hmmm . . . what?"

"Earth to Duff. Where are you, man?"

"Eh? Sorry. I'm distracted."

"Too distracted to eat, apparently, which for you means it's something major. Do I need to get you to a hospital?"

"Could be," Duff said, wanting to talk about it, but not knowing where to start. "You ever have that feeling in the pit of your belly, like it wants to turn over like an engine full of fuel?"

"I'm assuming you're not describing a stomachache from eating too much jambalaya?"

"I'm not. I'm talking about . . . fuck, I can't believe I'm saying this—me!—but I'm talking about Layla."

"Well, well. How the mighty have fallen."

Was this what it was to be falling? If so, he was going down like a fucking ton of bricks. But there wasn't a damn thing he could do about it. He rubbed a hand over his shaved scalp. "Fuck me," he grumbled.

"You're not my type, cousin. *And* you're my cousin, which is just sixteen kinds of wrong."

"Fuck *you*, Jamie."

Jamie swung his legs off the desk and leaned across it, hands splayed. "All right, I'll stop giving you a hard time. So, tell me what's going on."

"I can't stop fucking thinking about her. Can't stop touching her. I don't want my goddamn *space*, for God's sake."

"You've got it bad."

"You say that like it's a disease," he muttered, tossing the napkin he'd been holding onto the desk, since it seemed Jamie was right about him not being able to eat. "So what the fuck do I do?" he demanded.

"Do? There's not much you can do. You either go full throttle and give things a try with her, or you run."

"I don't think I *can* run," Duff said. "But I'm not ready to deal with this. It's been nearly a month. I need more time. I need to figure this shit out. I'm not good relationship material—I'll only fuck it up."

"Most of us do. Welcome to the human race, cousin."

"Fuck. You're not much help, you know."

Jamie shrugged. "Maybe not. But let me grace you with some wise words once spoken by 'an old bastard who knows nothing about women.' Don't wait too long. Women only have so much patience, you know."

"Ah, that's charming, to throw my own words at me."

"Not my fault that you were right. You were overdue."

"Thanks and fuck you again, cousin," he grumbled.

"You're welcome," Jamie told him cheerfully. "You going to eat that?"

"Nah, have at it."

Despite his grouching, he couldn't be too pissed off, because Jamie was right. But he didn't feel any better, any more comfortable with feeling this much for someone. He still had it in the back of his head that he was a bad seed, that he couldn't give any woman what she deserved, and certainly not a woman like Layla. She deserved everything. But he also wasn't ready to give her up.

That thought made his stomach turn.

Give her up? He'd rather cut off his left nut. And that settled that—neither was happening anytime soon.

"Hey, Kitty, it's me."

"Well. I thought I was going to have to call out the search party and dredge the swamps, girl," Layla's friend told her. "Hang on a sec, honey. Yes, she needs to have lowlights, Chelsea, not more highlights. Good Lord, the woman is going to bleach herself into brain damage—you make sure she understands that. I'm not having anyone leaving my salon with hair like straw, even if it is almost Halloween. Sorry, Layla, hon. Work issues. So, you gonna tell me where the hell you've been? And I'm hoping it's in his bed so I don't have to be mad at you."

Layla grinned, leaning toward her bathroom mirror and smoothing a stray curl away from her headset. "Of course it's been his bed. And mine. And his kitchen counter and his shower and his dungeon room."

Kitty lowered her voice, hissing at her, "He has his own freakin' dungeon room? You've been holding out on me! We need to get together if you can manage to tear yourself away from him for five minutes so we can catch up. It feels like it's been a million years since we've had a good sit-down. How long have you been seeing him now?"

"Almost a month."

Kitty let out a low whistle. "Boy, do you sound smug about that."

"I do not," Layla protested with a laugh.

"Okay, but yeah, you do."

She couldn't argue the point any further. "It's good to hear your voice, Kitty."

"It's good to hear yours, and to hear you sound so happy. So, what are you doing now?"

"I'm standing in front of the mirror and kind of grinning at myself like an idiot, and hating myself a little bit for it."

"Aw, you need to cut yourself some slack. Not that I want to lose my best friend to another relationship—"

"That won't happen again. Ever. I swear it."

"—even for the honeymoon period, but I'm trying real hard not to be selfish."

"This isn't a 'honeymoon' kind of thing, Kitty."

"Isn't it?"

"I can't even think about it in those terms," Layla said.

"Maybe it's about time you do. I have a feeling this one could be good for you."

"Well, we'll see."

"I haven't heard a single reason for you not to trust him. Except for that part about him being the biggest playboy at The Bastille since Finn arrived from the club in Atlanta, but Rosie cured him quick enough. Why shouldn't you be the one to cure Duff?"

"I'm not about to cure anyone of anything. I've hit my head against that wall often enough, and I'm done."

"Crap. I always manage to say the wrong thing, don't I?"

"No, it's not your fault I have so much relationship baggage. And I didn't mean to be so defensive."

"That's okay, honey."

"So . . . what I really called about was to see if you're going to be at the Halloween party at Midnight Ink this weekend? I can't believe we haven't talked about it yet."

"Of course I'm going. Wouldn't miss it."

"That's good. Because Duff is coming with me, and I'd really like for you to spend a few minutes with him."

"Mm-hmm. Because he's not that important and you're not getting emotionally involved? Oh, stop your sputtering— you know I can't resist teasing you. But I'll be more than happy to check him out close up. I need to be sure he's good enough for my best friend."

"Thanks, Kitty."

"It'll be fun. I can tell him all the embarrassing stories about you."

"Oh, yeah, that's exactly why I wanted you to come. On second thought, maybe you'd better stay home that night."

"Not a chance. I'll be there with bells on," Kitty said. "Well, not literally, since it's not a costume party. But . . . you know what I mean."

"You can always make me smile."

"That's my job, hon. Okay, I'll see you and your new man Saturday night at the tattoo shop. And since my life has been supremely dull lately, maybe one of you can introduce me to one of his hot Dom friends."

"I'll see what we can do. See you there."

She hung up, knowing she'd sort of just bullshitted her way through the conversation. And she knew just as well that Kitty saw right through her, which was the beauty of their close friendship. She only hoped Duff couldn't see it, too. Because she still couldn't trust that this was right, no matter how utterly right it felt—or maybe because it did.

But it had only been a month. She didn't need to worry about all that yet, did she? Even if the intensity of kink in a relationship had a tendency to step up the pace, the sense of connection—if the people involved let it.

Was she letting it? Or was it so far beyond her control there wasn't a damn thing she could do about it?

She didn't like that thought. She never liked being out of control, except when she *did* like it, with Duff.

Leaning over the bathroom sink, she asked her reflection in the mirror, "What am I going to do with you?"

Unfortunately, she didn't have an answer. She was going to have to live with the fear nagging at the back of her mind. Luckily, most of the time, the sheer pleasure of being with Duff, under his hands, in his bed, talking with him, joking with him, kept her distracted.

"Oh, yeah," she said to the mirror. "You just keep telling yourself he's nothing but a distraction. Especially since you just now thought of this thing with him—whatever it is—as a 'relationship.'"

Since she had no reasonable reply, she turned away and headed out to her studio to work. And hoped she wouldn't end up sculpting yet another clay phallus modeled on Duff's.

It was Saturday night and Layla had been thrilled when Duff picked her up for the party wearing his black utility kilt with his big black boots—one of her favorite looks on a man, and the combination had never looked better than it did on him. He'd lifted her into the SGR Motors truck—apparently he didn't like to ride his Harley in a skirt, either—and they'd driven down to Canal Street, where Rosie's tattoo shop, Midnight Ink, was located. Well, the shop was owned by her cousin, Christi, a successful indie musician who had bought the place when their uncle, the infamous tattoo artist Henry Lee, had passed away. Layla hadn't had the opportunity to meet Christi before, and she was looking forward to it, as well as to the evening ahead.

They'd somehow found parking a block away, and were walking down Canal Street, Duff's hand at the small of her back. The weather was just cool enough to wear a light coat, but even through her short leather jacket, she could feel the heat of his big hand, something she'd come to love—that and his protective nature when they were out in public, which surprised her. She'd always been the kind of woman—even the kind of girl as far back as middle school—who watched out for herself. But she had to admit there was something very girlish in her that appreciated having someone watch over her. And suddenly, the idea of that made her breath catch in her throat.

Never had this before. No man's ever wanted to treat me this way—as if I'm something precious. Maybe it's about time.

"Hey, lovely, what's on your mind?" Duff asked.

"What? Nothing," she fibbed. "Just checking out this area of town. I haven't been down here in a while."

"I like it. I like all of this city. Which is a good thing, since I intend to call it home."

"Yes, it is," she agreed, trying to ignore the small voice rejoicing inside her head that he wasn't planning on heading back to Scotland anytime soon. Instead, she asked, "So, who do you know from the shop, aside from Rosie?"

"I met a few of 'em when I was in there getting my bio-mech piece done a few months ago—Christi's girl, Etta, dropped in to see Rosie, although he wasn't around. Declan was there—great guy and amazing artist. And the huge guy with the shaved head . . . Caliph is his name, yeah?"

"Yes. His work is incredible, too. Have you met Eli, their piercer? You know, in case you wanted to have another piercing done."

"Fuck no—the one nipple was as much as I could take. I'm a big baby when it comes to having needles jabbed in my body. Ah, here we are."

He swung open the door and held it for her, and she was greeted by music, then by the hulking blond Finn taking her in a big bear hug that nearly smothered her.

"You're a pretty sight for sore eyes, Layla," he proclaimed, his Aussie accent lending good humor to everything he said.

"Oh, 'cause you're not getting enough pretty at home, you monster?" Rosie teased, coming up behind him and elbowing him out of the way to wrap her arms around Layla.

"Always, my girl. The prettiest girl in town." He leaned down to give Rosie a loud, smacking kiss on the cheek and a pat on her bottom. "And Duff—good to see you."

He and Duff gave each other a manly back-patting embrace, and as they stepped back Layla saw Finn also wore a black utility kilt.

"Aw, you two dressed to match," Rosie said. "How cute."

"You'll pay for that later," Finn told her, grabbing her and picking her up in one arm. "Or maybe right now."

Rosie pounded on his huge arm with her fists. "Put me down, you beast. I have a party to run."

"All right, all right. But later." He kissed her cheek again and set her on her feet.

"I actually did think we were cute," Duff said, sending Rosie a wink and making them all laugh.

"There are so many people here already," Layla remarked.

"It'll be a good crowd tonight," Rosie said. "And have you noticed nearly everyone is dressed in black? That's what we get for throwing a party that's almost all tattoo artists and kinky folk."

Duff let out a big laugh. "Right enough. But I hear black is the new black."

"It is in my book," Rosie answered. "There are drinks in the cooler in the back hallway—beers and soda—and some harder stuff and snacks lined up on the reception desk. You two help yourselves to whatever you want.

"Thanks—and don't worry. We're self-sufficient enough," Layla said, giving her friend's arm a squeeze. "You get back to hostessing."

"I will, but there are a few people I want to introduce you to first. My cousin, Christi, is in town, and I've been dying for you all to meet. Come on. Finn can hold down the fort for me for a minute."

She grabbed Layla's hand and led her through the crowd, Duff sticking close by in that protective manner.

"Christi, come and meet Layla's new man, Duff—he's Jamie's cousin from Edinburgh."

Her man? Was that what he was? She didn't think it was anything so official, but she was too momentarily stunned by the title to protest—it left her reeling a bit.

Duff shook hands with the tall, dark-haired shop owner and famous indie rock star.

"Great to meet you, man," Christi said. "I need to come down and see the shop as soon as you're open. I don't know if anyone's mentioned my love for a good Harley, but I'll have some work for you as soon as you're ready."

"Good man. Come anytime."

Christi grinned. "That's an offer I can't refuse."

"Hello, Etta," Duff said, taking the beautiful young woman's hand and giving it a brief, respectful squeeze. "Nice to see you again."

"You, too."

Etta smiled shyly at Duff, then at Layla, then at Duff again, her lovely brown eyes lighting up, leaving Layla to wonder what Rosie had been saying about their relationship. Or was she wearing her ridiculous teenage giddiness over Duff on the outside for everyone to see?

Suddenly she felt a hand on her shoulder and turned to find Kitty there, dressed in what she called her "power suit"—a waist-hugging corset in black satin with a deep blue damask pattern and a short black skirt. Layla hugged her friend, particularly happy to see her after the small shake-up she'd just had.

"Kitty!"

"Hi, honey. And this must be Duff. I've seen you before, but it's nice to finally have a formal introduction."

"Too formal to hug my girl's best friend?"

"Of course not."

As Duff pulled Kitty into his arms, Layla had to wonder at all the assumptions being made about her relationship with Duff. It had been a month, for God's sake! She knew they'd been kind of inseparable lately, but first Rosie, then apparently Etta, and now Duff himself. *Especially* Duff. What did this mean, if anything? Or did he call every girl he was seeing his "girl"?

"Okay," Kitty said, "which of these hot tattoo artists is single?"

"Um . . ." Layla looked around the room, spotting the enormous Caliph with his girl, Jennifer, the beautiful Declan and the lovely Sophie, as well as Eli the piercer with his partners, Rhonda and Burt. She'd always had a little thing for the darkly stunning Eli, but he was firmly and lovingly involved with his triad. "Honey, I think all the artists are taken. But there are plenty of guests. And you're looking extra hot tonight—I'm sure you'll have no trouble."

"Well, then, I'm off to mingle for a few minutes. Be back after I get a drink and look around. But don't think you're off the hook that easily, Duff—you and I have to have a little Q&A before I'm able to approve you as acceptable company for my best friend."

"Yes, ma'am."

Kitty grinned. "That's right." She winked at Layla. "I like that he knows his place in the hierarchy."

After she'd wandered off, Duff leaned in close to Layla. "She's a bit scary, that one."

"You'd do well to be scared. There are Kitty claws behind the soft curves and blond hair, and she's very protective of me."

He leaned closer to brush a soft kiss across her cheek, then pulled back and caught her gaze with his. "So am I, princess."

"I . . ." But she didn't know how to respond.

What was happening here? What was happening to her? It felt as if she were giving too much over, even though it felt good. Hell, it felt amazing. And seeing all the happy couples among her friends at the party made something in her want the same. But she'd fucked that up pretty well before—what made her think she could really choose any better this time around?

But when she looked up at Duff and saw the undeniably smitten grin on his face, that last wedge of resistance melted. And right there, in the middle of the party, she tilted her face up to be kissed.

His kiss was soft, just a pressing of lips, then again, then a third time—just enough for her to temporarily lose herself, which was what always happened when this man kissed her. When he pulled back she had to silently order herself not to sigh aloud. But she sure as hell was sighing on the inside.

His hand went to her hair, and he tucked a stray curl behind her heated cheek. The expression in his hazel eyes was soft, as if diffused by twilight. But the sun had already set, and the lighting in the shop was bright enough to tattoo by. What was going on with him? What was going on with her?

"Hey, lovely girl," he said, his tone low and husky.

"Yes, Duff?" she asked, breathlessly. Why had his voice, the words, made her heart flutter in her chest?

"It's good to meet your friends. I've wanted to, you know. Because I—"

"Hey there, Layla!"

She turned to see the shop's manager, Sassy, standing next to them with her hands on her softly flared hips, which were covered in snug black leather pants. Her hair—which was ever-changing—was black and orange for the occasion, and there was a wide smile on her face. Layla had always thought she was gorgeous, with her caramel skin nearly the same shade as her own and her wild hair. And her personality always shone through, making everyone adore her.

"Oh my God, Sassy—you are the only woman who could look this great after having twins."

"My partners, Ian and Rafe, between them keep me on my toes—I swear my two men are more work than little Ethan and Lily are. Not that I really mind. They find the best ways to burn the calories off me."

Layla grinned at her, glad to see her friend—and thrilled to see her so damn happy.

Maybe I can have that, too.

But she didn't trust herself to even think the words. Instead, she turned to Duff.

"This is Sassy, appropriately named shop manager. She's another one to watch out for," she teased.

"I'll be sure to keep my back to the wall from now on," he responded, making Sassy grin.

"I like this one," her friend said. "I think he's a keeper. And you've heard about my reputation for matchmaking—I *always* know these things."

Layla felt her tongue stall in her mouth—what could she possibly say to that? But Duff spoke up.

"She hasn't quite decided yet, but thank you for the vote of confidence, Sassy."

"Big, strapping dude like you who I could see from across the room treats her like a princess? Not even a question."

Treats me like a princess. Yes, he does.

"Ooh, have to go say hi to someone. You two stay out of the punch," Sassy warned. "I made it myself and I know for a fact it's dangerous stuff."

"We shall take your sage advice," Duff said, and Sassy stood on tiptoe to kiss his cheek.

"Yep. Keeper," she said over her shoulder as she walked toward the front door.

"Do you know everyone in here?" Duff asked.

"Not quite everyone. I haven't spotted Shea and Shep yet."

"So, all I have still to face is the intimidating Kitty?"

Layla laughed. "If you're lucky."

"This party should have come with a warning. Ah, don't look like that, lovely. I'm joking. I'm ready for anything, and your friends seem like good people. And here comes Kitty."

Kitty approached, a cocktail of some sort in one hand and fanning herself with the other. "My, oh my. I just met the hottest guy and he mixed my drink for me and asked me to come talk with him. I don't have long, so let's get down to it, Duff. You're Jamie's cousin and I know he wouldn't have invited you to go into business with him to represent the SGR name if you weren't a good guy. But you also have the rep as a bit of a womanizer at The Bastille, so I'm suspicious."

"I suspect you're suspicious by nature, yes? Yeah," Duff responded while Layla cringed a little. "But I'll admit to having been a bit of a man-whore since arriving in the States, so I can understand your concern. If you're worried about my intentions toward Layla, well, that I'm still trying to figure out myself, to be honest. But"—he paused, laying a hand over his heart—"I can promise you her well-being is my first concern, and that I've hung up my dancing slippers while we figure this out."

Kitty reached out and patted his enormous biceps. "Good Dom. Nice kilt, too."

He grinned, his dimples flashing. "Why, thank you, Miss Kitty."

"You about to tip a ten-gallon hat to me? Because if not, then I think we're done for the moment and I can get on with the evening's debauchery."

"I'm . . . not certain what a ten-gallon hat is, but I think not."

"All right, then." Kitty leaned in and kissed Layla's cheek, whispering, "He's a good one, honey."

Layla squeezed her friend's hand before Kitty moved back into the crowd. Duff immediately looped an arm around Layla's shoulders.

"I like her, I have to say. I take that sort of loyalty as a good sign. You know, I've always felt someone's friends tell a lot about a person."

"I've always thought so, too. What kind of friends did you have back in Edinburgh?"

"The truth? Not as good as they could have been. It's a small town, ultimately, and the guys I went to school with didn't necessarily take the best path—mostly they turned out to be a bunch of knobs. I was closest with Leith for a long time—and with Jamie, of course, although he was far away. I have a feeling I'll make better friends here. Finn is already becoming one of them."

"He's a great guy."

"Yeah, he is. And I like Rosie quite a lot. Do you think they'd want to have dinner with us sometime?"

"Dinner?" Her stomach tried to tie itself into a small knot. "Isn't that sort of a 'couple-y' thing to do?"

He was quiet for a moment, and she couldn't read what was going on behind his suddenly blank expression.

"I suppose it could be looked at that way. Would that be a bad thing?"

"I don't know. Is that really what's happening here, Duff? I mean, was that your intention coming into this? Because I don't think it was."

"Nah, you're right that it wasn't my intention. But it seems to be happening anyway." He paused, his dark brows furrowing; then his voice softened. "Wouldn't you say so, Layla?"

Looking up into his handsome face, she took a moment, allowing herself to explore every fine, strong feature: the cut jawline; the high, carved cheekbones; his beautiful deep-set eyes. The wide, lush mouth set off by his dimpled cheeks that seemed almost too sweet for his utterly masculine face. And she realized she wanted nothing more than to look at that face, as often as possible. But did she dare want that? Did she dare ask? Instead, she started to shake her head, but Duff grabbed her face in a gentle hand.

"Tell me, Layla. If that's what's happening here, do you mind so much? Because I don't. I like it. I like *you*. In fact, I care very much—much more than I expected to, but there you have it. Despite our worn and injured souls, this has turned into some sort of romance."

Her heart jumped, then soared to such sudden heights, she couldn't find the words to answer. All she could do was smile up at him, and lift her chin for his kiss. When his lips touched hers, the party and all the people in it melted away beneath the force of emotion that sealed their kiss. She knew only the caring between them and the warm press of his mouth. And maybe—just maybe, if she dared to even think it—what she thought could be the beginnings of love.

CHAPTER

Ten

THEY HADN'T BEEN able to get back to her place fast enough. There was something about that knowing moment, standing in the middle of the party at Midnight Ink with his girl—*his* girl—that made the rest of the world fade away—but not quite enough. He had to get her alone, and it seemed she felt the same.

They'd been quiet on the ride to her house, with Duff holding on to her soft little hand as he drove over the New Orleans streets, packed with the throngs celebrating Halloween. But he barely noticed. She was inside his head, her dark and utterly delicious scent filling him up from the seat beside him. He had to get his hands on her. But it was more than that. He had to get *close* to her.

When he pulled into her driveway he didn't even have to warn her to wait for him to come around and open the truck door. When he'd kissed her at the tattoo shop, something in her had truly relaxed for the first time, and he'd felt her give herself over not only to him, but to the moment, and in a way she never had before.

At her front door he took her keys from her and unlocked her house. Stepping into the warm amber light from one hanging lantern in the hallway, he swept her into his arms and carried her to the bedroom, setting her down on the bed. Then he had to stop and simply look at her—at the gorgeous curves of her body beneath her black dress, even the graceful arch of her foot in her high heels. He let his gaze roam his way up slowly, until he found the luscious rise of her breasts at the low neckline of the lace dress. Then to her face. And ah, Lord, that face. Had he ever seen anything like it?

"You really are exquisite," he told her, his voice a rough rumble in his throat. The words didn't convey enough. But he was hard and wanting—needing with more than his dick. Needing to touch her, to hold her, to be inside her not only as a form of satisfaction, but because he couldn't get close enough any other way.

He was afraid if he stopped to examine what the fuck was going on with him, it would all fall apart, so he chose not to.

Keeping his gaze on hers, he kicked his boots off, shrugged his way out of his shirt, unbuckled his belt.

"Are you going to spank me with that?" she asked. He could read the tension in every line of her body, but it wasn't fear.

"What? No, lovely. No, not tonight. Tonight I don't need any of that."

Blinking hard, her long lashes came down onto her high,

dusky cheekbones. She bit her lip for a moment. "You can, you know. You can do whatever you want."

Shaking his head, he knelt on the edge of the bed and began to undress her, leaving a trail of kisses over her shoulders, her hands, the unutterably graceful lines of her collarbone. Finally she was naked, and he was hard as stone looking at her, tasting her skin. "No," he whispered. "Right now it's just you and me. Nothing else." A surge of desire rippled over his flesh, so strong he could barely control himself. "I need you so damn badly, Layla. So badly."

There was a small, sobbing moan from her; then her arms went around his neck and he sank down onto the bed with her. Lying on top of her, he ground his hardness against her lithe little body, and she met his undulations with her own as he kissed her mouth, as his tongue found hers. He only grew harder, his need for her transcending the desires of the flesh. And yet it drove him on in a way he'd never known before.

"Christ, Layla. I am desperate for you. Fucking desperate." He drew his lips from hers only to press them to her throat, leaving small bites there, then to her lush breasts, biting her nipples, the softly rounded curves. He had to fill his mouth, his hands, with her gorgeous caramel flesh. With the flavor of her skin. "You taste unbelievable—do you know that? And I have to have you *now*. Right now, right this minute."

Somehow he got out of his jeans, and he was on top of her once more. She opened her sweet thighs for him.

"Yes. Please, Duff. I need you, too. I need you inside me *now*," she whispered, her mouth latching onto his neck and sucking hard. "Don't make me wait."

His cock pulsed—his entire body pulsed, hummed, vibrated, even his hands, his lips. What else could he do but comply with her heated, begging request? And the aching, driving desire was too wildly powerful to resist. Overwhelming. Undeniable.

He pulled her upright, and they came together, fluid, melting, desperate, their hands grasping, nails digging into flesh, kissing, sucking, biting each other. She spread her legs over his thighs as he knelt on the bed. Picking her up by the waist, he took a breath as he settled her open, wet sex onto his throbbing cock. It was too damn hard to wait—he couldn't do it, was totally out of control, and with one urgent, stabbing thrust, he was inside her.

"Ah, Layla."

"Duff! Yes, yes. It can't be fast enough. It can't be hard enough."

Her hips were pumping as he thrust up into her, his hands wrapped around her waist, helping her move. They were one writhing being—a being made completely of pleasure and sensation and a soul-shattering need neither one knew how to meet. He kissed her breasts, took one nipple into his mouth to suckle; then he bit down. She cried out, but held his head, urging him on, gasping with pleasure. And his own pleasure moved through his body in shattering waves that were already almost like coming. It was all intensity and mindless touching, kissing, fucking. Except that it was something else, something *more* he didn't have the words for.

She rose on his swollen, pulsing shaft, then lowered herself, impaling herself deeply. And nothing had ever felt so good as being inside her, wrapped up in her lovely flesh.

"Nothing, baby," he muttered. "Nothing has ever felt like

you. Fucking Christ, this is . . ." He gasped as the first tremors of orgasm shafted deep into his body—balls and belly and *heart*. He couldn't believe it. He didn't have the time or the breath to doubt it.

"God, Duff, you feel so good. So damn good. Oh, yes, just like that. More, please, please. Yes . . ."

She threw her head back, her sweet inner flesh shivering around him. And he felt her begin to come, that tightening and loosening, then tightening again, the heated clench of her climax.

"Duff! Ohhhhhhhhh . . ."

He fell over the edge with her, keen and sweet and so intense he could barely breathe through the pleasure. A cry was ripped from his throat, and he growled against her long, lovely neck.

"Ahhhhhh . . . Yeah, fucking amazing, my baby. Yes! Ah, yeah!"

He bucked into her—couldn't stop. And she moved with him in some mad dance of desire and satisfaction and rippling tremors of scorching heat. Eventually, their bodies slowed, but still pleasure coursed through him, slow and undulating, like a serpent in his veins. And it was like shivers and candy. Like rain and darkness. Like nothing he'd ever felt before. Because it was her. *Her*. And that was the important part.

Leaning into her, he pressed his cheek to hers. "Good Christ, Layla. You are the most amazing woman I've ever known. Do you know that? Do you know how much I need to be with you?"

She let out a small sob, and he thought he'd said too much. But then she grabbed his face in both hands and held on tight.

"Duff. Don't tell me that unless you mean it. Unless it's more than how intense the sex is. Don't tell me unless . . ."

"Layla. I mean it. I mean every fucking word. I do. Do you not feel the same way? Why are you so upset?"

"Maybe because I think I do feel it. And I'm sort of not sure what to do with it."

He drew back and held her face between his palms, looking into her eyes. "You only *think* you do? Seriously, woman?"

"That was a figure of speech. I do feel the same." Her face sobered suddenly. "What if we screw this up?"

"Let's try really hard not to."

He laid his palm over her chest, where her heart was thundering. He kept it there, his forehead pressed to hers, until her heartbeat evened out.

"Okay?" he asked, pulling back to lock her gaze with his, to make sure she really was all right.

She nodded. "Okay."

"Right," he agreed. "So, can I bring you flowers and shit now?"

She cracked a smile. "Let's not take it that far."

He leaned in and kissed her hard enough to bruise her. Hard enough to make his own lips ache. Then, pulling back, he told her, "Just for that you're getting flowers every damn day from now on."

She laughed. "No flowers. Just this. And spank me once in a while."

"Are you kidding? I'll fuck you right through the wall, then take my lovely wand to you. That's what made you fall for me, after all."

"Hmm. You might be right about that."

"As I often am."

"I hate to say it, but you're right about that, too. Which I'm sure you'll never let me forget."

He bent and kissed her plush mouth, then lifted her hand and kissed her palm over and over. "I'll never let you forget how I feel about you."

"Promise?"

When he glanced up, he saw how serious she was.

"Promise me, Duff?" she asked again.

"I promise. Yeah, I do. Come here now, princess. I need to do this again."

She laughed, a lovely sound. "Already?"

"Always. You've turned me into an animal." He growled and nibbled her ear. Then a thought struck him. "Fuck. Layla, we didn't use anything."

"Oh. Shit. But . . . I really don't think we have to worry— it's not the right time in my cycle. Okay?"

He shifted and let his softening cock slip from her body. "Damn it. I'm always so careful. I swear it. I'm clean—got tested two weeks before we got together."

"So am I. I'm sure it's fine. It was just once, right?"

"Yeah."

"Anyway, you just told me you need to be with me and you're going to bring me flowers, and now I need to be held, like a regular girl."

He wrapped her up in his arms, holding on tight. "You are a regular girl, you know, except there's nothing 'regular' about you. You're amazing."

She didn't respond, other than by snuggling into him, her head buried in his neck. And nothing had ever felt better than holding her. The warmth of her skin. Every sensuous curve of her body against his.

Except that she was right. Despite him having reassured her, this was bound to get fucked up. Only, he would be the one most likely to make that happen.

Buck up, man. Do it right, whatever it takes.

It was the first time he'd told himself that. He'd only ever given it a halfhearted try before, and he knew it. But he couldn't do that with Layla. This was the real thing—the real goddamn thing. He had to get it right, finally.

IT WAS A Monday morning and Duff had just kissed her good-bye and left for work. She usually hated Mondays, but she'd spent the last few days with ideas nagging at the back of her mind, things that had felt too complicated to talk to Duff about. She was dying to talk to Kitty, but it was only eight o'clock, and it was her friend's day off. She tried to busy herself by blasting Amy Winehouse while cleaning her kitchen, but soon enough the counters were sparkling, the sink had been scrubbed, and her mind was busier than ever. Sitting down with her second cup of coffee at the small wood table in a corner of her tiny kitchen, she brooded.

It had been just over three weeks since Duff had declared he'd give her flowers, and true to his word, flowers showed up at her door every single day—other than those nights when she saw him and he brought the flowers himself. It was adorable, really—if one could ever call a six-foot-seven man built like a wall "adorable." He'd stand in her doorway, a bouquet of roses or daisies or lilies clutched in his hand, a self-satisfied grin on his face. And those damn dimples. Okay, so maybe he really *was* adorable.

They'd done everything together in these last weeks—walked the French Quarter, gone bowling, climbed over the walls and explored one of the city's infamous cemeteries, made out in the back of a movie theater—even though he and Jamie were in the final stages of putting SGR Motorcycles together. The mural on the back wall of the shop was done, and it was gorgeous—a trio of vintage bikes against a background of smoke in blue and black and silver. Very fitting for the man she knew, and for the business. They'd been working hard, and although Duff had been tired, he seemed to be sailing through this, utterly fearless about the success of his business venture with his cousin, and Layla admired his confidence and positive nature, something she knew she needed more of in her life.

She got to see him on the nights he wasn't working late, and even sometimes when he did—some nights he'd come over at midnight and climb into her bed, curling up behind her and spooning her. And she liked it—*loved* it, which she'd been trying not to think too hard about. They'd played a bit, and he kept a toy bag at her place now since it was often easier for him to come by after his late work hours than for her to meet him at his place. Their sessions had been less rough, even when he used the violet wand on her, but she didn't mind. She knew that if things worked out and they kept seeing each other, they would have plenty of time to go back to the hard play they both loved. This was a time when he was investing his energy in his future in New Orleans. And she liked the fact that the break from the harder-core BDSM play was allowing them to explore each other on a deeper level than even the kink dynamic could take them. They were really getting to know each other, which was amazing, even when it made her want to run from the sense of vulnerability it created. But it was too damn good not to stick it out and see where this could go, despite the fear and the doubts.

The sex was unbelievable, and she was realizing it was because of the connection. Their meals together often ended up with them feeding each other bites, then with the food abandoned on the table so they could be naked and touching each other. She'd never felt such desperate *need* for a man's body before, for his hands, his kisses, as though she required him in order to breathe. That part really scared the hell out of her, but she was trying to move past the fear.

And that's where she was this morning—a confused mass of happiness and worried anxiety that it would be taken away from her. And the very real fear that she would be the one to do it to herself if she couldn't get her act together and wrap her head around the fact that a real relationship seemed to be developing, something she knew now she'd never truly experienced before. Which had kicked off all sorts of other complex thoughts about who she was, what she'd come from and what it all meant now.

By nine that morning she wasn't able to hold off any longer, and she grabbed her phone and called her best friend.

"Layla?" Kitty's voice was rough with sleep.

"Shit. I'm sorry. Did I wake you up?"

"Nope, I opened my eyes half an hour ago, but my brain hasn't kicked in yet. It's fine, honey. What's up? You okay? Do I need to get the shovel out?"

"I need to talk."

"Okay." Kitty yawned. "Sorry."

"It's okay." Now that she had Kitty on the phone, she wasn't sure where to start. "It's complicated."

"That's all right. Just let it come and you'll figure it out as you go."

"I love you for knowing me so well," Layla told her.

"Love you, too, honey."

"I know you do. Okay. This is about Duff and me. Or maybe more about *me*. You know I told you what he said to me a few weeks ago, about needing to be with me?"

"How could I forget? It was an important moment for you guys."

"It was. But now that I've sort of come down from the initial high, it's made me question some things that have come up since I've been seeing him."

"Like what?" Kitty asked.

"Like, am I even a Domme anymore? Because even to be a switch . . . I don't know if a switch can fall as deeply into sub-space as I do with Duff. So was I ever truly a Domme? I have to question the person I see within myself, what I am at this point."

"Layla, you were the one who taught me that no one else gets to define who we are in kink, and that there's an ebb and flow. You have both sides in you. Isn't it possible the side that's prevalent at any given time is simply a response to where you're at in life, and who you're with? Maybe this just happened at the right time, with the right man."

She let Kitty's words run through her brain and tumble around until they sorted themselves out. "You have a point. But there's more."

"You tell Mama Kitty, then, honey."

"I guess this thing with Duff has made me consider a lot of stuff I haven't wanted to look at too closely. He treats me so differently than the other guys I've been with. He made his interest clear from the start—there haven't been any guessing games with him. Nothing to chase, which I realize in looking back, I've always kind of liked. Something in me wanted the challenge, but this has been so much healthier for me. I feel like I've grown, you know? Because I wanted him despite him being so transparent with me. In fact, he was so up-front that at first I wasn't even sure if he was being genuine, but he's never given me any indication that he wasn't—he simply is who he is, and he let me know it. And now, when I look back at my past relationships, I can see the hundred red flags I chose to ignore because . . . why? It occurred to me last night in a sort of blinding flash that I haven't felt as if I deserved more. And . . . and this is the hard part. Because I knew instantly it was because of how my father's always treated me. *Less than*, you know? But fuck him. *Fuck. Him.* How could he have done that to his own daughter? His own flesh and blood? Unless, of course, he suspected I wasn't? Was that a factor? Did my mother cheat before? Or did he never really trust her because that's just the way he is? No one is ever good enough except for my brother the preacher—Dad's little clone. But I can't even deal with all that right now. Whatever the reason, I've just figured out why—finally—as strong a woman as I've always thought myself, I've let men walk all over me. And I'm fucking horrified."

"Oh, sweetie. Don't be so hard on yourself. We can be totally kick-ass in every area *but* relationships—it's not only you. And it doesn't change what you and Duff have, does it? You're having one of those 'dark nights of the soul' and it's lasting a few days, but what does it mean, other than you're doing some self-reflection, and learning from it?"

Layla shoved a hand into her curls, pushing them away from her face. "I guess you're right. But it's hard. I'm starting to panic, which isn't like me. And I actually *cried* during sex the other night, if you can believe it. I've been crying a lot, which *really* isn't like me. I cried a little this morning, mopping my stupid floors, and . . . Fuck."

"What is it? Are you crying right now, honey?"

"No." She sniffed as the small lie spilled from her tongue. "But I'm crying all the time, and I'm bloated and haven't been able to eat much, and I thought I was . . . lovesick, or something. But I'm not in love. I'm not. I'm just sick. And . . . Fuck, fuck, fuck, Kitty!"

"Layla?"

She could hear the alarm in her friend's voice, but it was nothing compared to the alarm in her own head. The tears spilled down her cheeks and she wiped them away with an impatient hand.

"Kitty, goddamn it all! I just realized . . . I think . . . I could be pregnant."

AN HOUR LATER Kitty had picked her up, driven her to the closest pharmacy to buy a pregnancy test, and now they were back at her place. Layla was standing in the bathroom doorway, reading the instructions on the box, her heart a small jackhammer trying to break through the wall of her chest.

"Kitty, how do I do this?"

"Haven't you ever taken one of these tests before?" her friend asked.

Layla looked up. "No. Never."

"Then you're the only woman who hasn't. All you have to do is pee on the stick, keep it level and wait for the results. It's easy, I promise."

"Easy for you—you're not the one who's pregnant."

Kitty came to put an arm around her shoulders, giving her a squeeze. "And neither are you. You're just going through a lot of emotions right now. This is simply to ease your mind. Okay?"

"Okay."

"Then go to it. I'll be right here."

Layla shut the bathroom door and read through the instructions on the box one more time before following the steps. Setting the stick on the bathroom counter, she opened the door. "Okay, start the timer, Kitty."

"Started. Come on, honey. Come sit by me."

Layla settled next to Kitty on the side of the bed and laid her head on her shoulder. "This is so stupid. I'm so stupid."

"Shh. I won't have you bashing my best friend like that. And I've taken these damn tests at least half a dozen times."

"You have?"

"You know birth control pills don't agree with me."

"Yes, but condoms—"

"Don't always work," Kitty interrupted.

"They have for me." Suddenly Layla brightened, lifting her head to look at her friend. "Hey. Maybe I can't even get pregnant."

"Is that what you really want?" Kitty asked quietly.

Her shoulders dropped. "No. No, I think I might like to have kids someday. I know I do. Just not now. I'm only thirty-one. I have plenty of time to figure that out, don't I?"

The timer rang on Kitty's cell phone.

"It's time, hon. Let's take a peek at that little pee stick."

They got up together and walked into the bathroom, leaning over the sink, where the narrow piece of white plastic shone like a beacon with its two pretty pink lines. Layla turned to Kitty.

"Fuck."

DUFF GLANCED AT the clock on the wall of the nearly completed shop and saw it was already ten at night. The new tool chests they'd ordered had finally arrived, as well as much of their supply of standard parts, and they'd been doing a lot of organizing. He wiped his hands on the rag sticking out of his back pocket.

"What do you say we call it a day, cousin?"

Jamie looked up at him from where he was kneeling on the floor, putting some metal shelving together. "You okay?"

"Sure I am. Just a wee bit tired."

"A new girl will do that."

"It's not as if I've been spending every night with her, cousin."

"Not *every* night," Jamie teased as he got to his feet. "But I can always tell when you have. You come in here with that sloppy grin on your face. You'd think this was the first time you'd fallen in love or something."

Duff's breath stuttered in his chest. "It is."

"What? What about Bess? I know Eileen was batshit crazy, but Bess?"

"Yeah, not even with Bess. It simply didn't ever happen. Didn't really think I was capable after that, to be honest, and was maybe a bit doubtful before. But Layla could change a man's mind on just about anything."

Jamie let out a low whistle. "You really do have it bad— every bit as badly as I did over Summer Grace. Not that I haven't seen it coming." Jamie grinned at him. "And not that I won't take great joy in every moment of your suffering. But maybe I didn't quite believe you were capable, either. Don't mean to insult you. I'm just amused at your expense, cousin."

"Gee. Fucking thanks for nothing, *cousin*."

Jamie gave him a firm slap on the back. "Personally, I think it's good for you."

"You wouldn't have said so a year ago."

"A year ago I still had my head up my ass."

"Ha! True enough. Still do a bit, in my humble opinion," Duff grumbled.

"Don't worry—Summer Grace has me on a training program. She'll have me in shape in no time. But don't say anything—I'm supposed to be blissfully unaware."

Duff shook his head, then ran a hand over his stubbly scalp. "All right. All joking aside, though, is it bad that I'm having a hard time going five minutes without thinking of her? That no matter how damn tired I am, all I want to do after we're done here is go see her? Curl up with her? And I want all that shit as much as I want to have sex with her, or even play with her. Does that sound right to you, cousin?" he demanded.

"Yeah, sounds about right for a guy in love."

"Fuck. That's what I thought. How do you handle this shit?"

Jamie shrugged. "You have to tell her, for a start."

"Ah, and that's fucking helpful. Like I don't already know that. It's making my stomach hurt *not* to tell her—eating a hole in my gut, if truth be told. It's like trying to hold mercury in your hands—all that'll happen is you'll burn the hell out of your skin before it slips out. I don't want it to slip out. I need to think about how to tell her, what to say. When to say it. And good Christ, I sound like a fecking girl, don't I?"

Jamie nodded, his grin wide. "And your Scottish accent just made you nearly impossible to understand."

"Great. Fine. You laugh your ass off while I'm here suffering and letting my heart bleed all over the floor."

"As long as you mop up, I don't mind. But, Duff, the only way to really clean up this whole thing is to let her know how you feel. Or you can keep on torturing yourself and bitching to me about it. Your choice."

"You sure there's no third option?"

"What? Afraid of a girl?"

"Damn right I am."

Jamie paused, nodding his head. "Yeah. Probably smart in this case."

"Like I said, you're a big help."

"I'm giving it my best shot. Seriously."

"Okay. Okay. I'll do it. I'm going to Layla's place, and telling her how I feel. Let the chips fall where they may."

"If you duck, they won't take an eye out," Jamie joked.

"Very funny."

Jamie patted him on the back once more. "All kidding aside, good luck, cousin. I mean it. She's pretty awesome. I think you guys are really good together."

"Yeah, yeah. This is too much girl talk for me. I'm going." He gave Jamie a good slap on the back. "I'll keep you posted, cousin. Maybe."

His stomach was churning on the drive over to Layla's house, and he blasted some old-school Sex Pistols to take his mind off it. By the time he arrived at her door he was feeling confident and driven—he *had* to tell her, and he felt fairly certain she was on the same page.

He knocked and when she opened the door he was surprised to see her looking wan and a little wrung-out.

"Hi, lovely."

He bent to give her a kiss but instead of standing on her toes to offer him her lips, as she usually did, she turned her head, giving him her cheek.

"You sick, princess? What's wrong?"

"I haven't been feeling too well, actually. But I'm glad you're here—I've been waiting for you to get done with work. I need to talk to you, Duff."

"All right. What's up?"

"Can we sit down?"

"Of course."

She sat on her big couch and he settled next to her.

"So . . ." she began. "I don't even know how to say this."

He reached out and took her hand. It was cold in his. "What is it? Are you all right?"

"Yes. No. No, not really." She paused, biting down on her lip. "I'm not okay, Duff. I'm *not*. And I don't know how I will be. Because . . . because do you remember that night a few weeks ago? The night we had that one little slipup? The one we agreed couldn't possibly do any harm? Not just that one time, you said. Or maybe I said it. I don't even know. But the thing is . . . we were wrong."

His gut did a hard flip as he took in what she was saying. "Are you . . . ?"

She locked her gaze with his. "I'm pregnant, Duff. I'm fucking pregnant and . . . I think my life is over. But don't worry. You don't have to do anything here. I can handle this on my own. And I think that's best. I really do."

A fat tear spilled down her cheek, and all he could think of at that moment was how utterly miserable she looked, and that he had to do something about it.

"We'll figure this out. Don't cry." He took her in his arms, and her body was stiff, resisting, but he wasn't about to let her go. And he still had something important to say—maybe even more important now. "Layla, it'll be all right. It will be. Because I have something to say, too. I need to tell you that I love you. I love you," he repeated.

LAYLA COULDN'T BELIEVE what he'd just said to her. And she couldn't answer for several long moments, or maybe it was minutes as a high-pitched ringing started in her ears. A million thoughts were racing through her mind, but the main thrust of it all was "I can't believe you're saying this to me now, Duff!"

"What . . . what does that mean?"

Shaking her head, she pushed her way out of his embrace,

and he let her go. She felt unable to articulate what was going through her head at a million miles an hour. He was going to tell her this *now*? When she'd spent the day agonizing over her decision to move on with her life without him, despite Kitty trying to argue her out of it. How could she drag him into this now that he'd said he loved her? It would be emotional blackmail whether he actually did, or if he was saying it because he thought it was the right thing to do under the circumstances, and she couldn't do it. She wouldn't do it.

Instead of letting him know what she truly felt—what she had to fight to swallow down so the words wouldn't spill from her lips—she cast her gaze to the floor, focusing on the grain of the wood as she murmured, "I think you need to leave, Duff."

Don't go.

"What do you mean I need to leave?"

She shook her head, biting the inside of her cheek.

Don't say it. Don't.

"Please. I can't," she pleaded.

"You can't what? You can't say it back? You can't love a big dolt like me? I get it. That's fine. Forget I ever said anything, and I'll do well to forget about it, too. But we still have something to deal with here."

She could hear the hurt lacing his voice, but she couldn't stop the caustic words from coming out of her mouth. "'Something to deal with'? That tells me all I needed to know. It tells me handling this on my own is the right decision."

"You'd already made that decision before I even knew about this?"

"Yes, I pretty much had."

"Why?"

"For obvious reasons, Duff. Come on. Are you really the kind of guy who wants to raise a child? And no, I never considered any other option. I can't, so don't even attempt to suggest it."

"What? *What*? I never would. *Never*, Layla."

There was a small rage burning in his eyes, and she knew in some distant way that she'd hurt him, although she had no idea why it was such a tender spot. But she couldn't get any closer—not to him, or to the situation—or she'd lose it completely.

"When did you find out?" he asked.

"Today."

"At least you hadn't been hiding it from me," he said quietly.

"No. But it's only been about twelve hours, and I've barely had time to digest it, so can you go now?"

"Layla, I—"

"Please? Please just go, Duff. I can't do this. I'm tired and nauseous and I want to go to bed. I don't have the energy to deal with this tonight, or with you."

His jaw went a little slack, and he looked as if he were trying to speak, but nothing came out at first. Then he demanded, "Seriously? That's it? I know you must be tired, but you're really set on locking me out of this? I get no say? Is that how you want things? And Christ, Layla, I just told you I love you. Does that mean nothing to you at all? *Nothing*?"

"Maybe it doesn't," she said wearily, looking away. She

couldn't stand the bleakness in his eyes. The hurt. She couldn't begin to understand what it was about. All she knew was that she had to be alone. *Had* to.

She got to her feet. "You have to go. Just . . . please. You have to go now, Duff."

"Fuck," he muttered, but he stood and moved toward the door. He opened it, but turned at the last minute to say, "We're not done with this discussion. And *we're* not done, even if you have yourself talked into thinking we are."

He slammed the door behind himself so hard it made the house shake. She heard his bike start up, then heard him driving away, leaving her by herself in the empty house. It had never felt so empty to her. She'd never felt so empty. Moving back to the couch, she curled up on it, pulling the throw blanket over her shoulders. And cried harder than she ever had in her life.

SHE STAYED MOSTLY on the couch for the next two days. She couldn't bear to be in her bed—the bed she'd shared with him, and that still held his scent on the sheets and pillowcases, which she only knew because she had to walk through there to get to the bathroom.

Kitty had been calling her three or four times a day, wanting to come over, but Layla refused to let her. She'd barely gotten up, ordering soup from the Chinese place down the street, and eating little else. She barely looked at television, and when she did, she could only watch action films. Anything hinting at a romantic subplot she immediately turned off. She didn't have enough focus to read a book, and music—any music—only made her cry. It was easier to blame it on the hormones than on her emotions. Because if she looked at the reality of it, she'd have to recognize that her heart was broken.

Duff had called, too, but she hadn't picked up. She couldn't bear to listen to any arguments. And maybe even more, she couldn't stand to hear the pain in his voice.

The sun was setting when she realized she hadn't bathed since Monday morning, and decided to take a shower. She shuffled into the bathroom, turned the hot water on and caught sight of herself in the mirror.

"Oh my God." Leaning on the edge of the bathroom sink, she peered at her reflection. "Wow, you look like hell. Let's hope the whole pregnancy isn't this rough."

Oh, God. It couldn't be. She couldn't take it.

"Just get in the shower," she muttered to herself. "One foot in front of the other, right?"

She stripped off her clothes and got under the hot water, letting it pound on her back. And as the heat worked its way into her sore muscles, she began to cry. Not the soft seeping of tears she'd been doing for the last few days, but long, deep sobs that wrenched her body.

"What am I going to do?" she asked aloud, not knowing whom she was asking. Herself, maybe? She didn't have any answers.

Frustrated, she wiped at her face, but the tears wouldn't stop. Not after standing under the water until it went cold. Not after she'd dried herself off and gotten into her warm winter robe. Not when she shuffled her way back to the living room to find her cell phone—which thankfully still had a little charge left in it, even though she didn't know when she'd last remembered to plug it in.

She turned it over and over in her hand, then got under the blanket on the sofa once more, hanging on to her phone so tightly the edge bit into her hand. But she knew what she had to do. She took a breath and dialed.

CHAPTER
Eleven

S HE HEARD KITTY use the key she'd given her when she moved into the house; then the front door opened and her friend walked in, her blond brows drawn together in concern.

"Oh, honey. It's worse than I thought." Kitty moved to the sofa and sat down, pulling Layla into her warm embrace. "Why didn't you tell me how bad off you were? Why wouldn't you let me come before now?"

She buried her face in Kitty's shoulder. "I couldn't stand the sympathy. I don't know if I can stand it now—I can't seem to deal with anything. Oh, God, Kitty, what a mess I've made. My father was right about me. I'm irresponsible."

"First of all, your father is an asshole. Okay? You may not be comfortable saying it, but I certainly am. And second, you are not irresponsible. Shit happens. You got lost in a moment of passion, and the odds were that nothing would have come of it. But, honey, you're having a baby. How can a baby be a bad thing?"

"But, Kitty, it's *me*. And shit . . . I told Duff to go away. I told him about the baby, and then he said he loved me and—"

"He did what?"

"He said he loved me. Right after I told him about the baby, so I knew he didn't mean it. He couldn't possibly." She pulled back to look at Kitty, wiping her runny nose on the sleeve of her robe. "Could he?"

"Why wouldn't he? *I* love you."

"I didn't just tell you that you're going to be a father."

"That's true, but it would have been kinda weird if you had."

"Don't try to cheer me up, Kitty."

"Okay. Let's talk logic instead. He came over here after a long day at work and you let him know you're pregnant."

She sniffed. "Yes."

"Then he said he loved you."

"Yes."

"But despite the fact the man can't keep his hands off you, wants to see you nearly every night despite working his admittedly big, tight tail off to open a new business—which is a lifelong dream, if I remember it all correctly—has taken you out, wined and dined you, spoons you in his sleep, has confided some pretty deep stuff to you and generally acts as if he's smitten—a word you yourself used to describe it—you still can't convince yourself that he actually might just be in love with you?"

"Um . . . I need a moment to absorb all that."

"Go ahead. I'm here."

"I'll admit it makes sense. Sort of. Except for the part that still feels I don't deserve it somehow." She paused, wanting to think about why she felt that way, but all she knew was that she had, for as long as she could remember. But her last conversation with Kitty had been the first time the idea had been conscious, and definitely the first time she'd said anything like that out loud. Which didn't make it any less true. And how sad and awful was that? "I know it's because of my dad—all those years of him being disappointed in me for no reason, really. I was a pretty good kid. And if I let that feeling make my decisions for me, then my asshole father has won, hasn't he?"

"Yep."

"If he wins, then this baby in my belly loses."

Kitty's blue eyes welled up. "Yeah."

Layla laid a hand over her still-flat tummy. "I don't know if I can let that happen. But, Kitty, what if I'm too late? I was kind of a raging bitch to Duff."

"Do you love the man?"

Layla smiled through her tears. "Yes. I love him. I do."

"I thought so. Then you have to try. For all of you."

"Where do I start?"

"By getting your damn hair in order, and I'm just the woman to do it. Come on."

SHE'D DRIVEN BY the shop first, but the lights were off. Granted, it was after nine at night, and the place should have been nearing completion, so the guys shouldn't have had to stay so late at this point. Pulling back onto the road, she headed toward his place on Kerlerec Street as a light rain began to fall. By the time she reached the pretty Victorian, the rain had started to really come down, and unfortunately there wasn't a parking spot open on his block. After driving around for ten minutes with her pulse racing so fast it was making her dizzy, she settled on a spot two blocks away, got out and ran down the street. By the time she reached his door she was pretty well soaked, but she didn't care—she barely felt it. All that mattered was what she needed to say to Duff, what she had to get through to him.

Ringing the buzzer, she waited breathlessly, praying he was home. Praying he would answer the door if he looked out the window and saw it was her. She waited. And rang again. Still no answer. Defeated, she turned to head back to her car, uncertain what to do next.

"Layla? Are you crazy?"

She turned, and there he was, standing in the open doorway to his building. He was so damn handsome her breath caught.

"Yes. I probably am."

"Good Lord, woman. Get out of the rain."

Stepping out onto the sidewalk, he grabbed her arm and pulled her inside, into the dark stairwell, then kept his hand at her elbow as they went up the narrow staircase, then into the flat.

"Hang on," he said, leaving her by the door while he disappeared, coming back a few moments later with a towel. He started to reach for her, as if to dry her off; then he seemed to think better of it and handed the towel to her instead.

She rubbed at her shoulders, then patted her hair, but she

was far too wet for the towel to do much good. And far too anxious to talk to him to wait any longer.

"Duff." Her nerves stalled her, making her throat constrict. She tried again. "I've come to tell you something. It's important."

"Yeah, I think you've told me the important stuff already. But go ahead." He crossed his arms over his chest, a gesture that made her heart ache.

She cleared her throat. "First, I need to . . . I need to apologize."

His dark brows shot up, but he didn't say anything, so she continued.

"I'm sorry. I'm sorry I launched this on you the way I did. I'm sorry I made the decision about what I was going to do without you being a part of the conversation. I'm sorry I didn't even give you a chance to show me the kind of man you are—the kind of man I already knew you were. Which makes it even more supremely stupid that I didn't believe it when you said you loved me."

"Huh." He stopped, and when he uncrossed his arms, she breathed a sigh of relief. "It's not past tense, you know."

"It's not? Oh, God, Duff," she said, then burst into tears.

As he took her into his strong arms, she muttered, "It's the damn pregnancy. I can't seem to do anything but cry. And it's *you*. And my utter stupidity. I tried to blame it on the hormones, but the truth is . . . the truth is, I'm so damn scared."

"Sure, you are. Of course."

"No, it's more than being pregnant. It's because I'm so in love with you, I can't see straight."

"Wait." He pulled back from her, holding her at arm's length, peering down into her eyes. "Say that again?"

"No, please don't look at me like this. I look awful."

"You look more fucking beautiful than any woman who ever lived. Say it again, Layla."

She started to shake her head, but even as she did, the words poured from her mouth, totally beyond her control. "I love you. Ridiculously. I loved you before I found out I was pregnant. I knew it when you said it to me. I'm just so damned stubborn."

"No kidding."

She tried to roll her eyes, but they were too swollen, so she looked up at him instead, at his beautiful face—the face of the man she loved. "Duff? Do you still love me? Really?"

"Yeah, I do. Two days and an argument don't change that, you know."

"I guess . . . I guess I didn't know. It's not something I know how to trust. And you were so mad at me."

"Yeah, I was. But there's a reason for that. A reason I haven't spoken to anyone about. But I think I should tell you now. Come sit down, lovely."

He led her to the couch, sat her down and covered her with a blanket, clucking, "You didn't even wear a coat."

"It's New Orleans."

"It's still November."

"I forgot about that part."

He gave her arm a squeeze, a small smile on his face. "All right. So. This is fairly awful, this thing I'm about to tell you. I've been carrying it around for a while. But some things you can't burden other people with."

"I don't know," Layla said. "I think if you have people in your life who care about you—and you do—you should be able to tell them anything."

"Yeah. I probably should have confided in Jamie, but I'm a guy, and we tend to think we have to behave like chest-beating cavemen most of the time."

"There seems to be a lot of truth in that. But tell me."

"I've mentioned my ex, Bess, yeah? The last relationship I had? Well, we broke up for a lot of reasons. But the kicker was this: she went to England, telling me she was going to visit her sister. And the day after she returned, I had to rush her to the hospital. She was bleeding. Hemorrhaging. Because she'd had . . . she'd terminated a pregnancy and wasn't going to tell me about it."

"Oh my God. Why not?"

He dropped his head, his hands curling around each other; then he looked back up at her. "Because apparently she didn't trust me enough. And to be honest, it made me question what sort of man I was—her assuming I'd be so averse to having a kid that she had to go and do that. And I wouldn't have been thrilled, especially not where our relationship was at the time, but it wore on me. It did. I've always felt as if I fucked up fairly badly to bring that about. And her guilt over it, it ate her alive. I feel responsible for that, as well. She couldn't stand to look at me after that, and I can't blame her."

"But you blame yourself? She didn't give you any choice in the matter. And I know, I know—I was about to do the same thing. Well, with not giving you any choice, but I was only ever going to keep the baby. You have to know that. But, Duff, how was it your fault that she didn't?"

"Because perhaps she was right about me. Same as my parents always said. I'm a handful. Irresponsible. Incorrigible."

Layla tried to smile at him. "Well, I'll give them the incorrigible part."

"You'd be right enough."

He was still wringing his hands, and suddenly she felt her own strength returning—she was strong because in this moment he needed her to be. Maybe that's what love was. She reached out and pried one of his hands free, hanging on to it.

"Now I need to tell you something. I've lived my entire life with that same message ringing in my ears. My father was always disappointed in me, and I thought it was because I was a disappointment. But I've just come to realize it was because I couldn't have *ever* pleased him. I've theorized about why, and maybe I'll never know the answer. But that's not the important part. The important part is that I know my own value, and that I stop allowing what happened between my parents to dictate how I handle my life."

"What do you mean?" he asked.

"Okay, I'm still a little vague on this part, but I'll try to make sense. My mom cheated on him. She was always the loving one, but when I was nine and I found out—and since my father was constantly raking her over the coals about it, it was no secret in our house—I felt like I had to . . . not love her anymore. I mean, I did. Of course I did. But I've felt like I had to sort of cut myself off from her love. From loving her. From letting her love me." A sob caught in her throat and she had to swallow it down. "It sounds so awful saying it out loud. It *is* awful, and I swear I'm calling her tomorrow to tell her I love her. Because that was so wrong of me. Even if the idea started when I was a kid, I never grew beyond it. What I did, in essence, was detach myself from the one source of love I had in my life. My father was always a hard man. My grandparents on my mom's side have been gone since before I was born, and my other grandparents—my dad's parents—were never demonstrative. My grandfather was a pretty cold man as well, which is where my father gets it, I guess. The sad thing is, I could have been so loved by my mother, if I'd only let her. This whole damn time. Why have I been punishing myself over this? Never mind the way I've punished her. But God, I owe her one hell of an apology."

"You were nine years old when you heard about the cheating. You were a child."

"Yes. But I never reevaluated things when I became an adult. Not until now. And now it's only because you've made me look at myself, question everything I thought I knew about myself. At first I was completely freaked out by that, but it's been a good thing. It's been necessary. Because I've spent my whole life not knowing how to accept love. I learned not to. It's taken me all these years to figure it out, and, Duff, I still can't claim to have it figured out. I only know I want to try— I need to try. But I think I've had to forgive my mom before I could forgive myself."

"Forgive yourself for what, my lovely?"

"I don't know, exactly. For the blame and judgment my father heaped on me that had nothing to do with me, maybe? I know it doesn't make much sense. That's maybe the saddest part about it. I never did anything wrong but be my mother's daughter."

"It's a terrible, terrible thing that that was what he held against you."

"Yes, it is. He made me feel happiness was beyond my grasp, that it wasn't something one could reasonably expect in the world. And I sort of manifested my own destiny by choosing a long string of the wrong men. Until you."

"You may be the first woman to ever think I'm the right man."

"You're right for me. You're exactly right."

He pulled her in then and pressed his lips to hers, then pulled back enough to tell her, "I love you, Layla. I don't care what we have to do to make this work. And it's not because of the baby. It's because of you. It's because of *us*. I cannot live without you, my lovely hardheaded girl. We'll help each other through this. I'll remind you that the world is a safe enough place to love and be loved—safe with *me*. I will love you hard enough for you to believe it, until the memory of your father fades away. Until we create new memories that will stand in that place. And I'll love our child. I'll be a good father. I'll learn how."

She looked up into his hazel eyes and saw the truth of his words. "Thank you. For making the world a safe place for me. For helping me to believe I can be happy, that I deserve it. For accepting this baby, despite the surprise of it."

"That part doesn't matter."

"But we've only been together for two months, Duff—less than two months."

"That doesn't matter, either. I knew it the moment I saw you, when you came cussing and sputtering into my shop. You were meant for me. I was meant for you. And I will be there for this child, and for you."

Reaching up, she held his face between her hands, tears

stinging her eyes. But this time they were happy tears. "I don't know how anyone could have thought you wouldn't be a good father, including me. Have you forgiven yourself for what happened with Bess?"

"I'm beginning to. But let me ask you, is it a bad thing, do you think, that I feel somehow this baby—*our* baby—is a sort of redemption for me? I know the other child can never be replaced, but that's how it feels to me. Am I some kind of bastard for thinking so?"

"You don't mean it that way. I understand, and it's not a bad thing at all. Sometimes the universe gives us a second chance."

He smiled at her, his dimples creasing his cheeks, and for the first time that night she saw real happiness in his hazel eyes. "Fuck, Layla. We're having a baby."

She laughed—and realized it was the first time she'd felt real happiness in several days. And what she felt was perhaps the most giddy happiness she'd ever felt in her life. "We're having a baby," she agreed. "Who would have thought it would have been us? Having a baby, and smiling about it?"

He stroked her face, gave her cheek a gentle pinch. "Are you happy, love?"

She pressed her cheek into his hand. "I am. I sort of can't believe it, but I am. I had no idea I wanted this until it happened. Duff, I know you said it didn't matter, but it has only been a couple of months since we got together."

"It's not that it doesn't matter—it's a reality, and I'm a realist at heart—but this is *our* story, yes? Yeah. We get to decide how we want to write it. I can't explain how right it feels."

"Neither can I. But it makes me feel a little crazy."

"You're pregnant. Aren't you allowed to be a little crazy?"

She smacked his arm. "Hey!"

He grinned once more. "And no less dangerous. You know I love that about you."

"I've suspected."

He leaned in and brushed a kiss across her cheek. "I love you, Layla Chouset. Tell me again that you love me, too."

"I love you, Duff Stewart," she murmured against his neck. "It may take me a while to learn to trust in it completely, and I'll just apologize in advance for that."

"Don't apologize. Just promise me you'll learn to like it."

She let out a small laugh. "I do like it, even if it's not exactly a familiar feeling." Then, her heart leaping in her chest, she pulled back and twined her hands behind Duff's thick neck, looking into his eyes. "Duff. I thought I'd loved before, but it wasn't . . . *this*."

"Yeah. It's never been this. Only with you."

"I just can't help thinking that it's *us*. The damaged ones."

His face sobered. "Maybe not anymore. Or maybe that makes us exactly the right ones for each other. Now come here and kiss me, woman."

She went soft and loose against him as he pulled her into his arms, and when his mouth came down on hers it was as if something in her was set free. *Everything* felt different with him, and different now than it had been before. But the one thing that hadn't changed was the chemistry between them.

He deepened the kiss, his hot, silky tongue exploring her mouth, passion in every press of his lips, in the way he held her. She pressed up against him—she couldn't get close enough—and sighed in disappointment when he pulled away. But it was only so he could stand up and lift her in his arms so he could carry her to the bedroom. There he laid her down gently on the bed, and undressed her slowly. His hands were so sweet on her skin, and she moaned in pleasure when he stroked her breasts. She realized then what she'd felt for the last week or so, and understood how much more sensitive being pregnant had made her. But her nipples were hard beneath his fingertips, aching in the most delicious way. He paused to draw his shirt over his head, and she hungrily took in the sight of his beautiful body—the impossibly broad shoulders and heavily built chest. His tattoos, which were like art on his fair skin. And the metal piercing his nipple, which always seemed insanely hot to her.

She parted her thighs without being asked, and one corner of his lush mouth crooked in a smile as he bent over her to kiss his way down her body. Pausing at her stomach, he circled his tongue around her navel.

"Your skin tastes like honey. Have I ever told you that?"

"I don't think so," she answered.

"Well, it does. I plan to tell you every day."

"Like the flowers."

"Hmm? You know what part of you tastes the most like honey, princess?"

"I'm hoping you'll show me."

He ran his hands over her thighs, then pushed them farther apart, and she loved being so open to him, as she always did. When he licked her, pleasure moved through her like liquid heat, and she wanted to close her eyes, but she couldn't stop looking at his muscled shoulders bunched between her thighs.

He licked her again, running his tongue up her wet, ready slit, and she needed to come immediately.

"Duff . . . I need to . . . May I?"

"Mmm, yes. Now, if you like. Again in two minutes. I'll stay here forever if you want me to."

"Yes, please," she murmured as he went back to work, his lovely mouth sucking at her tender flesh.

In moments her climax began, and it was like a warm wave, washing over her like water, then building into a tidal wave that carried her off, out of her head, as she shivered, filled with pleasure. Filled with joy. Only his touch brought her back to earth as he kissed her inner thighs, kneading her flesh with his hands.

"That was damn beautiful," he said. "Again, my lovely. My love."

He bent his head and this time he sucked her clitoris right into his mouth and held it there while he swirled his tongue over the tip. Pleasure built so fast she could barely comprehend what was happening before the waves crashed over her again, and she came in a liquid torrent of heat and need and emotion.

Before it was over, she panted, "More, Duff."

"Anything for you," he told her.

Once more he teased her to impossible heights with his clever mouth, his tongue pushing inside her while he massaged her swollen clit with his thumbs. And again passion built so quickly she barely had time to realize she was coming; then suddenly she was. She cried out, over and over, her voice going hoarse as her sex squeezed around his hot, wet tongue inside her, leaving her panting.

"Oh, God, Duff. I feel as if I could come forever."

"I'm happy to make that happen, love."

Reaching down, her fingers scrabbled at his shoulders. "Take your pants off and make it happen with you inside me," she begged.

He raised himself up, and his crooked grin was back. So were his dimples. "Anything for you," he repeated.

As he stood to pull his boots and jeans off, she had a moment to consider what he'd said. But it didn't make him any less her Dominant. It didn't mean she was any less his submissive. As he slid over her body, she said, "Duff? I'm yours, you know."

"Yes," he said, slipping her thighs over his.

"No, I mean, I'm really yours. I belong to you."

He held himself over her, watching her face. His brows drew together; then he smiled, and it was a beautiful thing. "Yeah, you are. Mine, lovely. *Mine.*"

"Tell me again," she begged.

He held her face cupped in his hand and said, "You belong to me. I won't have it any other way. And when you're ready, you'll wear my collar."

She would have cried if she hadn't been so deliriously happy. "I didn't know until this moment that it's exactly what I wanted."

Leaning in, he kissed her lips, his mouth demanding, telling her without words she truly did belong to him. And she understood that it really didn't matter what she called herself—Domme or switch or submissive—as long as what they had was real. All that mattered was what they were to each other.

He left her mouth only to kiss her breasts, and it felt as if he were worshipping them. It was amazing. She held his head there, savoring each tiny sensation, every press of his lips, every tiny nip of his teeth, every lovely, wet sweep of his tongue. But soon her need became too great.

"Duff, please. Now."

He looked down at her, his heated hazel gaze flecked with silver and gold and *love*. She had never seen anything so beautiful. And as badly as she needed him to be inside her, she needed to be able to see him.

"Duff, help me."

He instinctively knew what she was asking and, slipping his hands under her hips, he turned her, rolling onto his back, until she was straddling his body.

He smiled up at her. "Do your worst, princess."

She placed her hands on his chest, and he kept his hands on her hips, helping her to raise up, then to lower her onto his beautifully rigid shaft, pleasure thrumming like a humming vibration in her body as his heavy flesh pierced her.

"Ah, love . . ."

Sensation was something warm and sinuous, yet no less intense than it had ever been. It seemed to weave throughout her body, reaching her arms and legs, the back of her neck as she arched against him. Together they moved in a rhythm that was all about *them*, as if they were one being made of love and pleasure, heat and desire. She saw his gaze on her, watching her sway above him, and felt so completely abandoned to sensation she was going into overload. But she wanted it—she wanted everything. When he reached up to fill his hands with her full breasts, his touch brought a new wash of pleasure to her system. She was panting, cooing and sighing, and his breath was rough and raw, signaling his pleasure.

"I love you, princess," he told her.

"Ohhh, love you, Duff. Love you, love you . . . Oh!"

Then she had to bite her lip, trying to hold back. But he was coming in a heated rush inside her, arching up into her, and she ground down, taking all of him, needing every bit of his flesh, every bit of *him*.

"Layla. I belong to you, love," he gasped, pulling her down onto his chest, crushing her to him, but she loved it.

They stayed there, moving together, hips arching and drawing back, slowing until it was only the smallest motion, like water gently lapping at the shore. And everything felt that liquid to her. Soft and silky. Quiet and gentle. And outside, the rain was still falling, but the storm had passed, and it was nothing more than the sky weeping their joy.

"Layla," he said quietly, his voice a low rumble.

"Hmm?"

"Would it freak you out if I wrote you some poetry?"

She giggled. "Are you about to?"

"I just might. My inner Scotsman is coming out, and I don't think I'll be able to help m'self."

"Why is that?"

He kissed her cheek, then her jaw, and she reveled in every point of contact.

"Because I love you, my princess. *Mine*. All mine. But I'm yours, too, you know."

She snuggled into him. "Good. That's exactly how I want it."

"Anything for my princess."

"I love you, Duff."

"Good. Because that's exactly how *I* want it."

"Who would have thought?" she asked after a few moments. "The two of *us*, of all people? But the universe works in its own time, in its own way, doesn't it? And as you said, I think this was simply meant to be. I believe that. How silly we were to think we could resist the inevitable."

"I'm over being silly," he said.

She smiled, her cheek against his chest, his heart beating against it. "Why do I find that hard to believe?"

"Well, you know, not like that. I can't ever take myself too seriously. But you? This? I know what we've got."

"Yes," she murmured. "We've got each other. And whatever the future holds, I feel like that's the important part."

His arms tightened around her. "I knew from the start you were a dangerous woman—dangerous to my bachelorhood, as it turns out. But I'm damn happy about it."

"And I knew you were a dangerous man. But in the end, it wasn't a bad thing. Because the only thing we were ever really in danger of was falling in love."

"I like a dangerous ending, my love."

"So do I."

And she did. It was all so unexpected, but she'd needed some of that in her life. She'd needed a big dose of the unexpected, and they didn't come any bigger than Duff. Or any bigger-hearted.

Somehow, she'd found the man she'd been looking for, even if she hadn't been aware she was looking. Or maybe he'd found her. But it didn't matter. She had her dangerous man, and he had her heart. They'd figure the rest out. Together.

EPILOGUE

LAYLA LEANED INTO Duff's big body as the music started. She'd never been much of a girlie-girl—the type who'd dreamed of weddings since childhood—but this was Summer and Jamie's wedding and that made it special. And she loved the ambience of this place. The Chicory was a classic old New Orleans building, with its exposed brick walls punctuated by tall, narrow-paned windows, vaulted raw-beamed ceilings and gorgeous wood floors. It was a special day—special enough that she found tears gathering in her eyes as she watched Jamie shifting nervously, waiting for his bride at the altar beneath an arbor of white flowers and tiny faery lights. Or maybe the tears were the damn hormones again. She'd barely been able to stop crying since her pregnancy, and it had been even worse since giving birth three months earlier.

Her tiny daughter cooed softly, and Layla looked down at

the beautiful baby girl sleeping in her lap, the infant's long lashes resting on her smooth, round cheeks.

Duff leaned over and whispered in Layla's ear, "It's Joy's first wedding."

"Don't get started on the wedding thing again just because I'm crying." She sniffed and stroked Joy's dark, downy hair. "I can't help it. But it doesn't mean I've changed my mind."

"Woman, you are gonna marry me someday. You might as well get used to the idea."

"I wear your collar—that's enough for me."

"We'll see." He rubbed a big finger over their little girl's cheek. "This one may have other ideas when she gets a bit older, you know."

Layla sighed. "Well, if she wants us to . . . I'm pretty sure I won't be able to refuse."

Duff bent to pick up the sleeping infant's hand and kissed it. "Hear that, my darling girl? Have a talk with your mum for me, will ya?"

Layla shook her head.

"You're awfully sentimental today. Duff? Are you sure you don't regret turning down Jamie's invitation to have you as his best man?"

"Nah, Mick is doing a good job of it. Jamie understands I wanted to be with you and Joy for this."

She turned to him, smiling as she gave him a quick kiss. He'd barely been away from her side since she'd given birth, even taking two weeks off work to stay home with her and the baby. At the time she'd told him it was unnecessary, but she loved him for doing it—for *wanting* to do it enough to argue his way past her stubbornness, which, she had to admit, had been at an all-time high during her pregnancy. Duff was an amazing father—an amazing man—and her heart surged with love as she took in the sight of him gazing down at their daughter's sweet face. She had to be the luckiest woman on earth.

But today wasn't about her. It was Summer and Jamie's day, which she was reminded of when the music shifted. Adele's "Make You Feel My Love" began to play, and a new wave of emotion rolled over her. She glanced down at Joy, pressing her pinkie into her baby's tiny fist, trying to hold back tears as everyone stood to watch the bride walk down the aisle.

Summer looked like something out of a fairy tale in her sweeping vintage satin gown, her hair a cascade of blond silk dotted with tiny white flowers beneath the long veil. The pale December sun shone through the sheer white curtains on the tall windows, filling the room with a misty light as Summer moved down the rows.

Layla had to sniff back more tears at the expression on Jamie's face when he caught sight of his bride. There was such a profound and powerful happiness there, and it was a feeling she knew now, thanks to Duff being in her life.

She leaned her head on his broad shoulder, and he slipped an arm around her, kissing her hair as Summer joined Jamie, flanked by Mick at Jamie's side and Summer's best friend, Dennie, standing by her as maid of honor. The ceremony began, all of it a blur of emotion as the officiant talked about the nature of love and commitment. But Layla didn't need to concentrate on the words to revel in the beauty of the day.

The officiant—a large man with a lovely deep voice—said Duff's name, and he stood to read a piece from Kahlil Gibran.

She focused on the seriousness of his handsome face as he spoke, the rich timbre of his voice laced with the Scottish accent she adored.

"'Love one another, but make not a bond of love: let it rather be a moving sea between the shores of your souls . . .'"

Even she had to admit it was a lovely sentiment. She knew that sea, that ebb and shift of love between them, the swell when Joy was born. Duff sat down and the officiant turned to Jamie and Summer.

"Tell each other now the words you need to say on this most wondrous day."

Jamie took Summer's hands in both of his, gazing into her eyes, and he truly looked as if the rest of the world had ceased to exist.

"Summer Grace Rae, I love you more than life itself. I did long before I knew it. But you knew. And it wasn't until you'd given up on me that I saw the light—and the light was *you*. That light has let me see how amazing life can be, how amazing love can be. I will thank you for that for the rest of our lives. You mean more to me than I can say, and without the words, the only way I can think of to let you know how I feel is to spend the rest of my days *showing* you. And I promise I will do that."

"Jamie," Summer started, her soft voice shaking, "I always knew I loved you. I fell for you the moment I met you, when I was just a kid. I had no idea then how big this love would be, but I've discovered that it's endless, without boundaries, without limits. Love needs no limits, and that's something I've learned—something I could learn *only* with you. Thank you for that lesson. Thank you for loving me so thoroughly. Thank you for allowing me to learn to trust in love again."

Layla tried to hold it together, but the tears rolled down her cheeks, and there was nothing she could do to stop them. When had she become so unbearably sentimental? Maybe it was the poetic heart of her big Scotsman, whose hazel eyes had been glowing with emotion all day. Or maybe it was the almost unbearably sweet magic in becoming a mother that had opened her up like this. All she knew was being with Duff, and being Joy's mother, had changed everything for her.

"Damn it," she muttered under her breath.

Duff tucked a tissue into her hand, and she wiped her eyes.

"Everyone here can see the great love between you," the officiant continued, "but the important thing is to always see it in each other. I believe you will. But first, you must make your vows. Jamie Stewart-Greer, do you take this woman to be your wife? To love her and cherish her, to honor and respect her, in good times and bad? Do you pledge your life and your love to her?"

"I do. God, yes."

"And Summer Grace Rae, do you take this man to be your husband? To love him and cherish him, to honor and respect him, in good times and bad? Do you pledge your life and your love to him?"

"I do. I do."

Summer was shaking as Jamie leaned in to kiss her, a hard, long kiss full of passion, while their officiant laughed.

"I didn't say it was time to kiss her yet! But what the hell—have at it. That's a good man. He knows what he's got," he said, a wide grin on his round face. "Well, now, all I have left to say is, by the power vested in me by the grand state of Louisiana, I now pronounce you husband and wife!"

There was a hearty round of applause, along with some whistles and catcalls; then Jamie picked his bride up in his arms and carried her down the aisle, with a glowing Summer laughing joyfully as the crowd cheered.

"I have seriously never seen anything more beautiful," Layla murmured to Duff.

"Except for my two girls here," he said.

"You're such a romantic," she teased, but she couldn't help but smile.

"Yeah, I am. But that's how I reeled you in, princess, so it's not a bad thing, is it? That and my astounding good looks."

"I think it may have been your looks, period."

"Ha. Well, at least this face was good for something. Ah, time to clear out for the reception. Give me that baby for a moment—you're hogging her."

She handed Joy over as Allie approached them, and Layla smiled at the woman who was engaged to Jamie's best friend, Mick.

"Wasn't that beautiful?" Allie asked, her eyes gleaming. "Wasn't Summer beautiful?"

"It was," Layla agreed. "She was. I love her dress, and this place! It's perfect."

"It is." Allie bit her lip. "I hope everyone likes the cake."

"It's from your bakery," Duff said. "I'm sure it'll be incredible.

"It's a work of art, Allie," Layla told her. "It really is."

"Thank you, hon." Allie turned her attention to Joy, rubbing her tiny hand with one finger. "Is your father ever going to let me hold you or not, baby girl?"

Layla laughed. "You just have to grab her from him. Don't worry—she's a sound sleeper. She won't be disturbed."

"I was more concerned about Duff. He's bigger than I am."

"I'm bigger than most people," he said gruffly, but it was all an act. He handed Joy carefully into Allie's arms.

"I have to go show her off to Marie Dawn," Allie said, referring to her best friend. "I promise to bring your baby girl back in a bit."

"You will if you know what's good for you," Duff said, a mock threat in his tone.

"Yeah, yeah," Allie said over her shoulder as she moved across the room.

Layla smacked his enormous arm. "You are ridiculous."

"Ridiculously in love with my child." He bent to kiss her lips. "And with you, my lovely."

"Hey, you two, no hard-core smooching—leave that for the bride and groom," Kitty said, handing them each a glass of champagne, then pulling them back. "Oh, hell, I forgot you don't drink, Duff, and you're still nursing, aren't you, Layla?"

"I am. You can have my glass, Kitty."

Her best friend grinned. "I may need it. There's a hot guy over there and I have to grow the balls to approach him. Fingers crossed that he's kinky."

"That's Grant," Duff told her. "He's a friend from the club. So yeah, he's kinky—kinky as hell."

"Yay!" Kitty grinned, smoothing her dress and fluffing her hair as her gaze went back to the tall, dark-haired man on the other side of the room. "Single?"

"As far as I know."

"Meow."

Duff chuckled. "Layla, darlin', do we need to hold her down before she jumps the poor, unsuspecting bloke? Could cause a scene."

"What's a perfectly good New Orleans wedding without a little commotion? Anyway, Kitty can handle herself—and any man, I'm pretty sure."

"Damn right I can," Kitty said, her signature sensual purr in her voice. She tossed back the rest of the champagne "I'll call you two tomorrow if I don't make it through the cutting of the cake."

Layla grinned after her friend as she moved away. "He has no idea how much trouble he's in."

"He's a good Dom. He'll get her under control quickly enough if they connect—quick enough to make her head spin, maybe. I've seen him play."

"I actually think it'd be good for her. Our Kitty could use a little taming."

"The same as you needed?"

"'Needed'? Are you implying I've been tamed?" She dug her nails into his thick forearm to drive her point home.

"Only partially, love. Don't worry—I know exactly who my wildcat girl is."

They spent the rest of the afternoon smiling, eating and dancing. Joy was passed around and cuddled by nearly everyone at the reception, it seemed, but Layla knew she was always in good hands. Finally, the cake had been cut and it was time to leave.

"You sure you're up to going to The Bastille tonight?" Duff asked her.

"Absolutely. We haven't played since Joy was born, and I'm getting antsy."

"Then it's definitely time. You're certain Dennie's grandma Annalee is up to caring for her overnight?"

"Dennie will be there, too. They've been family to Summer forever, and that makes them our family now, too. And they're dying to get their hands on Joy."

"It's our first night without our baby girl."

"I'll be fine."

He grinned down at her. "I know you will be—I was more worried about me."

"I love that you're such a softhearted lug."

"Tonight I'm hoping to remind you what else you like about me."

He wiggled his dark, heavy brows, making her laugh.

"I'm sure you will—you've kept the beast locked up tight for months."

"Yeah, I have. It's past time to whisk you off to my lair. Are you scared?"

"Terrified," she said, knowing he didn't believe her. But her stomach was fluttering at the thought of playing with her gorgeous man. It had been far too long, and she needed play, needed that level of connection with him. It was going to be a very good night.

THEY'D MADE SURE Dennie and Annalee had all of Joy's supplies, and they'd kissed their little girl a dozen times before Duff took Layla home to rest and change. Home these days was the house they'd just bought and were planning to remodel—a beautiful old New Orleans shotgun style with three fireplaces and a large studio in the back for Layla. The kitchen had been done before the baby was born, as well as one bathroom. Bit by bit, they were making a home together. How had she never known she'd wanted this until Duff had come into her life? There was even a white picket fence out front.

She'd taken a nice, long bath, submerging into the ritual of preparing herself, her head already sinking into subspace as she rubbed lotion into her skin. She'd dressed for him in a little black dress that fit her curvy body like a glove, making her glad that nursing had helped her lose most of the baby weight. Her body would never be quite the same again, but it had made a baby—a new life—and somehow that only made her feel the sacredness of her form. She had a new appreciation for everything these days.

She was quiet on the ride to The Bastille, and Duff let her be, knowing this was part of her process, how she transitioned into subspace, readying her mind for play and for the roles they assumed even before Duff began to prepare their scene space.

The doorman ushered them inside, and they walked into the foyer of The Bastille, where Pixie, the club's manager, sat behind the enormous antique desk.

"Good evening, you two."

"Evening, Pixie," Layla said.

"No fee tonight for you guys. Go on in."

Layla glanced at Duff, but he simply nodded. "Thank you. Nice of you."

Pixie sent him a saucy wink, but Layla didn't have time to wonder what was up before Duff slid a hand across the small of her back and guided her into the club.

Ambient music and low lights in shades of amber and red shone on the highly lacquered black walls and created the rich, sensual atmosphere she'd always loved about this place. But the club felt different to her, maybe because they hadn't been there since the earliest days of her pregnancy. It took her several moments to realize the main play area was empty, then understanding forced its way through the momentary shock.

She turned to Duff. "What did you do?"

He slipped his big arm around her waist. "It's for you, my lovely. We have the place to ourselves all night."

"I can see that. But why?"

"Why? Because you deserve it. And because I could," he answered, looking incredibly pleased with himself. "I wanted you to be able to ease back into things—you've been away awhile. And I admit I wanted my girl all to myself tonight."

She looked up into his glittering hazel eyes. "I don't know what to say. This is amazing."

"'Amazing' hasn't even begun yet, lovely," he told her, one dark brow arched. Then, laying his hands on both her shoulders, he caught her gaze with his and held it. "How are you feeling?"

"Honestly? Excited. And oddly nervous. I guess because it's been a while. And the itch to play is . . . a little distracting."

"Then I need to make you focus." His tone dropped. "Look at me now, love. Hear my voice. I want you to breathe. Yes, you know exactly how—deep and slow, more slowly as you exhale. Look right into my eyes. Yeah, that's it. Be with me. Be a part of me. Align your breath with mine."

She did as he said, her body falling into rhythm with his breathing as he spoke, his low voice soothing her nerves, bringing her into the sphere of absolute connection he was such an expert at creating. When he pulled her black leather collar from his back pocket and buckled it around her neck, a shiver ran over her skin, arrowing deep inside her, and she sank deeper into subspace, feeling her submission to him in every cell of her being.

"You are mine, Layla. Say it."

"I'm yours, Duff."

She reveled in the sense of belonging as he took her through more synchronized breathing. It all went to work on her body as well as her mind, lighting her up inside with need. She had no idea how long it went on before he slid his hands down her arms, took her hand and led her to the play station in the center of the room, where two lengths of chain ending in a pair of padded leather cuffs were hung from a hard point in the high ceiling.

"I'm going to undress you now. To unveil you."

She nodded, her mind already in that lovely, ethereal space he'd taken her to—a space filled only by love and desire and utter trust.

He slipped her dress over her head, pausing to lean in and kiss her cheek softly, and she closed her eyes for a moment with a sigh. Then he kissed her wrist before buckling her into one of the cuffs, and did the same with the other before working the pulley that drew her arms over her head, elongating her body.

"Such pretty lingerie, I had to leave it on. The pink lace is so lovely against your skin. And let's leave your pretty heels on, too."

Her stomach went tight with need when he ran his hands

over her sides. He blazed a trail of hot kisses over her shoulders, the tops of her aching breasts, up one arm to her hand, where he kissed her palm, then her fingertips. Then, reaching into his back pocket, he came back with a leather blindfold.

She let out a small gasp, part fear, part anticipation. He was quiet as he slipped it over her eyes, adjusting it to make sure it was secure.

"Good girl. Breathe. Yeah. I like that you have no idea what I'm going to do to you. I love that element of surprise. Are you ready?"

"Yes," she murmured, desire running hot in her veins, in her pulsing sex, driving away the edge of panic that always came with being blindfolded. Panic, and a sense of freedom, of release.

He kissed her cheek, her jaw, then her lips, and she tilted her face, hungry for his mouth, but he pulled away.

"Ah, ah, don't be too eager, princess. *I'm* running the show right now, and you're in my hands. Give yourself over to me."

She sighed, her body full of wanting so keen it hurt. But she took another cleansing breath and tried to calm herself, to force herself to comply.

"Better," he murmured, running his hands over her skin. "So beautiful, my love. More beautiful than ever, I swear it."

He kissed her stomach, grazing her skin with his teeth, and she shivered.

"You like that, do you? That little bit of pain?"

He slipped a hand between her thighs, making her gasp, but just as quickly he pulled away.

"You are going to kill me, you know," she grumbled.

He laughed. "Oh, I think you'll survive."

"Don't tease me, Duff."

"What did I say about giving yourself over to me? You can't see, can't really move. And I may want to spend the entire evening teasing you. You may as well relax into it, since you've no other choice. Unless you want to call 'red' and end the scene?"

She groaned. "You're so mean to me."

"Yes, but you like it. And so do I. In case you've forgotten, I'm a bit of a sadist."

"As if you'd ever let me forget."

"Damn right," he said, chuckling. He grabbed a handful of flesh at her waist and squeezed, bringing her the pain she needed so badly. Then he pinched her there, making her yelp. "Aw, poor thing," he teased, but he kissed the small, hurting spot just above her hip.

He kissed her there again, then once more before moving lower, kissing and biting his way down her thigh. Her sex grew wet, but when she tried to squeeze her legs together, he forced them apart with strong hands.

Gears were turning in her head, like pieces of clockwork falling into place, and she knew it was that lethal combination of him tormenting her with pleasure and glimpses of the pain she craved. He knew exactly what he was doing, as always. There was a certain relief in that, even though she wanted him to really hurt her—needed him to. She felt as if she'd been left hungry for months, and was starving for sensation now. He knew it, of course. He would handle her need the way he chose. There wasn't a damn thing she could do about it.

That thought made her go loose all over, and she pulled in another long breath.

He continued his slow, lovely torture, kissing her skin, running his fingertips over her heated flesh, grazing the tops of her breasts, her inner thighs. He kissed his way down her spine, starting at the top of her neck and moving down an inch at a time, so gently she could barely stand it. Then he grabbed her and yanked her in so tight she could feel every hard muscle in his big body. She melted into him, her brain emptying out.

"Duff," she murmured.

"You need this, yes? Yes. But you know this will go *my* way, love."

He stepped away from her, keeping his palm flat on her stomach as he moved around in front of her and began those lingering, torturous kisses over her collarbone, her throat, brushing her lips with his before moving on to her shoulder. Her body was vibrating with need, desire a pulsing beat between her thighs. But it was as much the need to be taken over as it was the more animalistic desires. He was feeding one, starving the other, and it made her head spin.

It seemed to go on forever, a little pain mixed with the pleasure of sensual touch, driving her crazy. She realized she was panting, making small mewling sounds, but she couldn't help it. She wanted to beg for more. She couldn't let herself do it. There was a certain pride in being able to take whatever it was he would do to her, and she let that pride fill her up.

"You're doing well, my lovely," he told her, pleasure in his voice, along with stark desire and some tension she wasn't sure she understood. "But let's ramp things up a bit, shall we?"

She waited for him to act—to spank her or bite her, but there was nothing but several long, quiet moments in which all she could hear was her own heartbeat against the background of soft music. Finally, she felt his breath on her skin; then he bit into her neck, a soft bite, making her lean into him, but he drew back.

"Still," he ordered, and she struggled to obey.

He bit her neck once more, sinking his teeth into her shoulder, then the underside of her arm, but so gently—too gently—and she understood he really was going to torture her this way. The nibbling bites were followed by soft kisses and sweeps of his wet tongue. She was shaking, desire and the need to please a battle being waged in her system—one she knew she would lose one way or another.

When he gave her one good bite on the palm of her hand, she gasped. "Duff! Please . . ."

"I know you need it, princess," he said, his voice rough. "I always know what you need. You have to leave it to me, though, you know. Do you trust me?"

"Yes. Completely."

It was true. She'd never trusted anyone the way she did this man.

"Good."

He began to kiss her again, down her stomach, pausing at the apex of her thighs for a long, lovely moment. When he pulled her blindfold off, she was surprised, blinking hard in the dim light. She was even more surprised to see him down on one knee in front of her, holding a small black velvet box in his outstretched hand. She couldn't even look at the sparkling diamond gleaming against the dark velvet.

"Duff? What are you doing?"

"I'm proposing, my silly, beautiful, amazing girl."

"But I'm . . . Jesus, Duff. You're going to do it *now*? When I'm half naked and bound and out of my head?" She pulled against her chains, but they held her tight.

"I'm smarter than I look," he said, a small grin on his face.

"This . . . this isn't fair," she sputtered, her heart racing. "You're going to ask me to marry you after playing? While I'm in this state?"

"I knew this was the only way I could get you to listen. And I figured this would be the best possible form of aftercare. I'm brilliant sometimes, yes?"

"Oh my God. You're serious."

His grin faded, his expression somber. "I've never been more serious in my life than I am about you. I love you, Layla, my stubborn, wild girl. I love you so hard it makes me shake in my boots sometimes. That's how I know this is real. That's why I have to ask you to be my wife, to spend our lives together. Because I need you to be here with me. Wherever 'here' is, I need you at my side."

"But I'm already collared to you," she said, not even sure why she was protesting anymore.

"The collar is a lovely symbol, but I want the whole thing. That unbreakable commitment. I want to make that commitment to you, as Jamie and Summer did today. I want us to make those promises to each other, to our little girl, to any future children we'll have. Do you want that, Layla?"

"Goddamn it, Duff," she said, tears slipping down her cheeks. "Let me out of the cuffs."

"Only when you agree to marry me."

She started to laugh then, and her laughter mixed with tears as her system flooded with joy. "You crazy man. Of

course I'm going to marry you. Jesus. You didn't have to go
to such lengths."

"Didn't I?" he asked, his wide grin back as he got up and
released her from the cuffs.

She fell into his arms, and he pulled her close, kissing her,
his lips a warm, steady press before he pulled away.

"I need to put the ring on your finger."

"God, I forgot there was a ring."

"That's my practical girl."

She laughed as he slid it onto her finger, then looked down
at the large emerald-cut stone.

"Oh my God, Duff, it's perfect. It's so beautiful."

She started shaking again and leaned into his big body for
comfort—a comfort she knew would always be there for her.
He would always be there for her.

"It's you who's beautiful, my love. My love forever."

She looked up and caught his gaze in hers, her body melting all over again, her heart a liquid pool of need fulfilled and
filled again.

"Yes. Forever."

How many times lately had it occurred to her how lucky
she was? She had the most amazing man in the world, the
sweetest little girl ever born. And now this promise of perma-
nence, which was something she'd never dared dream about.
But it was real. *They* were real.

He wiped her tears with his thumb. "I like that you cry so
much these days, princess."

"Don't say that!"

"It's true. But I only like it because I know you wouldn't
do it if you didn't feel safe with me."

She sighed. "It's true. I think . . . I think this is really the first time in my life I've ever felt this safe. I know you'll be there to catch me, no matter what."

"I will. I will swear it to you now, and every day to come."

"I love you, Duff."

"I love you, my princess. So damn much."

"I can't believe I'm getting married—me, of all people."

"*Us*, of all people, my love, which makes us perfect for each other—don't you think?"

"Yes. Perfect."

As he bent to kiss her, letting her feel his love along with his command of her, she truly knew what absolute safety was. What absolute love was. And she knew she truly was the luckiest woman on earth.

ABOUT THE AUTHOR

Eden Bradley is a *New York Times* and *USA Today* bestselling author. She has written a number of erotic and romantic novels, novellas, and short stories, including *Dangerously Broken, Dangerously Bound,* and *The Dark Garden.*